Cover Art:
MLC Designs 4U

Publisher's Note:

This is a work of fiction. All names, characters,
places, and events are the work of the author's
imagination.

Any resemblance to real persons, places, or events
is coincidental.

Solstice Publishing - www.solsticepublishing.com

TROUBLESHOOTER FOR EARTH

A Novel by
Arthur Butt

*To all the Puddlefoots out there, and as always,
to my wife Susie.*

Part 1: Puddlefoot

Chapter 1

The *Thor* averted disaster, the ship rested, safe and secure in her berth on Luna base. The young rescue pilot reclined in his acceleration chair, waiting for the sickened passengers and crew to disembark. To pass the time, he amused himself by trying to give the ship's computer a nervous breakdown.

"I tell you, man killed off the dinosaurs."

A flat, female voice issued from the machine. "The dinosaurs died off in a meteor strike sixty-five million years ago."

Don checked the overhead. It still blinked amber and read, 'Disembarking'.

He returned to screwing around with the ship's brain. "No, really. They killed off the dinosaurs and had a big barbeque afterward. It caused global warming."

Lights flashed at him. "Caveman drew pictures of the animals they hunted on cave walls. There are no pictures of dinosaurs."

The overhead blinked green. It was time. All the passengers and crew had left the ship except himself.

Don tried to think up the most nonsensical thing he could to cause the machine to implode.

He had it.

"Doesn't prove a thing," he snarled in joy. "There are no pictures of '57 Chevys either, doesn't mean they didn't have 'em." He covered a light on his board before the computer could respond and the machine fell into sleep mode. "Gotcha." Don picked up his cap, checked the inside band, and left the control room.

The tunnel leading from the deep space landing bays, through Customs and Baggage, to the popular Earth-Luna shuttles was deserted. It hadn't been when the *Thor* arrived four hours ago, nor would it be a half-an-hour hence when the *Palmer* departed for Venus.

Don glanced around a corner. With the casual ease deriving from long repetition, he sauntered toward Customs. Whistling off key, he pushed his cap back and opened his collar, dragging his luggage bag behind him. He gave the Customs Inspector a cheery wave and walked through the gate.

"Hold it, bub. Let's see the bag."

"Huh?" Don tensed, but not because of the inspector's remark. Two Space Marine MPs had materialized in the causeway and strode with purpose toward him.

"The bag...let's see the bag," repeated the inspector.

"Sorry. I, er, forgot something." Don back peddled and pivoted. Two Spaceways security guards stood waiting behind him.

"Hi, boys," Don said, trying to produce a weak smile. "I was..."

They grabbed him in front and handcuffed him from behind. For a brief instant Don thought about fighting, until he looked into the eyes of the MPs, then he slumped.

"Ah, damn."

***

When Donald Weiss found himself in the outer office of his boss, the General Manager of Spaceways Inc., he commenced to worry in earnest. After the company finished with him, he'd be hauling ice cubes to Mercury, if he were lucky. What right did the military have to arrest him and turn him over to his employer anyhow? Standard practice called for confiscation, a fine. Maybe a short prison sentence where he could sit safe in a cell. Not this. Don privately believed the fates had it in for him.

A buzzer rang interrupting his thoughts. Don was ushered into the general manager's inner sanctum by a tight-lipped secretary, who glared at Don, already condemning him to the deepest reaches of hell.

Roberta Hershey waited for him behind her antique mahogany desk, the one pleasure she allowed herself in an otherwise utilitarian room. The old woman watched in silence as a cat might watch a mouse, while Don was uncuffed, and pushed into a straight-back chair by one of the security guards. Don shot his fellow employee a dirty look and bolted upright, snapping to attention.

"Don't hand me your fake military manner," Hershey barked, leaning forward. "You know why you are here." She stood and walked around her desk, her limp hardly noticeable in the one-sixth gravity.

"Why, Ma'am, I, I don't..." Don stammered.

"Sit *down,*" she snapped. "I don't need you towering over me." Hershey glared at the guards. "The rest of you, *clear out.*"

Don sat abruptly as the room emptied.

Hershey glared at the young man, but inside she was delighted.

"You've done it to yourself this time, my boy," she barked. "This makes things a whole lot easier."

She loved the lad even though she treated all her employees equally. Hershey respected Don also. The tall American always delivered in a pinch. Nevertheless, the boy sure was a handful.

"Transportation of Martian artifacts is now a National Offense. Parliament has put Mars under the protection of the navy." Hershey paused to let her words sink in. She added in a sarcastic tone, "I take it you have not heard?"

"Uh…" Don hadn't, but something no doubt was lasered while he was out. "Why, no Ma'am. If you'll recall, I was sent to rendezvous with the *Thor* on one of your rush jobs to drop off medical supplies. Then herd her back here because half the crew was down with the Martian flux or something." Don added, "You'll have to dispatch someone after my ship. By the way, how is Blackie?"

"The captain and crew are being shuttle-vaced to Johansasburg as we speak, and a salvage crew is out picking up your vessel," Hershey said off-handed, and glanced at her watch. She leaned against her desk. "Back to business. What you did was dumb, Weiss. The curator of the Phobos museum noticed the substitutes right after your ship lifted. The police arrested your accomplice within twenty-four hours." Don winced. "Once they gave him the needle, he blabbed every detail of your little scheme." Hershey smirked. "You can guess what happened to him afterwards."

Don blanched. Earth's justice was harsh, but on Mars, especially with a Martian citizen… He speculated on what it felt like slowly suffocating while left outside in sub-below freezing cold. For once, he was glad he was a member of the pilot's guild. Don reminded himself sharply to check and make sure his dues were paid up. He snapped his attention back to Hershey who was still talking.

"...By the way, your ship was searched and we couldn't discover the gems," Hershey said. She stuck her palm out. "Hand them over."

Without hesitation, Don pulled off his cap, flipped up the sweatband, and removed a strip of surgical tape. Stuck to the adhesive were three small gems, fire stars, Martian opals. One by one, he plucked the jewels off, cupping them in his hand. They glowed black, shimmering with a light of their own, like the depths of space. He gave them to Hershey without a word.

The old woman slipped the baubles into her pocket without a hint of how much they were worth. "If this had been your first offense," she said, glowering at Don. "Things would be different. I recall, however, an incident a few years back." Don winced again. "Illegal transport across planetary lines, wasn't it? Minor females from Granymede to Titan, I believe."

Don bolted upright, indignant. "I was set up. They flashed me military ID. How was I supposed to know they were...?"

"Shut up. No excuses, please, and speaking of the military, this is, of course, a matter for them." Hershey took a deep breath, pretending to calm herself. "I talked to Captain Sims. It seems charges might be dropped if you are willing to do the navy, and Spaceways, a small favor."

Don felt chills run down his spine. He knew it would come to this. He remembered his last conversation with the crusty Provost Marshal of

Luna Base. A one-way trip to the Lithium mines on Titan was one of the better vacation spots offered.

Don weighted his options. He was sure Hershey didn't mean to kill him, on purpose. Something hazardous, but not fatal. Maybe, his fate was flying into the photosphere of the sun to test a field generator to gauge if it would hold. Experiments in the genetic labs to see if he could adapt to the vacuum of space minus a spacesuit? Viruses did it, why not man? On the other hand, days, months, maybe years of deep space exploration without the benefit of companionship.

Don thought bleakly about the rock and the hard spot. He made his decision. He drew a deep breath.

"Sure Ma'am. What is it you need me to do?"

Hershey broke into a grin. She walked around her desk, sat, and waved to a leather-bound chair opposite hers. "Have a seat, my boy. Here…" She withdrew a cigar from an ornate wood box and handed it to Don. "Relax." She released a sigh, settling her leg in a comfortable position. "There's nothing to worry about."

Don winced. Nevertheless, he accepted the gift and cringed on the edge of his chair.

"You see, Don, we need a volunteer." The general manager withdrew a bulky manila envelope from her desk. "These are photos of the control room of the *Hope,* an unmanned, experimental starship Spaceways has developed." She passed the envelope over. "Go on, open it and take a look."

Don accepted the package but didn't open it at once. The excitement of a starship drove all other thoughts from him. "Ma'am, when did we…how?"

Hershey shrugged and leaned back. "Don't act surprised, Weiss. Experiments with faster-than-light drives reach back to the Twentieth Century. I dare say ten corporations right now are designing similar ships."

"Ma'am?" Don sputtered, "I thought interstellar was still years away."

She stuck up her palm and leaned forward. "I can't reveal secrets, Weiss, you know the rules. I imagine you'll learn soon enough, I suppose. Don't ask me how it works either. I haven't the math to explain the theory." Hershey raised her shoulders and dropped them. "I couldn't understand the equations if I tried. I'm a glorified file clerk." She gestured to the package. "Now, take a look at the pictures and tell me what you think."

Red string secured the envelope, which someone stamped 'confidential' across the front and back a dozen times. Don unwrapped the cord and began scanning the pictures, one by one. The first showed the control room of the *Hope* and was marked 'Pluto'. He examined the image closely but saw nothing wrong. The second photo displayed the same control room, this one marked, 'post-transition'. Still nothing unusual. Don placed it beside the first and picked up the third.

At first, he discerned no difference between this and the previous two. Then he noticed a hole punched through the main computer terminal the size of his fist. In addition, something was wrong with the communication gear. The mike was missing from its cradle. Don estimated the trajectory of the errant mouthpiece and concluded three things. A) An unseen agency yanked the mike from its socket. B) The mike shot across the control room into the computer with the force of a bullet. C) Both A and B were impossible in an unmanned ship.

Don studied the rest of the photos. In each, the wreckage grew worse. The last pictured showed the door of a utility closet flying toward the lens of the camera.

"My goodness, Ma'am," he said, setting the last picture alongside the rest. "I've heard of solar winds, but the control room looks like a hurricane hit the place. What happened?"

"Umm-m, don't know." Hershey scooped up the pictures with a snort, and slid the photos back into the envelope. "This is why we're sending you. To find out."

Coldness gripped Don's chest. "Say what, Ma'am? You faded."

Hershey scowled at him. "Don't be a smartass, Weiss. You heard me. The ships *Faith* and *Charity* embarked on trial runs and returned broken, gutted inside as if some wrecking machine ran amuck. It was our good fortune these pictures survived from the *Hope*."

Don's mind snapped into overtime. No way was he going on this mission. "Ma'am, if three ships went out and no one can figure out what happened..." He raised his hands and smirked pitifully. "I'm no expert on unexplained space phenomenon. I'm a pilot. What you need is one of those scientific Johnnies."

Hershey shook her head and stared him in the eye. "No. We need someone experienced in the unknown. A person used to dealing with problems at once. Whatever is happening out there must be corrected on the spot."

"But..."

"It can't be solved from a million miles away by a computer. What we need is a space pilot like you." The old woman sighed. "Even with all your faults, you're one of the best we have unfortunately. You've been elected."

Don knew a swindle when he heard one. *This is gonna be a rough one,* he thought. Without realizing what he did, his brain was already running subconscious scenarios of possible problems. *The boss wouldn't say something nice to me unless she was desperate.* "Come on, Ma'am. You could grab any pilot for this mission," he protested.

The old woman sat straighter in her chair and shook her head. "You're going," she replied dryly.

Don was feeling dry too, or at least, his mouth was. He remembered the last photo of the *Hope.* The next set of pictures might show *him* flying toward the camera. He shuddered at the thought, and wondered if it weren't too late to turn himself over to Captain Sims. He stammered, "Ma'am, you know I have three children…"

"No good, Weiss. One child, a son, and he doesn't know you. He was adopted by the man your wife remarried after your divorce."

"Two cats…" he said, desperately.

"Only one," she denied. Her lips twisted down. "She's in the West Tunnel Kennel." Hershey withdrew her palmputer from the drawer and surveyed the screen quickly. "And I see you've been billing the company for her rooming costs?" She shoved the device in Don's face so he could see the figure.

"Ma'am, those receipts are for legitimate expenses. I…"

"Enough." The general manager stood. "Pack your duffel, Weiss. You leave in two days."

Don protested his assignment. He complained as he lifted off Luna. He griped while in transit to the launching site. He even found reasons to bitch to the company clerk, a noncom, at Tombaugh Barracks.

"I don't want to be here in the first place," he yelled, waving his arms in exasperation. "If I have to wait until my ship is ready, I'm not staying in the barracks. At least put me in the BOQ. I belong with the officers."

"Sorry, can't help you," mumbled the sergeant, studying a roster.

"Speak up, soldier, you sound like a woman." Don gripped the edge of the desk until his knuckles turned white.

Sparkling brown eyes met his blue ones. "I *am* a woman."

"Oh." Don shaded to red, embarrassed, and then broke out in a foolish grin. "I'm sorry. It was the hair. I..."

The sergeant ran her hand over the top of her head. "Brush cut, regulations, and I still can't help you." She read the expression on Don's face, leaned back in her chair, and crossed her arms. "Look, you'll be here for twenty-four hours, will it be so bad?" She smiled.

At her smile, Don's anger melted. He felt his pulse quicken. "No, I guess not. I'm not gonna be doing much sleeping anyhow." Her eyes weren't brown, more hazel, he decided. They went with the freckles on her face. "Say, will you be here when I get back?"

"Well..." She inspected his lean body, took in the short, blond hair, and noticed a faint scar above his left eyebrow. Her gaze locked onto his. Then she blushed. "I don't know where you're going or how long. Your mission is classified. Besides, my boyfriend takes up most of my free time."

"Oh. Okay." Don slumped and turned to the exit. The ship would soon be ready to leave, and to tell the truth, so was he. The solar system had done him no good from the first day he left the Academy eleven years ago. Space took him away from his wife, child, and cost him his marriage. Maybe the galaxy would be a kinder place.

As the door swished closed behind him, Don heard the sergeant yell out, "My name's Samantha and I'm stationed here for the next six months!"

He grinned, straightened his shoulders, and went to inspect his ship.

Don dubbed her, *Last Chance,* or *Chancy* for short, because the flight he was undertaking was the last opportunity Spaceways would have to con him into a mission such as this again. Some things were too foolish to do twice.

As he gazed at her trim lines, he marveled at the craft. Built in space, she reminded him of a bird taking wing. *Pretty thing,* he thought. *At least I'll have a Fifty Billion credit coffin if I don't come back. I wonder why they didn't wait and buy a company manufacturing interstellar ships.*

Spaceways could not help but develop the stardrive. A fact Don didn't realize. Started in the late Twentieth Century as a space tourist company, the company absorbed many of the commitments of the American space program when the agency closed for lack of funding. Later it added Arianespace, and the Japanese program. The financial collapse of the world economic system in the twenty-first century meant the final disintegration of Russia, and their adventures in space. By the mid-twenty-second century, Spaceways left China in the dust.

Spaceways stayed in front by always beating the competition on research and development.

Others developed the lithium fusion engines. They made it to Mars first, but Spaceways made the trip faster, cheaper, and turned a profit on the Red Planet. After five years, their remaining competitor folded when Spaceways offered passenger service for voyages of a month's duration.

Spaceways was about to beat the competition again. With the successful completion of an interstellar trip, the corporation opened the gateway to the galaxy. The human race would profit. So would Spaceways.

At 0100 hours, Don went to bed. Blast-off was at 0800 hours, and he needed to be fresh. He'd spent the previous five hours pouring over blueprints, checklists, and pre-flight photos of the three unsuccessful missions. He was searching for something, anything, to explain what happened to the ships. At first, he thought the problem was something simple. Scientists, and even the most brilliant, possessed a tendency to concentrate on one thing to the exclusion of all else. Don pictured some engineer triple checking the radio to make sure the device worked to perfection, and forgetting to dog down the mike. He didn't laugh at the picture. The situation happened to him once, that time the mistake was oxygen tanks. He'd escaped with a mild concussion and thereafter double-checked the checkers.

Don discovered nothing wrong, however, with the preparations for blast-off. He searched for other reasons his long years in space told him could be culprit. He checked the specs of gaskets holding liquid and gas, and examined x-rays of welds. He even compared the itemized weights of all component parts of the ships, plus excess equipment, to the total weight at launch. He hoped a stowaway, be the offender person, rat, or fly loused up the operation of the flight. Everything proved negative.

As Don stumbled into bed, he was tired, bleary-eyed, and frustrated. He closed his eyes and relaxed. In reflex, his mind commenced to think on its own, constructing stories to amuse itself, an old habit acquired as a cub fresh out of the Academy. The stories and pictures served to pass the time during the long stretches between landings when he was alone in space. He started to give himself up to the daydreams, and then with a savage twist jerked himself away. No. He wasn't a cub. Dreams were for the young, but his youth faded in the starry void of space. He hadn't touched the stories for years.

Don rose, dressed, and strolled to the rec room, searching for something he knew was there. A beer machine. He bought two cans and sat in a plastic chair humming to himself:

If buttercups chased after the bees,

...as he sipped. He preferred classical music, but in times of stress, the English ditty lent him courage. When he finished the second beer, he returned to his bunk and slept.

At 0630, the charge of quarters woke him. "Sir, it's six-thirty, time to get up." The CQ shook his pillow.

"Umph," said Don, coming instantly awake, ready for action. "Go away. I bought a ticket."

"Sir, it's time. Grab your socks and get dressed."

"Okay, I'm up." Don rolled out of bed and stood. "Where's the mess hall?"

"Two flights down and turn to left," the private replied with a smirk. "You can't miss it, follow the trail of dead flies."

Don grinned back. "Typical army food then, huh? Thanks for the advice."

Nevertheless, Don ate a hearty meal. Three scrambled eggs, toast with butter and grape jelly, hash browns, bacon, and coffee. Lots of Army coffee. After which he ran to the latrine to shave. He ate a big breakfast because he knew how these missions worked. Abort...abort...abort, until all the lights showed green. He finished his toilet and donned his spacesuit.

As he left the barracks, he ran into the Company Clerk, Samantha walking the other way. "Good luck, Sir," she said.

Don winked. "Thanks. With any luck, I'll be back in two days." He grinned broadly and asked, "You'll be here?"

She spun away on the balls of her feet, hand on the door, smiling. "I told you I'm here for six more months, didn't I?" she said over her shoulder. "I'm not going anywhere."

"Good, I'll see you then." Don called after her. He wanted to add something else, thought better of it, and started to walk toward the pressure lock. A small, soft hand on his arm stopped him.

"Hey, I didn't get to say good-bye!" Sam's warm mouth met his in a quick kiss, her tongue probing into his mouth. "Good-bye," she breathed.

"Until later," he amended, and left for his ship.

Chapter 2

The scheduled called for blastoff at 0800 hours, but the time read well past 1900 before everything was set to go. Don missed lunch and wound up eating a corned beef sandwich for supper, which someone, Samantha, sent to the ship.

While he waited, he tried to make sense out of a report on how the stardrive worked. As far as he could tell, the ship wouldn't travel through normal space, but around the void in some weird, other dimension. He reread this part twice, each time formulating a different notion of what was to occur. Farther into the report, he discovered the jump would not be far, half a parsec, enough to test the drive. Nor was the time involved long, three hours, however, nowhere did he see written how much subjective time would pass.

Don caused part of the delay himself. Besides reading the report, he continued to speculate about the previous jumps. On a hunch, he called the tower and ordered the ship's lifeboat removed, after some argument, had the small craft replaced by a jumpship.

Launched from a mother ship, the tiny, maneuverable craft could travel anywhere in space, searching for mineral deposits, or survey asteroids and meteoroids between Mars and Jupiter. In this case, a jumpship claimed one advantage over a standard lifeboat. Built not to disturb the delicate instrumentations onboard, non-ferrous metals comprised the bulk of its construction.

Don developed a possible reason for the strange behavior of the equipment onboard the *Hope*. Magnetic fields. The whole ship transformed into one gigantic magnet, he reasoned, or it passed through magnetic bands in space. The jumpship provided him a control. It would also save his life if the *Chancy* disintegrated around him.

At 2000 hours, less than a minute remained until blast-off. A heady flush raced through Don's body. Aloud he intoned, "Oh Lord, let me live to see your glory."

He checked his radar and view scopes, the stars stood motionless. He had nothing else to do. The ship was out of his control, blast-off and retrieval were automatic. Only in an emergency would he take over manual operation. All he must do was wait.

The waiting was over.

He felt, rather than heard the thunder of the engines. The thunder changed to a whine, which grew higher until the sound was lost. The stars quivered. An invisible hand compressed his chest.

The hand pushed harder, then released.

The stars disappeared.

Weight but weightless, blood flowing in slow, ponderous pulses setting off a throbbing in his head. The pounding grew worse, and boomed until he thought his brain must explode. Struggling with his webbing, he tried to escape. Don bolted upright and screamed for the pain to go away.

It did not stop. Would not stop. Please God, make it stop.

STOP.

The stars returned.

Don rubbed his temple, sweat dripped down his forehead. He whistled. The engineers back on Earth still needed to get rid of some bugs.

With the return to space, he felt normal again. Don stood, stretched his cramped muscles, and prowled around the cabin searching for damage. "Nothing wrong yet," he muttered. Not a microchip out of place. Satisfied, he strolled to his couch and laid back, watching to see what would happen next.

The control room was warm. His suit cradled him with soft arms. Don checked the time. *Almost midnight,* he thought, suppressing a yawn, *the witching hour.* His eyes grew heavy and his head sank onto his chest. It had been a long day.

A video camera snapped off a bulkhead and crashed into the light panel over his head. His couch bounced up and down. Microphones, dials, and switches broke their fastenings and danced about the room. Don's eyes snapped open. He stared in confusion.

A loose screw whined past his ear. The computer screamed, *"Help me,"* and abruptly chopped off. Don considered his options and decided retreat was his best bet. He ducked underneath the couch for protection.

Events became busy after he hid. Nuts, bolts, and rivets shot in all directions. Larger objects they secured developed a life of their own, ripping through internal walls. Don followed in amazement, from the safety of his couch, as the first aid cabinet flew open and surgical supplies swarmed out. When his protection, the couch, leaped into the fray, Don saw red. He struggled to his feet amongst the wreckage of his control room. Sterile gauze gravitated to him, circling his waist like a hungry boa. He shoved it down and stalked to the middle of the cabin.

"ENOUGH," he bellowed. Bits of debris paused in their wild dance, started up again. "Oh no you don't. Enough is enough. Stop it, NOW."

One by one, the objects flying around the cabin dropped to the deck. Don stepped out of the circle of gauze tagging along around his feet. He nodded in satisfaction, hands on hips. The couch was settling back in place. "Good, now the rest of my control room," he shouted. "Come on...everything, don't hold back." In a few minutes, the air was clear. He swung in a wide circle and surveyed the mess.

"Well, somebody has a lot of explaining to do, and it's not gonna be me." Don squinted, surveying the cabin. Hell, the disruption wasn't a magnetic field. Those things came alive and obeyed his orders. Someone, or *something,* was playing tricks, but whom? He shrugged. *Well, it worked once.* "Okay...let's see you. Wherever you are, I know you're here, stop hiding. Show your face." He waited dubiously for the author of the destruction to appear.

At first, he saw nothing. Then a shimmer ruffled the air. With a POP, a figure materialized. Don rubbed his eyes, positive he was seeing things, but it didn't help. Standing before him was a three-foot tall man.

The midget wore a brown shirt and pants, both neat but worn, while a scarlet cap perched on his head. Don noticed the manlike figure was not wearing shoes. Instead, his legs ended in cloven feet. He also lacked a nose, but at first glance, his missing nostrils weren't apparent.

He beamed at Don with a mischievous smile. His eyes twinkled, and a smile touched his lips. Both deepened to amusement as Don's expression faded from disbelief, to astonishment, and settled into shock.

"What...who a-a-are you?" Don stammered.

The little man cocked his head and replied, "Ah...'tis Puddlefoot I'm called, and I am what I am."

Don's brow knitted. Something tugged at the back of his mind. He had seen, or read, a description of the little man before. The memory eluded him.

His surprise rapidly faded. He sighed. *Why do these things always happen to me?* "What do you mean, 'I am what I am'? What kind of an answer are you handing me?" The little guy wasn't making things easy.

The midget smirked. "What I said, O mortal man. I'm known as Puddlefoot from the lowlands of Scotland to the English Coast."

He giggled at Don's confusion and did a poor excuse for a Highland fling around the deck, which brought him in a circle to face Don again.

It struck him. Don remembered the cover picture on a magazine he'd read as a boy. The story was about elves. "You're an elf." It was absurd, but the miniature proof stood before him, snickering. "You can't be. They're not real. I must be dreaming."

Puddlefoot glanced at his diminutive body, back at Don, shaking his head. "Nay, mortal, for if this be true, thy mind must be weak indeed to dream up so poor an excuse for a creature as me." He paused and added, "But pray, call me not elf. I am a brownie, descendent from a long, noble line of brownies and proud to be one." Faint indignation rang in his voice and his eyes flashed a warning.

Don shrugged, rubbing his chin in thought. "Elf...brownie, what's the difference." He hadn't noticed Puddlefoot's look.

"There might not be one to thou, ye thick-skinned lout. Now, good day to thee." A small clap of thunder filled the void Puddlefoot occupied. He was gone.

Don leaped back in surprise and scanned the cabin. "Hey wait...Come back. I didn't mean to make you sore."

Sheesh, the little guy was touchy. He couldn't let him get away, though. This Puddlefoot character was the cause of the company's problems, and it was his duty to deal with the brownie. He faced the last spot he'd seen the brownie and yelled, "Hey fella...Puddlefoot...I'm sorry, please come back?" He felt foolish talking to thin air.

The shimmering returned, assuming humanoid form. With a mild detonation of displaced air, Puddlefoot stood before him. "Yes?" he inquired sweetly.

"Sorry about the name," Don apologized. "I didn't mean to offend you. I'm, ah, a mortal you know, not too bright...forgive me, will yah?"

Puddlefoot stuck out his lower lip and looked obstinate, but after a moment's thought, changed his expression back to impishness. "Aye...I forgive thee."

"Good." Don was relieved. He was back in control and planned to stay there. Studying the brownie, he said, "Well, dream or not, we still have a problem here, my friend." How to coax some information out of this little demon?

A strange expression passed over Puddlefoot's face. "Thou callest me friend, Sire?"

"A figure of speech, Puddlefoot," Don replied with caution. He watched the brownie closely. "Nothing personal. I don't collect friends."

"Oh, Sire, I meant not to rush thee, but please, do not say such words with haste. An acquaintance, nothing more." Puddlefoot gazed at him, hope flickering in his eyes, and sniffled.

"Well..." If it made this Puddlefoot easier to manage, why not. It couldn't hurt. "I guess so...stop snuffling. Here," he handed Puddlefoot his handkerchief, "blow your," Don noticed the brownie had no nose, "whatever, and tell me what your pranks are all about."

"Thank thee, Sire." Puddlefoot dabbed at his eyes. "I knewst not so wonderful a man as thee was aboard. I am sorry."

Maybe this pint-sized problem wasn't so bad after all. Anyway, he was making sense now. Don patted him on the back. "It's all right. Did you happen to meet three other ships on this spot?"

"Aye, Sire, but no one was aboard." Puddlefoot handed Don back the damp handkerchief.

"Why destroy them?" Don was perplexed again.

"Because they were neat." Puddlefoot beamed and started to sing.

"Neat is a treat to destroy,
No fun to assemble, my friend,
But oh, like a mischievous boy,
I do it again and again."

It matters not what kind,
Of thing it happens to be.
I take it apart. Reassemble again,
And that is my nature, you see.

Puddlefoot appeared crestfallen. "Only the ships wert taken away 'afore I could make everything right."

Don was smiling, picturing the son he'd never met, when the implications of what Puddlefoot said struck him. "By all means, make it right." He added to himself, *and let me get my tail to Tombaugh Barracks.*

"Yes, Sire, as you command." The brownie threw him a Boy Scout salute, and stared at the wreckage littering the cabin in concentration.

A miniature tornado erupted in the middle of the control room. Broken bits and pieces of plastic, aluminum alloy, and fiberglass welded themselves together and jumped back to their respective spots. The scene flickered like a motion picture in reverse, with each part of rubble having a purpose of its own. Within five minutes, the room returned to normal.

"Wow." Don blinked and scanned the room in awe. "Don't you ever get tired, Puddlefoot?"

"Nay, sire…not often." He sighed, "I suppose thou wilt leave me now?"

Don had the same idea. He'd checked the timer on the retrieval, and knew in fewer than two minutes he would travel home to a hero's welcome. The first man to make an interstellar jump, almost, he corrected. What the heck, it was close enough. The mission was over. The ship was again in good condition. The cause of the failures known. He remembered Puddlefoot waiting before him and replied,

"Yes, my little friend," he replied with a benign pat on Puddlefoot's head. "I'm afraid I must go. You be good, you hear? Don't take any wooden…" Don stopped short and slapped the abort button on the retrieval.

Don switched the controls to manual and slumped on his couch. He couldn't leave, not yet. His mission wasn't completed even if he did pilot the *Chancy* back intact.

Any other ship traveling this way would be subject to destruction by Puddlefoot, the three-foot wrecking crew. Worse, yet, the brownie might take it into his head to follow the ship back to Earth. Who knew what mischief the little terror would produce there?

Don's greatest concern was the question of his sanity. Not his question, but what others would say. He imagined himself reporting to Hershey, "Oh, yes, Ma'am, I solved your problem. Space is inhabited by little elves, three feet high, who destroy your starships by magic." He next tried to imagine how comfortable a straightjacket was while squatting in a padded cell.

No. He must neutralized Puddlefoot somehow, and make up a plausible explanation for what happened, before returning to Earth. "Puddlefoot…what are you going to do when I leave?"

The brownie did not hear him. The little man was preforming a strange dance in the middle of the deck. First, he laughed. Then he pranced and jumped high in the air clicking his heels. He repeated this combination twice.

"Whoa there, fella." Don seized an ankle as the brownie floated toward the ceiling. "Come back to Earth."

Puddlefoot touched down for a perfect three-point landing on the deck. "Thank thee, Sire, oh, thank thee." He caught Don's foot and kissed it.

"Hey, cut it out." Don snatched his leg back.

"Ye have labeled me friend, twice sire." Puddlefoot's eyes shone with worship. "Now I know 'tis true. A companion means the world to me, to have a friend. I have been alone so long. Thou art a prince among men, sire. I am yours to command."

A prince? Don smirked. *More like a joker, especially in the last few years.* What use was it? Return to Earth, a pat on the shoulder, and then back to the old grind with orders to pilot from point A to point B. *Why can't everyone leave me in peace?* He sighed. *The mission – always the mission.*

Don gazed at the little brownie kneeling on the deck. *Well, if you can't beat them,* he thought. The situation could be worked to his advantage, but he didn't like what he was about to do. "If you want to be my friend you have to promise me two things." He felt like a heel.

"Oh, yes…anything, anything at all!" Puddlefoot rose, worship in his eyes.

"Don't bother anymore ships from Earth."

"No sooner said than done, Sire." Puddlefoot bobbed his head up and down. "Your wish is my command."

"No." Don added, "There's something else. My friends on Earth wouldn't believe you're real. You must remain here, unseen. Understand me?"

Puddlefoot wilted. He gave Don a wishful smile. "Well, if it must be, it must be." He sighed. "I suppose thou wilt abandon me here, forever?"

"I have to." Don's guts knotted.

"I cannot comest?"

"No. I must go unaccompanied." Don hated himself for the act he was about to give. He took a stance, hands on hips, gazing off at something unseen. "Even if you are my friend and would stand beside me. I walk alone. Down the unbeaten trail, through the uncharted wilderness. I must make my way." He set his jaw. "It is my destiny to have friends and leave them. My road is hard, but don't weep for me, for loneliness is the path I have chosen. I..."

"I knowest of a mountain of gold," Puddlefoot interjected.

"...live alone, alone I must..."

"'Tis free for the asking."

"...go. Friendless, forsaken...*SAY WHAT?*" Don chopped off his monologue and handed Puddlefoot his full attention.

"Gold, my lord, piles of it. All yours for the taking."

Don swallowed hard. "Where did you see this g-g-gold? How far...how much? Gold, you said?"

Puddlefoot shot him a sideways glance. "Certes Sire, thou soundst like a greedy man."

"Who, me? Uh-uh," Don denied vehemently. "Gold makes me nervous, nothing more. I can't stand wealth that isn't mine. Besides," Don nodded to the controls of the ship, "if I move too far from this spot, the auto-pilot won't return me to Earth." He frowned. "I would have liked to have seen it, though."

Don perched on the edge of the pilot's couch and pondered his situation. Puddlefoot did likewise. Together they sat and shared unhappy thoughts.

"Say, Puddlefoot," Don exclaimed after a few minutes, "How did you sneak into the ship?"

The little man eyed him with a puzzled expression. "Why, I thought to come here and I did."

"You can teleport my ship where the gold is the same way," Don whooped. "We grab the gold and you pop us back here. It's as simple as landing in a space dock."

Puddlefoot grinned, and then his lips drooped down. "Nay, Sire, for I could not move so great a weight of cold iron. Even the attempt would prove disastrous to me."

"Oh." Don rubbed his chin. "You're telling me you can't handle steel, huh?" He applied his mind to this new problem, and in a split-second had a solution. "How about something smaller? Something made from a non-ferrous metal?"

"Non-fer – what's the word, Sire?"

"Not made out of iron," Don replied rapidly. "Could you transport a small ship not built out of steel, or," he amended, "not much steel? What do you think?"

"I knowest not, Sire," Puddlefoot answered. "I have never tried 'afore. Perhaps…"

"Sure you will, think positive." Don grabbed the little man by the shoulder. "You're Puddlefoot, worker of miracles, remember? Let's go."

He hurried the brownie aft, and stopped when they reached mid-ship, pressing a green button set flush on the bulkhead. A panel slid back revealing the hatch of a small boat, the jumpship.

"Ta-da!" Don waved with a flourish. "Hop aboard and let's get moving." He stepped into the airlock and undogged the hatch. Puddlefoot hesitated and did likewise.

Don touched a switch and the panel closed, hidden machinery ground into life, pumping air from the lock. Keeping his eyes on the instrument panel, he waited until a red light flashed green. With the dexterity of long practice, Don maneuvered the small craft out of the lock, away from the starship, and gave it a gentle nudge with the tail rockets. When they were a quarter mile away from the mother ship, he stopped their forward motion with a blast from the nose jet, leaving the craft motionless in space.

"Okay, Puddlefoot," Don said at last after he'd locked his board. "How do we do this? Join hands and recite the pilot's manual backward?"

"Nay, Sire," the brownie chuckled. "I told thee, 'tis a wishing, nothing more."

"Start wishing before someone else swipes the gold." Don rubbed his hands together in anticipation.

"Have no fear, Sire. Thy gold is well guarded."

"Huh?" Don stared at him in confusion. "I thought you said the gold was free for the taking. What's a guard have to do with it?"

"Hush, Sire." Puddlefoot placed a stubby finger to his lips. "'Tis time...we go now."

He moved his attention to the controls and focused on the stars in the view scope. The brownie's forehead knitted, and his eyes narrowed in concentration, as if he could move the heavens by force of willpower alone.

Don watched the 'scope also, but didn't see any change. He glanced at Puddlefoot and saw sweat dripping down the little brown face. "Hey, are having a heart attack? If you can't move the ship, you can't. Don't kill yourself." The little fella looked like he would drop dead on the spot.

Puddlefoot said nothing. Don looked back to the stars, but they all disappeared. Except one. A great light was drawing rapidly nearer.

Chapter 3

The jumpship swung around a small planet in three separate orbits. After completing the third, Puddlefoot showed him a large crater at the base of a mountain range.

"Yonder, Sire…at the far end. Look sharp, do you see it? Do you see the city? There lies our prize."

A city? Don strained to gaze out the tiny port. "Now it's a city?" Don pictured police with rifles. "First, the gold is guarded, and now it's a city? I thought this gold was sort of…" he waved his hands vaguely, "sitting out in the open." Don glared at Puddlefoot and said suspiciously, "Are you trying to pull shenanigans on me?"

"Why no, Sire." Puddlefoot protested. "I…"

"You mean to steal the gold, don't you?"

"Nay Sire." The little man stuck his hand up. "The Zorns, they name themselves, knowest not gold from granite. Gold is plentiful here. 'Tis used for building stones."

A city of gold? "You've got to be kidding, a whole city?"

"Oh, nay Sire. Not the whole city." Puddlefoot broke into a mischievous grin, "but there be enough buildings constructed from the metal so a few bricks 'twill not be missed."

Don frowned. Walking off with building material wouldn't be stealing *exactly,* but… "I don't know," he said at last. "I may be a smuggler, but I'm no thief. Besides, what if these Zorns have guns and take a dim view of aliens carting away part of their town?"

"Hold thy anger, Sire." Puddlefoot gave him a weak smile. "You shall have your gold and naught will be the amiss. The Zorns do not deserve respect. They are a base people, cheap and lazy." His smile faded. "Now please, land thy craft. I am feeling faint."

"Yeah, sure." Don said. Puddlefoot's face was chalky white. "I should have guessed you'd be tired after hauling the ship halfway across space. Hold on, we'll ground in a minute."

The landing was rough. The little ship bucked, and came to rest with a loud 'CRUNCH', but the jumpship took the beating. Casual encounters with rocks were common in the meteor fields. After emerging from the craft, Don inspected the hull and found the vessel unscratched. He secured the hatch and paused long enough to place a personal lock on the door, sealing the opening with his palm print.

Puddlefoot watched in mild surprise. When Don finished, Puddlefoot put up his hand. "Hold Sire...I must cast a spell on thee."

"A what?"

Puddlefoot didn't hear. The little man etched a symbol in the air. The sign hung, burning vivid green. "A little something," Puddlefoot said, "so thee may understand the barbarian's tongue." The fiery mark drifted toward Don, encircled his head, and disappeared.

Don froze while a hive of bees took up residence in his brain, then the sensation passed. He glanced around, his eyes resting on Puddlefoot. "Your way sure beats how they did it in the little red school house I graduated from," he muttered. "Let's start moving."

They hiked the quarter mile to the outskirts of the city. First, private homes dotted the landscape, small stores and shops appeared. Larger office building and factories sprang up next. Nowhere did they see signs of life. No light burnt in the windows, nor did traffic crowd the streets, but in the distance, the strains of music and laughter drifted faintly to their ears.

"Where is everybody?" Don asked.

"Huh...? Oh. Fear not, Sire," Puddlefoot replied. "No doubt the people are all at the festival. The Zorns are big on holidays. They celebrate five days a week."

Don whistled. "Regular party animals aren't they. What do they do for the rest of the time?"

"Oh...Saturdays and Sundays are days of rest. Sleep I guess, work in their private fields, gossip, have friends over."

It sounded like fun, but Puddlefoot missed the point. "No, what do they do for a living, services, manufacturing. What?"

Puddlefoot shook his head. "They do naught, Sire. I told thee, they art a lazy lot."

"I see." Don frowned. "A planet full of hedonists. What's the birth rate?"

"Sire?"

"Are there a lot of babies born?"

"Oh, aye Sire," Puddlefoot replied. "Siring babes is how they fund their pleasures. The parents sell the offspring."

"You're kidding, right?" Don looked aghast at the brownie.

"How else would the Zorns pay for their goods?" Puddlefoot shrugged his small shoulders. "I understand the bairns are considered a delicacy off-world."

Don's frown deepened with his stomach threatening to rebel. "Yeah." He spun away and plodded deeper into town, not feeling at all guilty about what he was doing.

***

They left the street and walked into an alleyway running between two factories. The noise of the festival was near. Don saw the reflection of firelight dancing off the walls of the taller building, but in the alley, all was dark. He paused to let his eyes adjust while the brownie kept scurrying ahead. When he could see, he hurried on, trying to catch Puddlefoot. He stopped, however, when he noticed strange objects lining the street.

Row upon row of drums stood against the walls. Don stepped up to one and peered inside. *This can't be where they keep the gold,* he said to himself, *but what the heck's in the barrels?*

His monkey ancestry got the better of him. He found a stick in the gutter and probed the bunghole of the mysterious container.

"Hey, what you doing, man?" The barrel sprang up on ten spindly legs, tentacles sprouting from the top, three of which held eyes. The barrelman ejected the stick with a loud 'PIFF.'

Don jumped back in fright. The Zorn took a few menacing steps toward him, waving its limbs as it approached. Don snatched up the stick he dropped and shouted, "On guard." A stick wasn't as good as a foil, but...

The Zorn stopped. "What are you, a wise guy? I'll shove a stick up your fromp and see how you like the feeling." He fumbled about, searching in the street for another stick, and then sat abruptly. He hiccupped.

The other barrels stirred, disturbed by the ruckus, confused mutterings raising into a roar. Don looked wildly around for Puddlefoot, but the little brownie had vanished. He had to do something, something fast, or he would be in the middle of a riot.

"Say, fella," Don dropped the stick, "sorry about the mistake. For a second I thought you were a payphone." He chuckled and sat next to the barrelman. "I was trying to get a dial tone."

The Zorn's eyestalks focused on Don, a grating sound issuing from its barrel-like body. "A phone? Yah thought I was a phone? You were trying to get a dial tone out of my..." the words broke off, but the noise continued.

Don realized the creature was laughing. He joined in.

"Hey guys," the barrelman addressed his companions, "dig this." He related the story to the others who crowded around and received a chorus of guffaws.

One of the others piped in with, "Which reminds me of the story about the seven tentacle salesman. It seems he stopped at a farmhouse, see, and the farmer had this daughter..."

This, Don said to himself, *is getting me nowhere.* When the joke concluded, he spoke up before another started. "Hey, I hear there's a party going on somewhere. Where is it?"

"Yeah, the festival," the storyteller said. "Come on, gang, let's have some fun." They laughed and joined appendages, dancing toward the middle of the city. Don followed on their heels.

The conga line emptied into the city square. Hundreds of barrelmen milled around under the light of torches. Dominating the middle of the square stood a pyramid two hundred feet high, stairs cut in from the monument's base to the top, on all four sides.

The barrelmen leaped around the structure. Hawkers threaded their way through the happy mob, selling bottled drinks and long, thin cigarettes. Don search for an inconspicuous spot from which to observe. He located one next to an unoccupied amusement booth. Lounging back against the counter, he tried to decide what to do next.

"Psst. Sire...Don, behind thee."

He jumped, startled, and peered inside the booth. The little brownie squatted there. "Puddlefoot, where the heck have you been?"

Puddlefoot grinned, tipped his hat in greeting. "In here, Sire, waiting for thee. When you became lost, I, er, decided to come ahead."

"I bet." Don hurried around the corner of the booth and sat next to him. "Remind me never to walk down any dark alleys with you again," he snapped in disgust. "You're definitely not the type I want guarding my back. Now," Don slapped his hands together, "about the gold you were talking about."

"Aye, Sire. Gold." The brownie waved in the general direction of the city square. "Have ye not noticed it?"

Don looked puzzled. Puddlefoot went on, "The pyramid, Sire. Yonder, 'tis fashioned of blocks of virgin gold."

Don peeked over the top of the booth's counter and whistled. The Brownie was right, the monument shone yellow in the torchlight. "How do you propose we take a three story megalith home with us, on our backs? Don't forget, you promised...no stealing. Besides," he said, gesturing to the crowd as he sat back down, "these crazy Zorns of yours will rip us apart if we touch it."

The brownie stood and waved Don on. "Haven't I told thee not to worry, Sire? Come, 'twere best be done quick."

Puddlefoot led the way to the base of the pyramid. He stood in silent contemplation while surveying the great geometric form before him. When Don drew near Puddlefoot said, "Sire, if you please?"

"Huh...what?" Don had never seen this much gold in his life. It left him mesmerized.

"Put out thy hands and close thy eyes, so I may give thee a great surprise!" recited the brownie.

"Oh...okay." This was the craziest way of treasure hunting Don had ever heard of, but he was past arguing. He put out his hands, feeling silly. At once, something dropped onto his palms, something heavy. Another weight nestled against the first, then another. His legs buckled under him. "Enough."

Opening his eyes, Don stared down. He clutched three small blocks in his arms. He glanced at Puddlefoot then at the pyramid. "Puddlefoot...where did you get these?" The surface of the structure was unbroken, not a brick was missing.

"Did I not tell thee, Sire? 'Twould never be missed?" Puddlefoot gave a throaty chuckle, noticed something behind Don. "Now away. I see the hounds approaching."

A mob of drunken Zorns had spotted them standing beside the pyramid. They converged on the two with yells. "There he is. Yeah, he's the one. Hey you, wait up."

"Uh-oh." Don gulped. He waddled away as fast as his heavy burden would allow, but before he ran more than a few feet he felt tentacles wrap around his arm.

"Slow down, buddy, slow down. I brought some friends of mine to meet yah."

One of the Zorns holding him swayed drunkenly. He peered at Don and tried to focus all three eyes. "What's the matter...yah forget the joke you played on me?"

Don realized with relief this was the barrelman from earlier in the evening. He hadn't recognized the Zorn in the torchlight. They all looked the same to him.

Don broke out in a weak grin. "Hi, how yah doing? Sorry, but I gotta run." His knees buckled as he tried staggering away before they noticed the bricks.

The tentacle didn't let go. "Say, what's the hurry, man?" The rest of the Zorns watched curiously. "The party's just starting. Besides, I told these guys about what happened. They want to hear the story from you, they don't believe me."

"Uh, I've forgotten what happened for the moment. Maybe tomorrow?" Don tried to shake himself loose.

"Nah...I promised the boys."

Don freed himself from the barrelman's grasp and edged away. Without warning, one of the Zorns jabbed a tentacle in his direction and exclaimed, "Hey look, what's he carrying?" The barrelman answered his own question. "They're blocks from our temple."

Don stared down at the bricks in surprise. "From the Temple? You're kidding. These are fakes. I bought them as souvenirs of the festival, cost me five ninety-nine each."

"Yeah?" replied the first Zorn. "They sell for ten bucks even, wholesale. Those are the real thing." The other barrelmen crowded around him. The second Zorn yelled, "Put them back."

Don studied the Zorns. Where was Puddlefoot when he needed him? To the mob he said, "Really, you're mistaken. Check the temple, you'll see. There's nothing missing." He attempted a casual step backward.

"He's taking off. *Stop 'em.*"

Don kicked the first barrelman in the bunghole as he drew near. The creature rolled away, screaming. Don tried to run and felt himself pulled down. "Oh hell," he growled, and dropped the gold. He fell, rolled, and came up kicking and slashing. Zorns went flying backward, right, and left. He scooped up one of the bricks and tucked it under his arm. Then, like a brokenfield runner, he took off down the street with the barrelmen in hot pursuit.

Away from the lights of the city square, Don slowed, found the entrance to the alleyway, and lengthened his stride once more. Soon the silhouette of the jumpship loomed before him.

Five Barrelmen, however, still managed to keep him in sight.

They'd forgotten the golden brick he carried, forgotten the insult to their temple, forgotten everything. The bloodlust of the chase caught the Zorns up, and they carried knives and chains.

Before he could release the personal lock, Don felt a searing pain rip across his back. He spun and stood at bay. The barrelmen formed a ragged half ring around him, and closed in. As the circle tightened, Don bellowed, "Puddlefoot, *where are you?*"

A thunderclap erupted and the little brownie appeared. He reached in his pocket, drew forth a red ball, and hurled it at the Zorns. It hit the lead barrelman, exploded, and scattered among the rest. The barrelmen went down cursing, itching, and scratching.

Puddlefoot gave Don his merry grin and shouted, "Sorry I was slow in returning, Sire. I stopped to fetch some fire ants."

Don had the hatch unlocked and was halfway inside. He shouted back, "You shouldn't have. This ain't no picnic. Hurry up, and let's get out of here." Puddlefoot zipped in behind him and Don slammed the hatch. "Get us back to the ship, quick, before these crazy aliens call out the Navy."

Puddlefoot nodded and stared off into space. Don strapped down and switched on the view scope. Pictured on the screen, a horde of barrelmen approached, carrying torches and dragging a large cannon. "Hurry Puddlefoot, they're bringing up the heavy artillery."

The Zorns and the gun loomed in the 'scope, then replaced by the stars. Those, in turn faded and the hull of the starship appeared. Don piloted the jumpship into the air lock bay and set it to cycling. When the telltales switched to green, he stumbled inside and fell to his knees.

"Home," he gasped, "never more to roam." He kissed the deck.

***

Don finished his final preparations for departure. The lone block of gold from the planet of the Zorns secured in a locker, a monument to folly. He had also solved his problem, what to tell

Hershey about the destruction of the previous starships. He first suspected magnetic fields. Let it be. A temporary magnetic band had been responsible for the destruction, but faded even as he discovered it. He worked on the idea, threw in a few useless facts he remembered to cloud the issue, and concocted a theory.

Large concentrations of monopoles, single poled magnetic particles theorized about but never seen, gathered in the regions between stars and disrupted nearby space, in this case also destroying Spaceways' starships. Further, they were the probable cause of the occasional meteorite showers, which plagued Earth. A good antithesis to Nemesis, Sol's dark companion, and equally hard to prove. By the time he finished, Don almost believed it himself. It was the thing to set Earth scientists arguing about for decades.

He had one last thing to do. Don gazed at Puddlefoot. While he prepared for the return voyage, the little brownie pulled out the ship's specs and studied them. Don wasn't worried. Puddlefoot read them upside down. Then the brownie amused himself by taking the ship's portable recorder apart and reassembling it, until Don put a stop to his antics. Now the time for departure was near, the brownie stood by, uncertain. Don turned away and strapped down in his acceleration couch. "Sorry, old son, but it's time each of us went our separate ways."

"My friend?"

"I can't help it, Puddlefoot," Don said. "You wouldn't fit in. It's too busy, to uncertain, with far too many people. You die on Earth."

"Perhaps thou hast the right of it, Sire," Puddlefoot's voice quivered, "but methinks 'twhen

I last saw Earth, 'twas not bad, blue skies, soft breezes, and the kiss of a bonny lass. Not bad at all."

Don tried holding back tears. "How can I bring you to Earth, and still protect Earth from you? How can I take you there and explain your existence?" He shook his head. "No. You must remain unseen. It's best for me and for the world as well."

Puddlefoot hung his head in sorrow.

Don's mind raced. After a fierce mental argument, he allowed his emotions to override his better sense. "No, dreams never die. Mine are fading, but my problems are no reason to kill yours." He hesitated, sworn silently to himself, then ordered, "Strap down."

Don engaged the automatic retrieval and set the timer. Puddlefoot hurried to the copilot's couch and lashed himself in. As the timer ran down to zero, he said to Don, "Sire, if thou wantest me to be unseen and friendly…"

The starship shuddered and shook.

"…all ye have to do…"

Don felt weight where none existed.

"…is to leave a bowl of milk on thy step."

The stars shimmered and disappeared.

"I will." said Don. He blanked out.

Part 2: First Contact

Chapter 4

The small white cottage stood in the heat of the afternoon sun, shaded by tall oaks. Spanish moss overhung the branches, which stirred when it caught a breeze. A lake reflected the light through the leaves, small waves lapping the shore. In the distance a dove cooed, and closer by, bees danced around a trestle overhung with honeysuckle vines.

In the backyard, Don sprawled in a hammock. A Siamese cat stretched out on his chest, her black head bumping against his cheek, her paws set upon his shoulders. Both cat and man buzzed with contentment.

Don heard a knock on the front door.

"Darn it all," he exclaimed, sitting up. "Bet it's another fool who wandered off the country road. I'll be glad when they finish repaving the Interstate." The cat leaped off his chest as he rose and moved slowly to the front yard.

"Weiss, Donald Weiss."

Don found himself facing his ex-boss, General Manager Hershey.

"Ma'am." He snapped to attention, and then relaxed. Don didn't work for the old woman anymore. The hectic, rushing part of his life was finished, but Hershey was still a friend, sort of. "Come on in. I'll fix you something to drink." He swung the door wide with an uneasy creeping up his spine.

After installing Hershey in a chair, with a frosted glass of lemonade on the table next to her, the creeping reached his chest.

He saw no reason why a busy major executive would visit an ex-employee, acquaintance or not. Could the company have detected the lies in his final report about the destruction of the other starships?

Don felt a trap already closing in around him, although Hershey had not yet uttered a word. As if to lend him moral support, the Siamese leaped into his lap.

"Why, you're a fine looking fellow," Hershey said. "I wondered when I'd see you." She looked up from the cat and said to Don, "What's his name?"

"Peter, ma'am. Only he's a she." Before Hershey asked, Don said, "It's a long story, call her name a family tradition." He wrinkled his brow. "How did you know I had a cat?

"Humm...? Oh, most spacemen keep a cat after they retire. Reminds them of shipboard life, I suppose. I recall asking you about a boarding bill for her. Besides," she chuckled, "I noticed the empty saucer for her food on the stoop."

Don winced. For the last six months, he'd placed a bowl of milk out every night, and every morning the saucer was empty. Once he stayed awake all night to see who the robber was, but no one approached it. He'd convinced himself Puddlefoot was a figment of his imagination, but after that incident, he wasn't sure. Then he realized no matter how dirty he left his cottage when he went to bed, the following morning it was spotless, the floor vacuumed, the dishes washed, and the small hearth where he burnt a fire on cold nights, swept.

Oh, yeah, ah, the saucer," he replied.

"Which reminds me," Hershey said, crossing her legs, and settling back in her chair, "You caused a stir in the company, resigning like you did. I'm sorry I was not there at the time. I had to attend the triplanetary conference on nuclear waste disposal, couldn't send anyone else." She leaned back. "Why *did* you resign?"

Don muttered under his breath, but said, "You read my notice, didn't you? All my reasons were there. Incompatibility with the management, for one."

"Yes, I read it." Hershey leaned forward. "For years you've been the best troubleshooter the company's had, a topnotch pilot, good astrogator, loyal employee. Sometimes you show flashes of genius like on this last mission."

Don fidgeted in his chair, debating a reply. "I carried out my orders, ma'am," he replied carefully.

"Yes, you did, and you left half the scientific minds of the solar system debating your findings. Two astronomers from Tombaugh Barracks have confirmed your hypotheses. They've discovered similar phenomenon in other parts of space." She watched him steadily, waiting for a reaction.

"Really?" Don tried to remain calm. Maybe his lie would hold up after all. He sat back and relaxed.

Hershey reclined also, disappointed by his reaction. "Really. This is why I don't believe your resignation. You're still young. No one your age would quit the career you had, after finishing the greatest mission of his life." She pursed her lips. "Somehow it doesn't sound right." The old woman stared him in the eye. "Now tell me the truth."

Don tried to stare back, discovered it impossible to do. If she wanted the truth, he would hand it to her. The way he figured it, some was her fault anyway.

"Okay, ma'am," he said, releasing a deep sigh, "I'm fed up...there's nothing more to the story. They take, years of it. When I first entered space I had a wife, child, dreams, that was ten years ago. Now I have nothing. I said to hell with space."

"Who takes?"

"You. The company. Space." Don said, confused. *Didn't she understand?* He never tried to put his feelings into words before, but it must be plain. "Space takes everything and gives nothing back. Left to itself space will kill you. I figured it was time I took something for myself, peace and quiet." Don breathed hard. "Did I do something wrong?"

The old woman answered quietly, "No, I never said you had."

"You're darn-tootin' I didn't," Don declared, pacing in front of Hershey, his outrage mounting. "I did everything you asked. Crash priority runs to Titian, special missions to Mercury, back to Trition and Nereid. Drop everything and try matching orbits with Mars, for what, I ask you?" He glared at his former boss. "It was driving me crazy." Don sat, his anger spent.

"Feeling better, son?"

"Yes, ma'am, thanks."

"Good. Since you've got it out of your system now we'll put down these last six months as a leave of absence." Hershey glanced at her palmputer. "On to more important things. Project Starsearch is ready to begin."

Don raised his hand up in protest. "You don't understand me. I've quit. Finished." He grinned. "I'm no fool."

Hershey smirked back. "It seems a rock specimen was in your ship. One of the onboard cameras captured you placing an unidentified rectangular stone in a utility locker." Don's grin faded. "The specimen was never reported in your debriefing, nor, did it appear on the ship's manifest at the end of the voyage."

Don felt the teeth of a trap close in on him. He'd been careful to edit the inboard cameras on the *Chancy*, erasing every trace of Puddlefoot before their return to Tombaugh Barracks. In his haste to make the brownie disappear, he'd forgotten to delete the recording of the gold.

"We believe the rock specimen was valuable," Hershey continued. "Actually, though, it's not important by itself. I might overlook the disappearance, call it a bonus, let's say, if the person involved was still an employee of Spaceways." She looked straight at Don with a small smile spreading over her lips. "Otherwise I would consider it larceny. Everything in the ship was the property of the company. The police would be interested."

The trap snapped shut. Don slumped but in a way, he felt relieved. At least he kept the cash from the sale of the golden brick. A nice bonus indeed. "Uh, when do I leave, ma'am?" he sighed.

Hershey glanced at her palmputer again. "We have a shuttle standing by. It leaves Earthport in twenty-four hours, just enough time for you to close up any affairs you have here." She stood. "Don…"

"Huh?"

"If I ever visit you again, don't give me lemonade." Hershey grimaced at her still full glass. "I drink scotch, straight. Don't forget."

"Yes, ma'am."

***

On the ride up to Luna City, Don reflected he wouldn't miss Earth. The gravity was handing him fits. His feet hurt all the time and his back ached, not to mention the runny nose he'd acquired from the weather.

After disembarking from the shuttle, he headed straight for the main offices of Spaceways, taking Kennedyway to the heart of the underground city, and riding down three levels to the business district.

By the time he arrived, he was whistling. The stress he'd felt for so many months vanished. By god, it felt good to get back in space. Maybe he'd give Hershey's secretary a pat on her fanny and liven up the day even more.

He sauntered into the main lobby and strolled to the receptionist's desk. "Hershey's office, please. She's expecting me."

The young woman looked up and her eyes widened. A smile transformed her face. "Don."

"Samantha." It was the sergeant he'd met in Tombaugh Barracks and taken out once on his return from his last mission. "What are you doing here? When I saw you, you were bucking for Staff Sergeant and talking about making the Army a career."

Sam shrugged her shoulders. "Well, after you left, a lot of Spaceways VIP's hung around. I started talking with a few and one offered me a job working in Luna." She flashed her smile. "Here I am."

"Doesn't look glamorous," he commented, taking note of the lone snake plant and mass of computers in her cubicle, "but I'm sure you'll work your way up the ladder as time goes on."

"Oh, this is a makeshift job until the person I replace retires," Sam replied with a shake of her head. "They're bouncing me around from station to station, so I can get the feel of the place. What about you...?" She studied him with concern. "I heard through the grapevine you quit, gone crazy, or something."

"Bouncing off the walls," he agreed, "but I'm back on the job, mean as ever." He bared his teeth in a mock snarl. "Sam, it's good to see you, but I gotta run." He bent over the divider and gave her a peck on the cheek, receiving another smile in return. He turned to leave, changed his mind, and said, "Say...think you could do me a favor?"

"Nothing illegal, I hope," she quipped.

"Nah. Do you like cats?"

Peter was a problem vexing Don. Right now, the Siamese was in transit between Earth Station Five and Luna. He wouldn't be taking the cat with him, and didn't want to leave her in a kennel again. Sam was the perfect solution, if she was willing.

"I'd love to keep your cat," she declared after Don explained the situation to her.

"Great. We'll talk about it tonight, over dinner? Okay? Now you'd better tell Hershey I'm coming, should have been there five minutes ago."

Hershey met Don in the hall and ushered him into a conference room, saying, "You're late. Everyone is waiting."

She was right. Others crowded the room before him. Most he knew, his friend Blackie Johnson off the *Thor,* Penny Garcia, and Brad Henning. All crackerjack pilots. Don found a seat between Blackie and Penny.

"Hey, you sky bums," Don greeted them, "what's happening?"

"You see it," replied Blackie, gesturing around the room, "flew in from the *Thor.*"

"You're still herding that cow?"

"He likes the way the old widows slobber over his stories," Penny said loud enough for everyone to hear. "Oh, you're sooo marvelous." she mimicked, imitating a female passenger.

"Hey, can it, guys," Henning said. "The boss is ready to begin."

Two men sat apart from the spacemen at a separated table whom Don didn't recognize. They spoke in low tones to each other.

The general manager stood behind a podium facing the pilots. She waited until they became quiet, and then addressed her audience in her usual hurried tones.

"Gentlemen," Hershey tipped her head to Penny, "and lady, I will come straight to the point. I'm sure you have a lot of last minute ends to tie up. You have all received a briefing on what we're about to discuss." Don chuckled to himself. His was an e-mail he'd read on his way up in the shuttle, "so let me hit the highlights."

"Each one of you will pilot a Spaceways' Sparrow-class spaceship, equipped with the new stardrive. Each ship will travel in a different direction to survey the suns, planets, and space therein, of the closer solar systems."

Don smelled something rotten. It didn't make sense to send out one man exploration ships. Not that he minded. He was used to it. Still, dispatch a robot or a full crew.

"Let me make this plain people, no heroics, no landings, except for emergencies, and no, I repeat no, dealing with aliens. My one regret is we have not developed a way of communication with you." She scrutinized each face staring at her to make sure they understood.

Brad Henning spoke up. "Ma'am? What happens if we do meet one? Take their name and code?"

A titter ran through the pilots breaking the tension, but the very question was on all their minds. Hershey laughed along with the rest and held up her hand for silence. "No…not on the first meeting. You're not on a date. Let me rephrase my statement. You will not communicate with aliens unless it is necessary, then you will take whatever action you deem expedient." She sat on the edge of the table and continued: "You go in, take some photographs, run a spectral analysis, and maybe eyeball the world from space. Then you leave. You're scheduled to visit three solar systems." Hershey pounded a fist in her palm. "You need to hump on this mission, people. We have no time to dilly-dally."

She removed her glasses, and rubbed her eyes. Don realized the boss looked tired. The pressure must be getting to her.

Hershey put her glasses back on. "I would like to introduce Doctor Thomas from our psychiatric laboratory, here in Luna, and Doctor Smith, who was instrumental in the design and programing of your computer systems. Doctor Thomas?" Hershey sat.

One of the strangers stood and strode to the podium. "Good day, people. Some questions have arisen about the advisability of sending one pilot on these forthcoming missions. I personally opted for at least ten people per ship but was overruled." He looked depressed. "It is difficult for a person to remain stable, mentally, when he is by himself over long periods of time. He tends to, uh, go crazy, if you will for a better term, from loneliness." He shot his audience a grin. "You pilots habitually operate by yourselves in your profession. You have made an apparent successful adjustment to being isolated, or so my colleagues claim."

They don't know what they're talking about, Don thought. *We're all crazy as loons. We just haven't been caught yet.*

As if to confirm Don's thoughts Thomas said, "I don't believe it. At my urging, the company is including a series of tapes in your shipboard libraries. They contain possible psychopathic disorders, which might arise during this mission. Their warning signs, causes, and ways to combat them. Good luck." He sat without another word.

The other man, Doctor Smith, rose without introduction. He spoke from where he stood. "Hi guys, I'm Doc Smith and…" His words chopped off as the pilots chuckled. The man sounded like a Munchkin. Doc Smith blushed pink but retorted, "So fine, maybe I have a squeaky voice. Don't forget, I'm the guy who programs the computers. Maybe I should program them to drop you into a sun."

The spacemen became still. "Sounds better. About your equipment. Everything is preprogramed, you guys are along for the ride. Lift-off, the flight, and entry, are all automatic. If you need to record something, press a button. Or, better still. go to sleep. When the computers sense anything unusual they will record it. In fact, recorders and cameras will run the whole time. You're along because the company wanted the human factor included on this mission." He resumed his seat in a huff.

Hershey stood again and tried to act cheerful. "About the human factor. If we could send more people we would, but time is of the essence. You're all capable. In any situation, your responses are worth five of someone else's, or any machine. I don't think there will be problems. Any questions?"

Don spoke up. "Yes ma'am. Doctor Thomas? You said a man can't go for long periods of time by himself, but we can. We're adjusted. What does adjusted mean? We're crazy already?"

Thomas smiled and put up a hand. "No, not at all. It means you've developed ways of entertaining yourself without becoming bored. In interviewing seventy-five pilots, I've discovered seventy-three say on long trips they invent or write stories to amuse themselves." He waved a finger at Don. "Be careful when the characters become real, though."

"What about the other two pilots?" asked Penny out of curiosity. "How did they pass the time?"

"Nothing...they were committed." Don couldn't tell if he was joking or not. Thomas added, "If you have problems, check the tapes. They may help."

After the meeting, Doctor Thomas called Don over. "Weiss, I would like to have a word with you."

"Sir?"

"I almost gave you a down check for this mission, but the general manager would not allow it."

Don drew back in surprise. "Why, sir? I'm fit."

Thomas cleared his throat. "I don't know. You've got me there. In the last two years, you have displayed strange behavior. Not any one thing. Hmm, little things, like this smuggling incident."

"How did you learn I messed up? It wasn't placed into my records," Don snapped. *Geez, he would never live that down.*

"None of your business," the doctor replied with irritation. "After the mission, I am going to sit down and review your profile. There has been something happening inside you causing a change."

Annoyed, Don shook his head. "Uh, sir? I don't change. I keep rolling along."

Thomas picked up his briefcase. "So does an avalanche, Weiss. Remember what I said."

"Huh?"

He patted Don on the shoulder. "Keep your mind occupied on this mission. If you enjoy daydreams, do it. It's good therapy."

"Yes sir."

***

Don left the meeting trying to hold down his rage. The doctor had no right to said he'd changed in the last two years. Sure, he'd stopped dreaming then, but…

When he arrived at the lobby, he talked to Sam and made plans for dinner. Then he left going back to his hotel. After speaking to Samantha, he felt better, almost happy again. It was good to be around her while dirtside, and soon, he would have his first love, space, again. Don looked forward to it. Maybe he would even see Puddlefoot.

Chapter 5

Six months, Don reflected, was too long a layoff from work. It took him ten day to adjust into his shipboard routine. He finished making his log entries for the 'day', checked the telltales on the control panels, and glanced at a computer printout. He relaxed then. It would be another four hours before he repeated the operation.

Early in the voyage, Don dubbed his small ship, the *Sparrowhawk*. Although unarmed, she was sleek, fast and graceful. He fell in love with her the first time he gazed on the ship hanging in space, waiting for him. "You and I are going places, baby," he said the day he entered her airlock.

The temperature control in the cabin kept him comfortable at all times. Even so, he felt warm and drowsy. Don stretched out, snuggled deep into the acceleration chair, and slowly drifted off toward sleep.

"Sire, I hath missed thee for a fortnight. I am glad thou art well."

Don's eyes snapped open. Without moving he replied, "Puddlefoot, where have you been, and what are you doing here?"

Puddlefoot scurried close and peered down at him. "Why, waiting at thy home, Sire, for thee."

Don sat up and said in a skeptical tone, "Were you really there, or are you a dream?"

"Why, Sir?" A smile cracked Puddlefoot's face and he spun on his heel. "Did ye not tell me to stay unseen on Earth? I was always there. Did I not takest thy token of milk and clean thy house?"

"I guess so." Don shook his head in mock despair. He surrendered. Puddlefoot won.

The little brownie hadn't finished yet. "How was I repaid, ye might ask?" he declared. "You leave. No milk, no Don, nothing, and I must go a searching for thee." The corners of his mouth drooped as he gazed at Don, and swung up again. "'Tis bolts or shafts to me, Sire. Where art we bound?"

Don cursed the Dogerson kid. He'd paid the little squirt twenty credits to pour some milk in the saucer every night, in case. *Can't find good help anymore,* he thought. "We're taking a trip. What do you care? You're along for the ride."

"Aye, Sire, 'tis true," Puddlefoot nodded in agreement. "Hast ye heard of Finvarra and Ethna his bride?"

"No, tell me."

***

The voyage itself, via the stardrive, was short. Sol to Barnard's Star a mere eleven hours. What took time was the first leg of the journey and the last. Entry and exit of the new dimension was dangerous within the solar systems, the first part better executed away from Sol, because the powerful gravitational forces of the sun affected the operation of the drive, i.e., the physicists theorized the ship might blow up. The second was advisable, for the developers feared a collision with a heavenly body. It was safer to exit the dimension with plenty of elbowroom.

The journey continued. Don didn't notice when the ship's drive kicked in. He'd become immune to the soul churning feeling of the jump. The *Sparrowhawk* entered the solar system of Barnard's Star and decelerated. Cameras sprang to life photographing the outer worlds and recorded their orbits and satellites, but the gas giants of the double star were uninteresting, a mere replay of Sol's system. It wasn't until a buzzer rang, alerting him to the discovery of an Earth type planet, that his attention turned to the events around him.

Don switched the controls to manual and assumed operation of the ship. He swung it into a pole-to-pole orbit and prepared for a detailed investigation of the planet below.

"Let's see what we have here, Puddlefoot." Don tapped a few keys on the computer board.

Puddlefoot gave a quizzical glance. "'Tis a planet, Sire. Not much different from Earth, I'd say."

Don tapped two more keys and hit one marked, 'ANALYSIS'.

"I know what it is, Sherlock, but first let's check the atmosphere." Don drummed his fingers while the computer did its work, and again while it digested the results. A green and white paper spilled out of the printer. He ripped it across and studied the results.

"Hmm...not too different from Earth is right. Lower percentage of nitrogen, though, but a higher amount of inert gases, mostly helium."

"Aye, Sire, surely," Puddlefoot nodded in agreement, "but what doth all of this mean?" His eyes were round in amazement.

"It means whoever comes here next to explore, or live, can breathe the air." Don stopped and cracked a smile. "They'll sound like Doctor Smith, though. Who knows, he might even move here himself. He'd fit right in." Don turned away, "Let's check the cameras and see what's developed."

The ship's computers had been busy photographing the lithosphere of the planet, but no pictures emerged yet. "Puddlefoot," Don instructed the brownie, "wait here and let me know when the photos are ready." He sat the little man down and nodded to a tray cupping a slot. "I want to recheck our orbit."

Don reviewed their progress around the planet. When he finished, Puddlefoot appeared next to him. "Here Sire, as you asked."

"Thanks." Don accepted the picture and sat at his combination work/dining table. "Bring the rest over as they come out, will ya?"

"Aye, Sire."

Don studied the picture for signs of life, but all the image showed was an empty expanse of water. He grew so absorbed he hardly realized more photos piling up on his desk. When he noticed, he picked up the next and stared at it.

"Hey, Puddlefoot," he glanced around, "come her...*WHAT ARE YOU DOING?*"

Puddlefoot bolted upright from the deck of the cabin. Machine parts surrounded him. He'd kept himself busy bringing the computer enhanced pictures to Don as they appeared, but became fascinated by their production. One second, nothing, then *sprung.* they popped out. Finally, the temptation overwhelmed him and he dismantled the printer, piece by piece. "Sire, I did but want to see..." he began. His voice trailed off as he caught the look in Don's eye. "Oops, sorry Sire." He stared at the parts. They drew themselves together. "There," the brownie said brightly, "no harm done. Now, thou wert saying?"

"Ah, yeah." It took getting used to, this magic stuff. Don glanced at the picture he still held. "Come here and take a gander of this."

"Aye Sire." Puddlefoot hurried over, glad Don had forgotten the incident so soon. "What needs thee?"

"You'll never believe this." Don pushed the photo over. "Pangea."

"Pangea?"

"Yeah," Don traced the strange coastline, "the primeval land mass. No other continents. One huge hunk of earth surrounded by water and ready to split apart." He set the photo down. "Let's see if we can get some close-ups."

Don placed Puddlefoot in charge of photographs again, with strong warnings about leaving the machinery alone. The wait, however, wasn't long, and soon they studied the lone continent again.

"Yup...as I thought." Don ran his finger down a photo. "I may not be up on plate tectonics, but this baby looks ready to crack." He showed Puddlefoot a rift valley hundreds of miles across, and thousands of miles long. Others crisscrossed the continent like a fractured window. "Maybe it wouldn't be a good idea to send friend Smith here after all."

Puddlefoot was lost during this lecture. He saw something that might interest Don more than some silly photographs, a red light blinking on the pilot's board. It seemed very important. "Sire, a moment, please. Yonder, see the light? It flashes."

Don turned as the collision warning shrieked. "Puddlefoot, strap down." He hit his couch while the brownie jumped into the co-pilot's seat. They braced themselves for the surge pushing them out of the way. *"One Mississippi, Two Mississippi..."*

Don counted. When he reached sixty, he repeated the operation, and then once more for good measure. When the thrusters didn't fire, he reached out and readjusted his radarscope.

"Puddlefoot, flick the switch to your right and activate the viewer." Don pointed to the co-pilot's board. "Good. Tell me what you see."

The brownie searched his 'scope. "Sire, there *is* an object, but I knowest not what." He paused. "It follows us, I'm sure, 'tis not closer or farther away."

Don activated his own viewer and compared the two. "What the heck can the blip be?" he asked. "It zoomed at us like a meteorite on a collision course. The autopilot's ready to shove us out of the way, and then the darn thing falls into orbit behind us. Say Puddlefoot..." He had a flash of inspiration, "I think we met another spaceship."

Don switched on the radio and received a transmission from the other craft. Strange clicks and whistles repeated themselves in a distinct pattern.

"Sire, dost thou understand this gibberish?" Puddlefoot tried mimicking the noise without much success.

"No." Don hummed a tune, "but I bet the computers do. Let's press a few buttons and see what appears." He played with the keys, made a few adjustments, and turned to the printer to watch as a translation appeared:

"...Stand and identify yourself...Do not try to flee, or we will fire...Stand and identify yourself..."

"Well, I guess we landed in their backyard, Puddlefoot." Don grimaced. "What do we do?"

"Why, talk to them, Sire, what else?"

"The else is I was given special orders not to communicate with aliens." He paused, narrowing his eyes as he thought. "Those guys are talking nasty, too," he muttered to himself, "if they have so much as a laser cannon we've had it. This bucket of bolts doesn't contain a peashooter." Don fell quiet, thinking. He slammed his fist on the keyboard, cleared it, and began tapping:

"Alien vessel, this is the survey craft, Sparrowhawk, *over."* Don recorded the message and let the ship's computer repeat it while he waited for a reply.

"Survey craft, Sparrowhawk, *is this your home world?"*

Don pursed his lips, replied: *"No. We are on a routine mapping mission of this system. Who are you?"* At least he now knew the aliens didn't live on the planet below.

Nor did they answer right away. Don could imagine the discussion happening over there.

The alien vessel came back. *"We are the Vas. We too, are surveying planets. We search for a certain planet. What is the location of your home world?"*

Yeah, right. Like I'm going to tell you, Don thought. *"My world is not located in this part of space,* he evaded. *Maybe later we can compare maps."* He tried to change the subject. *"Do you find this planet attractive? You must remember, I was here first."*

"The atmosphere is too thick for our taste," came the noncommittal reply. *"The planet we seek is much like this one, however. Have you heard of a planet called Earth?"*

Don said to Puddlefoot, "Well, it's hit the fan. Somewhere, somehow, we acquired an enemy." He returned to the keyboard. *No. The planet is strange to me. Please supply a more accurate description.*

While the aliens transmitted a fair depiction of Earth, Don and Puddlefoot held a hasty conference.

"Puddlefoot, can you pop over to the alien ship and learn what's really going on? Without being seen, of course."

"Aye, Sire." The brownie looked perplexed. "What use 'twould it be? I cannot speak their language, nor have I the time to concoct the necessary spell to learn it quickly."

"Here." Don opened a cabinet beneath the pilot's couch and withdrew a flat metal disk. It was the newest edition of Spaceways general issue recorder-transmitter. He fiddled with the back and handed it to the brownie. "It's all set. Place this on the underside of anything close to where they're speaking. It'll pick up and transmit what's said."

Puddlefoot accepted the wafer and with a *pop* disappeared.

Don made the change enabling the computer to receive the broadcast. Next, he called the Vas. *"Ship Vas…I am having problems with translation. Please repeat your transmission a few times."*

The Vas started repeating their description of Earth.

Behind him, he heard a noise. Puddlefoot stood there. The little brownie's face was red. He released a blast of air. "Pretty noisy for such a little guy," Don remarked.

"Ahhh, Sire. But they breathe the most foul air."

"You placed the tap, didn't you?"

Puddlefoot's body stiffened and his eyes widened. "Aye, Sire. Most assuredly I did, 'neath the table they all sit about. Small creatures they are, with eight legs apiece like spiders, and eyes, Sire.

Terrible eyes, glowing red like the Hounds of Hell themselves." Puddlefoot shivered. "I fear them."

"Let's see what they're saying," Don said grimly. "I have a feeling I won't enjoy these critters much either." He activated a small auxiliary printer displaying the results of his bugging.

"...Kill slime. This gutter worm knows nothing of Earth. Destroy him, and all Earthlings. We rule space. The pack rules. The mother-queen of all rules."

"Not yet. We must locate his home world first. We cannot have unknown races on our flank, not at this time, not before the attack."

"Rape his planet, and crush his bones. Destroy this slug, I say. We will locate Earth and annihilate it too. They will send no more Voyagers to proclaim their advent into space."

"Not until we discover what this one knows, and where his world lies. This has been too carefully planned."

"I told you, this slime knows nothing. You know where Earth lays, one point eight parsecs from here. I told you so myself. When I am shown right this ship will have a new captain."

"At our next stop you may be proven correct. If so, you will have your chance to try for leadership. Then I shall suck you blood, until you are a dry husk. Enough bickering. You are right on one issue. We must make an end to this. The pack approaches soon."

Puddlefoot shaded white listening to this ghoulish discussion. He said to Don in a hushed whisper, "Sire, my God. What shall we do now?"

"We fight," Don replied. "We fight and try to warn Earth. Maybe we'll die, or escape, or get captured, but Earth must be warned."

"Sire, didst thou not say this craft was unarmed?"

"Yes, but still we must..."

"How, Sire? How?"

"I don't know." Don breathed hard. "I don't know," he repeated, reining in his emotions, "but I'll figure something out."

The Vas were trying to get the *Sparrowhawk's* attention. They had broadcasted their description of Earth three times, and waited for a reply.

"Sparrowhawk *to Vas. I have checked our computers and found information, which may be of interest to you. I show a planet fitting your description. Its coordinates are...* " Don stopped transmitting.

"Sparrowhawk, *come in. Your transmission faded. Please repeat."*

Don winked at Puddlefoot. *"This* Sparrowhawk... *checked... computers... information may...planet, which... coordinates are... Over."* He sat back and placed his hands behind his head. "That'll confuse the nasties for a few minutes, Puddlefoot. What are we receiving on the transmitter?"

"Sire, they are confused indeed. One blames our equipment, and another doth knowest not whom to blame, but knowest 'twas not their machine." Puddlefoot read, "From time to time a third adds 'tis sunspots."

"Sunspots. We can use his idea." Don bent over the keyboard. "Let's see if they bite." He typed, Sparrowhawk... *maneuvering... please wait... solar interference. Repeat.* He grinned from ear to ear as he told Puddlefoot, "Scoot over there and create a diversion. You know what to do. You've done your tricks before."

The brownie issued a throaty laugh. "Aye, Sire." He took a deep breath, held it, and disappeared. Don eased the *Sparrowhawk* over to come in below, and tilted toward, the Vas ship.

During this maneuver, the aliens did nothing. Don chuckled to himself. The little critter must be handing them an interesting time. Don thought of what Puddlefoot did to the *Chancy,* and her sister ships, and then he laughed aloud.

In a few minutes, Puddlefoot was back. The little brownie wore a deep, satisfied smirk on his face.

"Okay, baby, let's test your metal." Don patted the bulkhead of the *Sparrowhawk.* He strapped himself down. "Puddlefoot, brace yourself. I'm gonna ram them." He prayed the ship had enough thrust to disable the alien craft, then break out of orbit, knowing on a straight run she could outdistance almost any other ship. He kicked the engines into overdrive, feeding them every erg of energy they would take.

He prayed a final time.

The *Sparrowhawk* sprang ahead like a racehorse from the starting gate, her bow aimed straight at the underbelly of the alien craft. The distance was short. Don struck the Vas before they could react.

A scream of tortured metal tore through the ship as it bucked at the impact.

The *Sparrowhawk's* forward motion slowed.

"Come on baby, come on. Don't fail me now." Don changed the angle of thrust with the bellowing of a thousand gongs resounding. The ship leaped away from the crippled alien and gained speed.

Acceleration pressed Don back in his couch. Bells rang, and the smell of burning insulation filled the air. He tried twisting toward Puddlefoot, but mounting pressure held him in place. "Puddlefoot...Hey, Puddlefoot, you okay?"

He heard no answer from the brownie.

Don felt himself blanking out. He attempted to raise his finger the inch it would take to activate the autopilot, but couldn't tell if he succeeded. The last thing he remembered before darkness closed in was the cabin filling with smoke.

"Sire...Sire, please, wake up." A small hand shook him. Don unstrapped himself and sat on the edge of the couch. A shoulder jammed under his arm to steady him. It was Puddlefoot's. "Ye wert unconscious, Sire, but 'twas only for a minute. The spirit steering thy ship hath taken over, and we flee to safety."

Don's eyes focused. "Good, at least the auto-pilot still works." He coughed. Smoke lay heavy in the cabin, the air conditioning had broken down. Lights blinked once, twice, and then half flickered out, leaving him and Puddlefoot in semi-darkness.

In the resulting gloom, Don scanned the walls and ceiling in mounting panic. "Great. I can't see what's not working now anyway. Puddlefoot, help me up," he sighed. "Maybe we can jury-rig some of this stuff back in order again."

With assistance from the brownie, Don staggered to his feet. He groped his way to the main electrical panel, but the murk made it impossible to tell what was wrong. He coughed frequently from the smoke, and cursed steadily under his breath. When he'd given up hope of ever finding the trouble Puddlefoot, took his arm. "Here Sire, try this. 'Twill help thy sight." The brownie rubbed a thick salve in Don's eyes.

For a moment, they burned and grew cold, and then his vision cleared. The cabin was still murky, but he could see through the haze to the panels. Don switched over to emergency circuits and power. The lights and air conditioning systems snapped back on.

"What is that stuff?" Don touched his eyelids and held his fingers to his nose. "Pooo."

Puddlefoot shrugged and placed his hands on his hips, surveying Don in dismay. "Oh...a something, Sire, I keep for emergencies. But from the looks of thee, mayhaps' thou should have been kept in the dark."

Dow stared down. Blood and soot covered the front of his jumpsuit. *Where did the red stuff come from,* he wondered. An inspection in the control panel told him. He'd bled from his nose and mouth during the heavy acceleration. "Ain't I a mess," he told the brownie.

Other than gore and dirt, he was in good shape, and he itched to know if pursued followed. He wasn't too hopeful on picking up the Vas ship with the transmitter. It was a short-range mode. He glanced at the clock on the hull, pleased to see it still ran, and noted only twenty minutes had passed since ramming the alien. Maybe it was worth a try.

"Puddlefoot, check the printer and see if any transmissions are coming through."

A short while later the brownie called out, "Sire, I receive them, only faintly."

Don strode to the printer and sat next to Puddlefoot. "What are you getting?" He read over the brownie's shoulder.

"...fool. I told you to destroy the slime. Now he has holed us and slinks away."

"Quiet. You have wasted enough of my time with your prattling. Gather a repair party and see to the hull."

"I will, but later I shall drink you blood."

"You will drink space if you do not move. The pack shall be here soon. If we show signs of weakness they shall rip us apart."

The signal faded and disappeared. The *Sparrowhawk* had past the limited range of the transmitter.

***

"Well, Puddlefoot…we didn't stop them, but we slowed 'em down." Don slapped his hands on his knees and stood. "Anyway, we bought some time. I'm going outside and inspect the hull. Maybe we'll chance the jump."

Puddlefoot maintained a look of disbelief as he scanned the man before him. "Don, is venturing into space wise in your condition? You art weak and hurt."

"So it's Don, is it?" He smiled. "Don't worry little friend. I'll use a snap link and life-line so I won't float away." He clasped Puddlefoot on the back and climbed into his space suit.

As Don prepared to go outside, he reconsidered his choice. His reasoning was sound. It was bad enough he'd decided to chance the jump while still in Barnard's Star system, but he didn't want to try it with a damaged hull. Then again, he didn't have much choice. Either way, he needed to know the condition of the ship before he did anything.

As Don stepped out into the blackness of space, his magnetic boots clicked onto the hull of the ship. He hooked the snap-line on the first set of steel rings spreading over the hull.

Going forward, he felt like an insect treading on flypaper. When he reached the bow, he discovered what escape cost him.

Steel was twisted and pushed back onto itself like a flattened out tip of a nail. A pang of sorrow welted up inside when he saw the beautiful lines of his ship broken, and realized the *Sparrowhawk* might never survive the jump to Earth. He turned with misgivings and reentered the ship.

"I don't think we'll make it, Puddlefoot," he told the brownie. "She's taken too much of a beating. I'm surprised the ship is still holding atmosphere."

"Nay, Sire," Puddlefoot disagreed. The little man ran his hand over a steel panel. "Thy ship is not dead. She lives, I can feel it. The *Sparrowhawk* is part of you. She is of thy flesh and soul." He fingers traveled to a spot of Don's dried blood splattered on the bulkhead. "You have both been tried in battle and won. She is only defeated if you are."

"Maybe," Don replied dubiously. "Anyway, I wanted to find out why I couldn't make the jump so close to a planet. This is the easiest way." He reached for the controls, and began reprograming the computer. When finished, he rubbed his hands together and told Puddlefoot, "This is it, next stop, solar system Sol."

"Aye Sire, 'twill feel good to be on Earth again, would we possessed glad tidings to bring."

"Let's hope we have good news when we finish this trip." Don felt his stomach tightening into a knot. He shook off the feeling. "I still think we're going to end up as space junk."

Puddlefoot raised his hand sternly. "Faith, Sire. Faith."

"Yeah, right. Let's get going."

Don started the program running. The *Sparrowhawk* banked, gathered speed. It sped onward and outward, conveying a message of peril.

Chapter 6

"We made it buddy, we made it." Don unstrapped, stood, and stretched. "In two days we'll be within radio range of Tombaugh Barracks, and then we're home free."

"I told thee, Sire, the luck of the Irish is with us." A grin spread across Puddlefoot's face. He hopped around the cabin, singing as he went.

> *Fiddle-de-a, fiddle-dee-dee,*
> *I am as happy as can be.*
> *Over stars and comet tails,*
> *Off to Earth, we will sail!*

Over stars and comet tails? Don frowned. "Puddlefoot, did you make that up?"

The brownie was still bouncing around the cabin. He stopped in mid-flip and replied, "Aye, Sire. Why?"

"Next time, stick to something less taxing, like limericks."

Before the brownie could make a retort, the air conditioning whispered off. Next, the light failed, and the ship's engines sighed to a halt. The *Sparrowhawk* coasted on in silence.

Don scrambled into his spacesuit. A glance at the controls, before the lights blinked off, showed the cabin pressure sinking. He switched on his suit's headlamp and saw Puddlefoot. The brownie was unaffected by the loss of air, but he stood in the middle of the cabin looking about in bewilderment.

"I am sorry, Sire," he wailed. "I fear I danced with a heavy foot. I did not know."

Don made an impatient gesture and released a groan. "It's not your fault. More likely, it was the jump. Too much strain on the hull, too much strain on the whole system." Don cleared his throat. It sounded too loud in the silence of the cabin. "I hate to admit defeat, chum, but I've had it. It's time to abandon ship. Puddlefoot...pop us back to Earth."

The brownie contemplated him in surprise with raised eyebrows. "Sire, dost thou think I have so much strength? I cannot bring us a hundredth of the distance."

It was Don's turn to act surprised. "You go here and there. I thought..."

"Sire, perhaps I can travel a thousand miles, no more."

"Huh?" Something didn't sound right. Don exclaimed, "The first time we met, you moved the jumpship to a planet."

"Oh, aye Sire...but 'twas easy to do. The planet of the Zorns is not in this universe."

"What?" The Zorns were out of this world, true, but... "Where the heck is it?"

"Far away by their reckoning, Sire, but close by mine."

Don dropped on his couch. The conversation was getting out of hand. Different universes? He heard of such things, but he'd never really believed it. "You're not making sense, Puddlefoot, explain yourself."

The brownie spread his hands wide as if the explanation was obvious. "'Tis easy, Sire. The Zorn's world belongs to the realm of Fairyland, not in this space at all."

"I still don't follow you," Don said.

"Sire...Fairyland belongs in another time," the brownie explained, "far away, but easy to achieve by one who knows how."

"But if you can bring us there," Don argued, "why can't you transport us to Tombaugh Barracks?"

Puddlefoot was beginning to sound exasperated. "'Tis hard to explain, Sire. How did ye get us away from the Vas?"

"Why, I..." Don's voice trailed off as he realized he didn't have the technical knowledge to explain the jump between stars. "I see your point," he said at last. "So how did you travel so far out in space when I met you?"

Puddlefoot's face lit up. "Oh, 'twas simple. Space doth not bother me. I moved a certain distance and drifted. It took me a thousand years, Sire, but I am from a long-lived race, time doth not mean much to us."

"You could always duck back into Fairyland if you got bored, right?" Don nodded. "Well, time means something to me. I've got about twenty hours of air, and then I suck vacuum." He checked the electrical panel. It seemed like a habit. "Well, let's see, maybe I can fix this girl and make her crank again."

He couldn't, as two hours of back breaking labor showed him. In the meanwhile, the remaining atmosphere leaked away, the power was gone, even emergency power for the radio was low. The ship could but coast on until eventually the sun would pull it into its grip. Unless, Don mused, a planet grabbed it beforehand, or the ship crashed into an asteroid.

"It's no good, Puddlefoot," Don said at last. "The ship's had it. We've juice left in the power packs, I'll put a Mayday on the air, but pickings are slim out in these parts. I doubt there's anyone to hear us."

"If there is anything I can do, Sire," the little brownie answered. His mouth tightened in thought. "If you wish we could go…"

Don cut him off with a wave of his hand. "There's nothing. Don't worry about it. I'm going to lay back and relax. I'll use less oxygen if I'm not moving around." He settled back on the deck with a sigh. "Say, Puddlefoot, there is one thing you can do for me."

"Yes, Sire?"

"Tell me another story. It'll make the time go faster."

Puddlefoot started on the tale of Habertrot the fairy.

***

The hours passed by. Puddlefoot fell asleep, curled into a ball, but Don refused to follow suit. He changed to his last air bottle and waited. His Mayday had gone unheard, but it didn't matter.

Don closed his eyes and tried to imagine what he'd be doing right now if he were back in Luna. *Ah, the parties, fun, the girls he would miss…heck of a way to die….Lonesome place, still twenty-four hours outside of radio range…Too far….No one comes out here much, not even the Navy. They only orbit this way to bust some smuggler. Smugglers…?*

"Puddlefoot. Hey, Puddlefoot, WAKE UP"

"Huh…? What Sire?" The brownie stumbled to his feet rubbing sleep from his eyes. "Who attacks? A sword. A sword. Where is a sword?"

"Calm down, buddy. No one's attacking," Don said. "I thought of something. There has to be smugglers around here. They use this route for non-perishable items from the outer planets." His voice rose in excitement. "They swing the stuff outside the solar system, and then when things are quiet, run it in on tramp miners. There's even supposed to be a base around here."

Puddlefoot replied, "Why do they not answer our signals, Sire? Surely they art human with a human's heart."

"Hummm...you've got a point. Maybe robot freighters? Nah, more likely, they think we're some Navy plot to sucker them into a trap. I recall something though..." He paused and leaped to the radio and adjusted it, and then fell back to the deck with a contented grunt. "We're not out of the running yet. I'm playing an old smuggler's signal over our Mayday. If there's anyone here listening, they'll pick us up. It's part of the code. I hope the signal isn't too out of date."

Puddlefoot put a finger to his mouth, perplexed. "I knewest not 'twas a pact amongst people such as they."

"Oh, yeah," Don nodded vigorously," but we're supposed to hand over half of what we're smuggling in return. This is part of the code, too."

When Puddlefoot heard this he said distressed, "Sire, we are not smuggling anything."

Don shrugged. "I know. We'll cross that bridge when we come to it."

Puddlefoot stared at the deck studying his feet. "Sire? How dost thou knowest a smuggler's code? Surely thou weren't..."

"A smuggler?" Don gave a gruff laugh. "Well, you see it's like this, all pilots are smugglers to some degree, nothing illegal, the tax laws usually. Anyway, I know this guy, he gives me information for a price."

Puddlefoot stared at him wordlessly and didn't reply.

"Hey, don't look at me as if I were a criminal, Puddlefoot," Don hastened to say. "It was for my rudders, I swear."

The brownie shrugged, looking back at the deck. "'Tis your business, Sire, not mine."

"So it is." Don cocked his head. "Guess what I heard, another ship locking onto ours."

"Your friends, Sire?"

"No friends of mine, but they have power and oxygen. For small blessing I'll kiss their feet."

They heard the airlock cycling. Don tried to rise but found he was too weak. He checked his air gauge. The dial read empty.

"So close," he muttered. "So close." His vision became dim. The cabin grew dark and fuzzy. It became harder for him to breath.

"No, not yet I don't." He struggled to his feet.

"Hey, in here, I'm in here." He banged on the bulkhead.

"I live."

***

Don yawned, rolled over. He was laying on a mattress with clean sheets over him. He debated returning to sleep. It felt so good to lay there.

His eyes snapped open.

Where was here?

Don jerked erect and looked around. He was in a ship's cabin, he was certain. A fold-down writing desk and chair the cubicle's only furniture.

His clothes rested on the chair, hung and washed. He scrambled to his feet and put them on, silently thanking whoever laundered the garments. After he was dressed, he tried the door, and found the hatch locked from the outside.

"Hey, anybody there?" He heard no answer.

He banged and shouted again, "Anybody out there? Open up." He kept pounding until he heard a muffled answer from the other side.

"All right already. Calm it down, will yah? It's open." A short, heavyset man of about forty faced him. He wore a wrinkled flight suit and smoked a twisted black cigar. The man sized Don up, removed the cigar and flicked the ash on the deck. "You're looking better, fella," he said. "When they first brought you in, you weren't fit enough to feed the cat. By the way," He stuck out his hand, "my name's Matty."

"Don. Don Weiss." He took the other's hand and shook it. Matty's small piggish eyes were fixed on him, his grip hard as iron. "I'm feeling much better thanks to you people" he said honestly. "I thought I was a goner. Say…" Don realized he was still a long way from home, time was running short. "Matty, I gotta get out of here. I have to make it back to Tombaugh Barracks in a hurry."

"Yeah?" Matty stuffed the cigar back in his mouth. "Maybe we'd better sit down, and you tell me about it." He straddled the lone chair, indicated with his eyes for Don to sit on the bed.

Don outlined the events of the last few months, only omitting the existence of Puddlefoot for obvious reasons. Matty was silent, but occasionally showed interest by raising an eyebrow.

"So you see, Matty," Don concluded, "I've got to hurry back. The Navy must be warned before the Vas attack."

Matty puffed his stogy. "Let me get this straight," he said. "The biggest shipbuilders on Earth sent you out to explore the galaxy. You fought a space battle with little green spiders. Now you have to warn the human race about this, ummm, menace."

Something told Don his credibility was in doubt. "Well, yeah, but it's not like you make it sound. It's…"

"What do you think I am, a stupe?" Matty stood and pointed his cigar at Don. "I'll tell yah what happened. This whole thing is a setup by your buddy. When we nabbed him, you came in to spring him. We've captured both of you, and you're handing me this cock-n-bull story to save your hide."

"What?"

"Yeah." He shot Don a humorless smile. "Pretty cute playing our distress signal, too. Who'd yah sweat the code out of?"

Don's mouth worked wordlessly for a moment before he said, "Matty, I came by the signal fair and square. I do a little smuggling myself. You gotta believe me, I…"

"You're a smuggler?" Matty snorted. "What's your guild code number?" When Don sat mute in confusion, Matty added, "You don't know the secret handshake either."

Don made a sudden motion to run past Matty. As fast as he was, Matty moved quicker. A small hand laser replaced his cigar. He leveled the pistol at Don. "Don't make a move or I'll hand you a twinge of this. We're moving you from the presidential suite to someplace less pleasant." He motioned with the laser. "Start walking." Without taking his eyes off him, Matty called out, "Hector, Bob, get in here."

Two men came into view. "Take this guy and toss him in with the other."

They held Don on either side and dragged him out of the cabin. Five minutes later, and two flights down, the three stopped before another airlock. The bigger of the two smugglers, Bob, produced a key. Unlocking the door, he pushed Don inside to go hurling against a wall.

"Well, if it isn't the flyboy."

Don picked himself up. In the far corner of the cabin a man squatted against the wall, his knees drawn up to his chin, his grey hair tousled. In the darkness, Don couldn't make out the man's features.

"Who the heck are you?" he asked with irritation. Don had expected to find Puddlefoot. Confound him, where was the little guy? He was sick and tired of running. All he wanted was to find the brownie and escape. This stranger, whoever he was, better not try giving him a hard time.

"What happened, Weiss? You're friends' play you dirty, or did you screw up somehow?"

His voice, it was familiar. Don peered at the figure. Under the dirt and stubble of beard, he recognized the man. "Captain Sims." He checked again. "Is that you?"

The Provost Marshal grinned. "In the flesh, Weiss. I always knew you were crooked. If nothing else, this excursion of mine has turned up one interesting fact."

Don started to bluster, and then quieted down. "Listen Sims, let me tell you something." He found himself retelling his adventures for the second time in an hour. When he finished, Captain Sims whistled.

"You have been a busy boy, haven't you?" For the first time the captain studied Don with something of admiration. "I knew about project Starsearch, but I didn't know you were involved. Spidermen. Hmmm…Maybe I was mistaken about you, Weiss. Tell you what, let's play a word game to pass the time." When Don hesitated, Sims pulled him down. "Sit. We have to do something while we wait. We're going to be here a while."

Don settled next to Sims. The captain grabbed his shoulder and said, "Closer, I can't see you. Half the fun is watching the other guy's expression. There, much better. I'm thinking of a five letter word meaning fast. What is it?" Sims watched him.

Don tried to think. *Fast? What was this nonsense?*

Sims rested his hand on Don's shoulder, the captain's fingers tapping. Touching annoyed Don. He didn't like people who were familiar. "Hey, do you mind?" He pushed the hand away and said, "Quick."

Sims put his hand back. "I'm trying to steady you. I think you're still woozy. No, quick isn't the word, but I'll give you another chance." The tapping started again.

Damn Sims and his nervous habits, Don thought. Then it hit him. The captain was sending Morse code. He translated the message as Sims tapped, "T-h-e-y w-a-t-c-h."

Don chuckled and punched Sims lightly in the ribs. "I think I figured it out. Rapid." His hand came to rest against the captain's hip. He tapped back, "W-h-e-r-e a-r-e w-e?"

"I guess you're catching on. You're right. It's your turn." "A-b-a-n-d-o-n-e-d f-r-e-i-g-h-t-e-r. T-h-e-i-r h-e-a-d-q-u-a-r-t-e-r-s."

"I've got an easy one for you. A five-letter word meaning short. Y-o-u- h-a-v-e p-l-a-n?"

"You're right...You gave me an easy one. Small. Y-e-s w-e l-e-a-v-e."

H-o-w?

"Here's a hard one you'll never figure out – a six letter word meaning cold." Sims tapped out, "T-u-r-n y-o-u-r b-a-c-k c-o-v-e-r e-y-e-s."

"I'll have to think this one over for a minute." Don swung his back to the captain and pretended to study a cockroach on the deck. The next thing he knew a small explosion rocked the cabin. The door blew outward, and Don's ears rang from the sound of the blast. The dazzle blinded him even though he had not been watching.

"They didn't search me as well as they thought," Sims laughed. He seized Don and half-dragged, half-carried him, passed the ruined door. "Come on, let's make some tracks."

Don shook him off. "Lead on, MacDuff. I'm right behind you."

Sims glanced up and down the hall. He pointed to the left. "Let's see if we can find my ship, Weiss. Follow me." The captain sprinted down the corridor. Overhead, alarms clanged and loudspeakers bellowed directions. They ignored them all.

Sims kept searching out stairwells leading lower into the ship. When they could go no farther, he paused and entered a corridor.

Hector and Bob appeared at the other end from a side passage, laser pistols at the ready. Without hesitation, Sims raced forward and threw a body block at the nearer. Don hit the other with a French kick. This slowed the bigger man down long enough for Don to grab his right wrist and jam his shoulder under Hector's armpit. Don raised his right fist and bent at the waist. He let go and Hector sailed away.

The captain had made short work of Bob. The man lay senseless on the deck in a pool of his own blood. Don scooped up one of the lasers and tucked it in his pocket. "We go that way," Sims pointed down the passage where the two smugglers had appeared. "We're not far now." He snatched the other laser and led the way.

They faced no further opposition until they reached the launching bays. Three separate laser bolts hit the bulkhead over their heads as they peeked around the hatchway.

Don and Sims fell to the deck and wormed their way backward to hold a council of war. "Damn," Sims said. "I see my ship over there." He pointed to a small spacecraft a hundred feet away across the open hanger. "She hasn't been disturbed yet. I can tell the personal seal is still intact. We need a diversion, so I can open her up."

"What good will getting inside do?" Don asked. "The launching bay doors are closed."

"Who cares?" Sims grinned. "Once we're aboard I'll blast the hatch with a rocket. That, plus explosive decompression will shoot us out of here."

Don hoped so, but blasting away sounded like a chancy way of escaping. He prayed Sims knew what he was doing.

"We still have to figure out a way of getting over there," Sims continued. "Any suggestions?"

Don took a deep breath. "Yeah, one." Before Captain Sims could protest Don stood and took a few running steps. "Here's your diversion," he yelled over his shoulder and dove through the hatch.

Don landed in a roll and came up running toward the shelter of metal packing crates. Laser bolts ripped through the space he'd vacated and nipped at his heels. He sprinted faster and ended with another flying dive, which brought him to safety. Drawing his pistol, he fired in the direction of his adversaries to keep their heads down, and then he was up and moving.

A bolt flashed by his head singeing his hair. Don ducked and whirled, firing from the hip. A piercing scream told him his shot landed. He didn't stop to congratulate himself. He wanted to finish this before reinforcements arrived.

To confuse the situation, Don took careful aim on a lighting panel. His pistol flashed once and a row of lights blew out. He fired on another row, and another, leaving the bay in semi-darkness. He stopped firing and listened. "Come on, Sims," he breathed. "I hope this is enough of a diversion for you. I don't know how long my lucks gonna hold out."

A shoe scuffled. Don climbed a stack of containers making a passable staircase and peered down the opposite side. One of the gunmen was sneaking around a row of insulated barrels, the smuggler almost beneath him. Don steadied his pistol on his forearm and took aim, but the man below chose this moment to glance up. He flung himself sideways as Don fired. The laser missed, struck the barrels instead. A violent explosion flashed and hurled Don backward.

He landed hard, his right leg twisting. Don's perch, the containers, rained down – their restraining straps snapped by the blast. Two barrels slammed into Don, knocking the wind from his lungs, and driving him to the deck. Around him, more explosions erupted, and the launching bay grew brighter. Rolling to his knees, he crawled in the direction he thought Sims' ship was.

To his right he heard his name called. Don swung to starboard, but the light and pain confused him. For some reason he thought of Puddlefoot. The brownie was never around when he need him the most.

Don stopped to catch his breath. It was the wrong thing to do.

A fog rolled over his brain as toxic fumes engulfed his chest. Don felt himself drifting away. His situation did not seem to matter. This was his final resting place. The battle was over. The mist swirled thicker, and in it, he thought he could detect motion, as if a person walked behind a screen.

"'Twill do you no good to stay here, Sire. Come…follow me. Let us away."

"Puddlefoot?" Don tried piercing the haze, not knowing if it was real, or in his mind. "Where? I can't find you."

He heard the brownie chuckle. "Fear not, Sire. Follow my voice."

Don started crawling again, creeping after the voice through the haze. Puddlefoot spun a tale about the Pixies' fair, drawing it out, describing the wares. He was still crawling when a hand jerked him to his feet.

"There you are, Weiss. Get up and let's haul our asses out of here."

Don wavered to his feet, made it, but collapsed as his leg gave out. The captain picked him up and tossed him over his shoulder. "Don't crap out on me now, kid."

Don fainted. When he came to, Sims was strapping him in an acceleration seat. "Where are we?"

"Don't worry, old buddy…we're in my ship," the captain replied, scrambling into the couch next to Don. "We're about ready for takeoff." He flipped two switches on the instrument board and the engines fired. Sims taxied the small craft around until it faced the bay doors. He flicked another switch and the front view scope flashed to life. Over the 'scope was a grid with crosshairs. Sims zeroed it on the slit between the door and said to Don, "Hang on, buddy, this little bugger is gonna do some bucking."

Sims depressed a button on the yoke. A Bright spot sprang up on the bay door and the lock exploded outward. The ship trembled, shook and slid forward. He kicked in the engines and started his takeoff. The craft blew out through the ruined door with the rest of the contents of the bay, the interior of the freighter replaced by the cold brilliance of space.

The ship gained speed, showing off her legs. The craft was a 'Dragonfly', small payload but tremendous acceleration. The Navy used a similar version to chase blockade-runners, but this was a civilian model. How Captain Sims managed to fit her with rockets Don didn't want to know.

"Nice work you did back there, kid," Sims commented as he settled back on his couch.

Don ran his hand through his hair. It came away red. "Thanks. I'm glad those three didn't get help. We never would have escaped."

"About ten guys did show up right before the fireworks started," Sims gave a wolfish grin to Don. "When the place went up they didn't stick around long."

"Oh." To change the subject he asked, "Captain Sims? What were you doing on the freighter in the first place? Was it a navel raid?"

The captain shook his head. "Nah, not really. I had some leave time saved up, so I thought I'd take a run out here. I always suspected smuggling in this region, but never had the time to prove it. When I found the freighter, I played dumb and came aboard, pretending to be short on fuel. They got wise to me. You know the rest of the story."

Don shook his head in amazement. This was a vacation? Dedication was a strange thing.

Part 3: the Mission

Chapter 7

Don was back in Luna, this time in a navel infirmary. Captain Sims dropped him off before going to make his report. He stopped back once to bring Don up to date.

"The admiral took your story seriously, Weiss. They're assembling a task force and dispatching it to wait for your spider friends." Sims grabbed a chair and spun it around, straddling it. "I guess it was a good idea to radio Tombough Barracks then come ahead in person, even though the ships around Pluto should be able to handle the Vas." He reached over and patted Don on the shoulder. "It's too bad you're laid up here and can't join in on the fun."

Don winced and pushed himself higher in the hospital bed. "I'll leave space battles to you big, hairy types," he joked feebly. "I'm not the type to go looking for trouble. Trouble always finds me. Are you going?"

"Nope. I'm collecting a party of my own. Your boss wants her ship back, and I want to hang some bad guys, so we made a deal."

Some difference in Sims' tone made Don study the captain closely with distrust. "What deal?"

The captain chuckled and stood. "Never you mind, Weiss." He sauntered to the door. "You get some rest and heal up real well, you hear me. I'll see you later."

The next day Samantha paid him a visit. "Hi, cutie," Don said when he saw her framed in the doorway. "Drag up a chair and sit down."

Instead, she stood with her hands on hips and shook her head, her mouth drooping in mock sorrow. "Look at you. Mamma can't let you go anywhere by yourself, can she?" She melted into giggles, strode forward, and embraced him, sitting on the edge of the bed. "What hit you, a truck or a spaceship?"

"Neither," Don quipped back, "but you should see the surface car I was driving."

They both laughed.

"Serious Don, I'm glad you're all right. As soon as I heard you were here, I rushed right over to see you, but they wouldn't let me." This time her frown was for real. "You must be a VIP."

"Uh-uh. Not me. Must be a mistake." He didn't mention the twenty-four hour Marine guard mounted over him during his debriefing, and the warning to say nothing about his mission until the navel operation was over.

"How are you doing at dear old Spaceways?"

Sam brightened. "Oh, I love it. All the people are so nice, especially my boss." She lowered her voice, leaned forward and whispered confidentially, "She's the reason I managed to get in here to see you. I was able to pull some strings." She leaned back and crossed her legs. "By the way, Peter says to say hello. She misses you."

"The only thing my cat ever missed was a bird. Once."

"You miss her too." Sam eyed a saucer of milk pushed under the hospital bed. "Were you expecting me to bring her here?"

"Well, er..." Don's mind raced, trying to think up an explanation. "They say petting animals makes you heal faster, and you never know who's going to stop by."

Sam gave him a strange look. "Tell you what, next time I come, I'll try to smuggle her in." She checked her palmputer. "Oh my. I've got to get back to work, or my boss will skin me alive." She grabbed him gently by the shoulders and kissed him, her tongue probing lightly. "There, a quickie will have to hold you."

Don reached out and pulled her down to him. "You don't have to be so fast with me."

Sometime later, she bit his earlobe. "Don, I must be leaving."

"Oh, okay." He released her. "You're coming back?"

"Nothing could keep me away." She stood and brushed back her hair.

"Hey, Sam," Don asked, "You never did tell me what you're doing at Spaceways now. Still at the receptionist's desk?"

"No silly. I told you the front chair was a temporary job." She moved toward the door. "I'm the personal secretary to the general manager. She's such an old doll."

***

During the next few days, Sam's 'Old Doll' kept Don busy writing reports. Reports about alien contact, reports on how the ship functioned, reports about the system he had visited, Don was the first of four to return. Sam was a frequent visitor, once she brought Peter, disguised as a basket of fruit.

Eventually the doctors discharged him. Don received orders, via Sam, to report to the headquarters of Spaceways.

"They don't allow a guy much time," he groused to her. Nevertheless, he obeyed and

Hershey herself greeted Don at the door and escorted him into her office.

She surveyed him as if checking over a repaired ground car and said, "I've got progress reports on you every day."

Don was surprised. He hadn't known the old lady cared for his physical well-being.

In way of explanation, Hershey said, "She's a good girl, one of a kind," nodding to her outer-office where Sam sat at her desk. "I hear there's an arrangement between the two of you?"

"Oh, no ma'am," Don said, embarrassed. "We're pals, nothing more."

"Hmm…yes, quite. Well Don, let's get right to business. Captain Sims came to us with an idea. Illegal activities, smuggling, drugs, etc. cost the government trillions of credits a year. Now Spaceways has opened up the galaxy, we'll see more of these activities."

"Isn't customs and the Coast Guard supposed to go after the criminals, ma'am? I'm not a cop," Don said, mystified. What did this have to do with him?

Hershey snorted and then her face turned serious. "Oh, yes, and a fine job they do, but they are strained to the limit. What we need in the interim is a point man. Someone who understands smuggling, places of origin, bases, lanes of operation, until the government can pick up the slack. If left unchecked, these dangers would destroy our trading system."

Don smelt the cheese long before he saw the trap, and he didn't like it. "Now hold on, ma'am. I see what you're driving at. You want the person to be me." This was ridiculous. He'd been out of the hospital for less than one day. "Well, I don't work for the government. I work for Spaceways and…"

"I am Spaceways." Hershey's face clouded over as she cut him off, "about three billion stockholders and I." When she saw the set of Don's jaw, the old woman sighed. "Let me explain.

"Spaceways is many things to many people. We grow the wheat we ship to other planets. Then Spaceways hauls back the pharmaceuticals, heavy metals, and radioactive materials for the industries Spaceways owns. Spaceships aren't our only business.

"Twenty years ago the government made us diverse ourselves of all our holding except Shipbuilding. We did, but it didn't work out. Maybe three hundred years ago it might have, but not now. After five years, the government asked us to buy back the independent corporations we'd created. Parliament now understands the role Spaceways plays in society." Hershey drummed her fingers on her desk. "What I'm saying is what's good for the state is also good for the company."

"I still don't like it," Don complained. "I'm a pilot, not some super-secret agent. I herd ships from one place to another. That's why I joined Spaceways. I told you, I don't work for the government."

Hershey grinned. "You do now."

"Huh?"

"Or at least the Navy," Hershey amended. "They activated your reserve commission and bounced you two grades higher, because of your pretty face, Captain."

"WHAT? Oh, no."

The old woman studied her nails. "Look on the bright side. You receive two checks. You still work for me." Hershey continued, "Which brings us to the second part of your new job."

"Second part?" Don echoed.

"Yes. The outer fleet met the Vas and sent word back. The Navy found themselves fighting with inferior weapons, but they outnumbered the invaders. They won, but with extreme casualties, and only made the aliens retreat by exploding one of our own ships in the middle of the Vas formation."

Don's mouth dropped in horror. "My god, ma'am! That's terrible."

"So it is," agreed Hershey, her face blank. "There's more. If our best could only defeat a small exploratory force, what do we do if they return with an armada? Remember, we don't even know where they came from."

Don was mute. What could Earth do to stop these creatures?

"This is only the tip of the iceberg," Hershey continued, after letting her words sink in. "The Vas are one race. The galaxy must be filled with hundreds more who we'll meet. How do we deal with them, hostile or not?"

Don didn't know.

"This is the second part of your job. Find new races and make friends with them if you can, warn us about their hostile intentions if you can't, or stop the threat if you must."

Don gulped. "Aren't you asking a tall order for one person, ma'am?"

Hershey put her hand up. "Oh, don't get me wrong, Weiss. You may be the first, but you're by no means the last person to be assigned this job. Eventually there will be hundreds like you."

Don thought about what Hershey asked. It was worthwhile work, not exactly what he did, but he always considered himself a general specialist anyway. To explore new worlds, meet strange aliens. The thought excited him. This was the reason he'd ventured into space to begin with. The dream was coming alive. Don fought down the growing excitement inside him. "What is my first assignment, ma'am? Don't I get a course in alien affairs or something?"

Hershey heard the change in his tone and rushed to assure Don. "You'll receive all the instruction you need and more, my boy, but your first mission is to discover the home planet of the Vas."

"You want me to locate the aliens who tried to destroy us?" It was a big galaxy, a lifetime could be spent searching and still not find their planet. Meanwhile the Vas would return and lay waste to Earth.

"Yes, Don, but there's more. After you locate the Vas you must turn them into allies."

"You're kidding," Don gasped. "Do you realize you're discussing the meanest, most vicious, malicious creatures I've ever met? They back-tracked a hundred year old space probe to destroying us. Once they found our system, they plunged headlong into an attack." Don shook his head, still not believing what these monsters had done. "You want me to make peaceful allies out of them?"

Hershey chuckled. "Well, my boy, if you don't think you can turn them into nonbelligerents, there's one other thing you can try."

"What's the alternative?"

Her voice lowered. "If you can't tame these aliens, save the Navy a lot of heartache and destroy their planet."

"No."

"Oh yes, Don. You see, you're Earth's only hope."

***

Finding the planet of the Vas wasn't as hard as Don thought it would be. Analyzing records of the exchange between Don and the aliens, and the subsequent information gathered during the recent battle, the Navy pinpointed their location to a fair degree, somewhere in the constellation Bootes. Further information was scant, but at least he had something to go on.

As an added bonus, Hershey had the *Sparrowhawk* brought back to Luna Base and refurbished, a surprise to Don, as he confided to Sam one 'night' over dinner.

"I never thought I'd see the old bird again," he exclaimed. "Not only is she here, but she's beautiful again." Don knocked his wine bulb over in his excitement, while Sam hid her mouth trying hard not to laugh. "I remember the way she looked when they first brought her in. The bow was crushed, her hull pitted and blackened. She hung dead in space. Now she's alive. The *Sparrowhawk* lives."

Sam couldn't contain herself any longer. She burst out laughing. "I think I'm becoming jealous," she gasped at last. "You think more of your ship than you do of me."

Don's face drooped. "Ah, come on, Sam. You know I don't mean the *Sparrowhawk* is more important than you."

She placed a hand on his shoulder. "Oh, I know you're a big, overgrown boy playing with your toys. This is why I love you."

Don stared at his plate. "Sam, if it was a good idea for spacemen to marry, I'd ask, but I tried it once and it didn't work."

"Don't worry, dear." She reached out and patted his hand. "I'm still working on my career, and I don't know if I'm ready yet, anyway. Everything will work out." She hurriedly changed the subject. "Did I tell you, Hershey said the navy installed an over and under weapon system on the *Sparrowhawk?*"

"You're serious? Really?" Patrons at the closer tables stared at Don. He ignored them. "They've made a warship out of the old bird?"

Sam put her finger to her lips. "Shhh. It's supposed to be a secret. But…" She glanced around, the other diners had returned to their meals. Sam said in a lower voice, "Sure as taxes, rockets above and lasers below. Hershey said, 'Extra protection'."

Don made a rude noise. "If she wanted me protected she'd send a battle fleet along."

"You know the reasoning. One man might accomplish what a fleet can't. Besides, who wants to strip our defenses by having the navy chasing all over space? I wish they weren't sending you, though." For the first time her real emotions showed and she sniffed back a tear.

"Oh, stop crying, babe," Don hastened to say He took out his handkerchief and whipped her eyes. "I'll probably become lost before I get anywhere near the Vas."

She brightened and said, "I'm being silly. When do you go in for surgery?"

Don sighed with relief. These days they had very few opportunities to be alone together, and he didn't want them spoiled with unhappy thoughts. *She's taking this like a trooper,* he thought. *Beautiful woman.* "Oh, for the universal translator, you mean? Day after tomorrow." Spaceways was having one implanted behind his right ear. Don grinned. "I'll know what Peter is saying even if she doesn't."

"I'm glad you're taking her with you," Sam said, unhappy. "I'll miss her, though."

"Well, it was Hershey's idea. She insisted I take a cat in case of infestation. Still, I don't like stealing her away from you."

Sam wiped her lips, folded her napkin, and placed it on her plate. "It's okay. Make sure you both return home to me safely."

***

As the *Sparrowhawk* readied to blast off two weeks later, Don was thinking the same thing. The ship blasted from Luna, outbound for Arcturus, his first port of inquiry.

He fell back into his shipboard routine with the addition of being in charge of Peter's litter box. This detail attended to, he figured it was time for some rest and recreation. He placed a disk in the ship's player, fetched himself a can of cold beer, and stretched out on the couch to relax. As the music swelled in his ears, he became lost in a world of his own, soaring, leaping, carried to the heavens by the sound. The music cleaned his soul, returned his strength.

"Sire, did thy cat catch its tail in a gear?" Puddlefoot stood at the foot of the couch, his hands clasped over his ears.

Don startled, sat up. "Critic. Next time I'll wear the earphones. Where have you been?"

"Oh, here and there, Sire," the brownie replied, shrugging. "Not far. I'm always nearby."

Don nodded sourly and grunted, "Yeah, I know, except when I need you. When the going gets tough, Puddlefoot is nowhere to be seen."

"Aye, Sire. I said I wast nearby, not visible. Was I not there with thee in the smuggler's lair?"

"Yes, but..."

"Didst thou needst me 'afor or after?"

"No, but..."

"Didst thou not tell me to act like a mouse when others art about?"

"Yes, but..."

"Yes, but what, Sire?" The brownie threw his hands up in triumph. "Have I not done all ye asked?"

Don said nothing because Puddlefoot was right. "Let's drop the subject, can we?"

"Aye, Sire, as thou will. Where art we bound?"

"To locate the Vas," Don replied with a grimace. "Does hunting spiders suit your fancy?"

A shiver ran through the little man's body. "Nay Sire. Would I never meet those fiends again. They art depraved, Sire, to wish so much evil on so many." Puddlefoot scratched his chin. "'Tis strange. I have roamed these stars for many centuries and never afore have I heard of the kind."

"Not enough of the species to go around," Don mused. "If they're all out chasing spacefaring races, there's no one home to make a name for himself?"

"Sire, what you say may be true, but surely their name would be spread across the galaxy for the very reason you speak?"

"You've got me there, little buddy, but I sure know they exist."

Puddlefoot shivered. "Indeed they do, Sire."

"Well, you might as well make yourself at home," Don waved at the cabin. "We'll be kicking around in this old bird for a while."

"Aye, Sire. Sire? Dost thou enjoy the music of bagpipes?"

Don stared back at him in horror. "I should say not."

The little brownie sighed, put his hands back over his ears as Don's music played on. He'd listened to worse stuff, he supposed.

***

From their previous trips together, they knew what to expect from each other, and passed into a domestic routine suiting them both. Sometimes however, the little brownie tended to rub on Don's nerves.

The voyage finished. The star that was their destination loomed large in the view scope. Don settled back for his rest time, wearing earphones out of deference to Puddlefoot. In exchange, the brownie refrained from making wisecracks about his taste in music.

Don reached out for his beer, eyes closed, as the music roared in his ears. Bringing it to his lips, he took a sip. "Yeck." He bolted upright and spit the liquid onto the floor.

Puddlefoot appeared at his elbow, mop in hand, scowl on his face, and started swabbing the deck. "Sire, 'tis bad enough to waste good grog. 'Tis worse to spew it into our living quarters and make a pigsty of it."

"It was you." Don tried grabbing the mop handle, meaning to give Puddlefoot a rap on the head with it. The little brownie stepped nimbly out of the way. "Why you little imp. What are you trying to do, poison me?"

"Nay, Sire. 'Twas but a boon I paid to your palate." Puddlefoot rinsed the mop out and placed it in the utility closet. "Perhaps tomorrow, if you like, I can make some mulled wine."

"You'll leave my beer alone," Don lectured, "and if I wanted wine, I would have brought wine along."

"Sire."

A shrill beeping from the radio interrupted them. Don flipped a switch, and a message broadcasted into the cabin.

"...Mayday...to any ship of registry..."

Don said to Puddlefoot, "Well, it sounds as if someone's in trouble. Let's see if we can find him." He hurried to the radarscope. "Good lord, we're right on top of him!" he exclaimed. "There, see the flashing light? She's our baby." He picked up the radio mike and called back, *"Distressed vessel, this is the* Sparrowhawk...*come in."*

The other ship replied, *"This is the* Hell-be-gone, Sparrowhawk...*Do you see me?"*

"Hell-be-gone, we have you in our sights...What is your need?"

"Sparrowhawk, my engines have gone dead...Can you give me a tow?"

"Hell-be-gone, that's a negative...Repeat....That's a negative...This vessel

is not equipped for towing…Can you come aboard?"

"Sparrowhawk, *That's affirmative…I am abandoning ship…See you in a minute…Out."*

Don put the mike back. "Well, Puddlefoot, it appears we're going to have guests. Shall we greet him?"

"Aye, Sire. 'Twill be a most interesting experience."

They watched the radarscope. A small blip detached itself from the larger one, and floated their way. They heard a ship clamp onto theirs, and a noise in the airlock. When the lock finished cycling the hatch slid back, and a strange creature waddled out. To Don the alien resembled a truck tire with a silver bubble at the hub. He paused in the middle of the cabin, swiveled on three stubby legs, and revolved three hundred and sixty degrees, surveying the room as it turned. The alien stopped when it faced Don again.

"Whoee. You've got some nice place here. The atmosphere is breathable, too. You boys don't mind if I take off my spacesuit and set a spell, do you?"

"No…not at all," Don said, bemused. "Set all you want."

"Thank yah, kindly." Ropelike tentacles surrounding the hub sprang into life. The creature stripped off its suit. "My name's Frik, and I sure want to thank you! I never thought anyone was going to hear my Mayday." Frik finished shedding his garment. He folded his suit and placed it on the floor next to him. Minus his space gear, he looked like a shaggy truck tire, with long brown hair covering him to the floor. Three eyes stared at Don and Puddlefoot, sprouting up from the hub on short stalks.

"Uh, my name's Don Weiss. This here is, ummm, this is my friend, Puddlefoot." Frik waved tentacles at them. "Where are you bound?" Don gestured to the co-pilot's chair and sat.

"Don't worry about it, I'll make myself at home right here." Frik settled down where he was. Two eyes continued to gawk at Don, the third swung back and forth, searching for who knew what. "I was inbound for Arcturus before my engines quit, must have been the last overhaul two years ago. Goes to show you, never trust a Vegan. By the way, where are you boys headed for?" All three eyes swiveled to stare at Don.

Don shot Puddlefoot a fast glance. The little brownie looked back and raised his shoulders. "Well, it happens we're traveling to Arcturus, also," Don replied.

"Well then," Frik said with glee, "I guess we're going to be shipmates for a few days. Anybody got a pinochle deck?"

Chapter 8

$\mathbf{F}$rik, not his real name, but this was how it came out of the translator, was a trader. He started his voyage a year ago, stopped at two ports of entry in different solar systems, and was on the last leg to his homeport.

He was from Arcturus, but claimed to be a citizen of the universe. "Arcturus is a great place," Frik told them one 'day', "a real down home place. Everyone in this part of the galaxy passes through, one time or another, but it's only a *small* part of the galaxy. It's a big universe, with lots of interesting thing happening. Once you've had a chance to mosey around, one spot grows so boring."

They finished eating. Frik promised them a better meal once they grounded. Don lean back and picked his teeth while Puddlefoot hastened to clear the table. Don asked, "On your travels have you ever run across a race calling themselves the Vas? Little guys, shorter than you. They have red eyes, eight legs, and hate everybody, including each other."

"Maybe," Frik replied at last, "but it's hard to tell. There's so many races fitting your description. Not by the name you're using, anyhow. It sounds like you're talking about a Procyian, or maybe a race from out Argus way."

"No," Don interrupted. "The race I'm searching for comes from this region of space. The problem is I don't know which star."

"I'll tell you what," Frik replied. "Once we get to Arcturus I'll ask around. We'll see if we can dig up your Vas for you, okay?"

The next day the ship landed on the fifth planet from the sun. Don was glad to have the Arcturian along for the ride to cut through all the red tape. Before they planeted down, two challenges came their way, and Don babbled in confusion when the controller of the port demanded to know the ship's landing code. Frik took over. *"This is ZPQ753. Landing code number 278253, under license to His Majesty, King Gargo the Third. Permission to land?"*

"Permission to land, ZPQ753. Haven't seen you in a while."

"This is ZPQ753. Haven't been here in a while, but it's good to be home."

The port of entry Frik chose dealt in commercial traffic. They landed at docks stretching out on a barren plain five miles from the outskirts of a bustling town. A dozen freighters berthed there, and three smaller trading ships of the type Frik owned.

"What about Customs and Immigration," Don asked Frik.

"No problem," replied the Arcturian. "We go ashore with no questions asked."

"Huh? You mean to say anybody can land here without showing identification, or bring in any cargo they want?"

"Not really." Frik scratched his head and two of his eyes winked at Don. "You see, the landing code covers most of my ship's information. Without one, you'd have to go the regular route. Decontamination, and inspections, includes a three day quarantine."

"Oh." Don mulled the implications over in his mind. "The landing code you used was for you and the *Hell-be-gone.* Won't the port authorities catch on to the switch?"

"Don't worry," Frik waved a tentacle, "I'll straighten things out at the tower before we go. Leave everything to me."

As the three left, Don recalled some forgotten business. "Go ahead," he told the others. "I didn't feed Peter. I'll meet you outside."

Don hurried to the galley and opened a can of cat food, leaving it on the deck where Peter would find it. As an afterthought, he dug out his service pistol, checked the charge, and tucked it into his space boot. He didn't think he'd need it, but felt better knowing the laser was there.

Outside, Don searched for his companions. He spotted Puddlefoot standing near the bow of the ship. "There you are. I couldn't spot you hiding." Don glanced around. "What happened to Frik?"

"Over yonder, Sire, across the field." Puddlefoot waved vaguely to his right. "He is in deep discussion with someone."

Halfway to the tower Don spied two Arcturians arguing. One was Frik, the other dressed in a dark green uniform with web gear. Don could not tell what they were discussing, but he noticed green and blue bills flying from Frik's hub into the official's.

"Well, the contribution wasn't too bad," Frik commented as he rejoined Don and Puddlefoot, "didn't even have to walk all the way to the tower, either."

"Who was the bozo?" Don asked.

"Chief administrator of the port. I made you and your ship official." Frik searched the sky and raised a tentacle. "Yo, hey." He let out an ear-shattering whistle. "Over here."

A small airborne vehicle painted orange glided toward them. It stopped three feet away and hovered. "Hop aboard," Frik said, "and let's get some chow. Shipboard rations are okay, but there's nothing like some good home cooking."

He leaped onto the flat, saucer-shaped taxi, Don and Puddlefoot scrambling behind. The driver looked them over and said to Frik, "Where to, bub?"

"You know where Mamma's Place is, in old town?"

"Yep. Gotcha Mack." The little craft sped away toward town.

The taxi gained speed, dodged other vehicles as the traffic grew thicker. The ride turned rocky, and a few near misses made Don cringe in terror. He debated whether to bail out, until he peered over the edge of the cab. They flew two hundred feet in the air. Afterward, he contented himself by repeating Om…Om…Om, over again until the ride finished.

The craft landed outside a decrepit building in the worst part of town. The sign outside read, "M MMA's P CE".

"All out," Frik called. He handed the driver a silvery bill. "Here, keep the change." The cab zoomed off leaving the three standing alone in front of the doorway.

From inside the grill the raucous sound of music flood into the street. The place throbbed with concentrated movement. Frik grinned in delight.

"Ya'll gonna have some fun now. Wait, you'll see." He pushed the door open and they stepped inside.

Acid smoke swirled around Don obscuring his vision. Frik grabbed Don, who in turn, snagged

Puddlefoot. They wormed their way between throngs of aliens until Puddlefoot spotted an unoccupied table and touched Don's arm. They sped to it and flopped down.

Frik knew all the staff. He kept waving and calling out names. After they'd settled in their seats an Arcturian scurried over. "May I take your order, please?"

"Manny, have you forgotten me already?" Frik asked, heartbroken.

"Who? Frik, have you dragged yourself back here?" Three eyes dilated wide. "You did." She waddled around the table and embraced him in a bear hug. "Frik, it's been *so* long, you naughty boy. Where have you been?"

"Oh, flew in from a voyage. Out trading, you know. How are things? How's Mamma?"

Manny shrugged, two eyes centered on Frik, while the third roved the room. "Everything is fine here, and you know Mamma."

"Yep, well…Say, I almost forgot. This here is Don and Puddlefoot. Guys, this is Manny," his tentacle snaked around her, "the sweetest gal in ten systems. Now, let's get some dinner."

Frik ordered drinks and food for all of them. When he finished, he said, "It's my treat boys. Manny, put it on my tab. I'll be back in a minute. I have to make a few calls." He hustled away.

"Well, Sire," Puddlefoot said, "we art here. 'Tis this your destination?"

Don leaned back in his seat and cross his legs. "No, but we're one step closer in the right direction. We have a native who knows the local setup and area." He checked over the mixed races crowding into Mamma's Place, and nodded to the packed dance floor. "If the Vas exist, someone here is bound to know. I've never seen so many different people in one place before."

"Aye Sire," Puddlefoot agreed. "Neither have I observed such a throng since I last attended the Fair at Blackdown. There ye could see all manners of strange and wondrous things. Why, once I saw this fellow…"

Don hastily put up a hand before Puddlefoot started on one of his long tales. "Enough, please. I get your meaning." Don cocked his ear. "Say, do you hear the music?" A band had started playing. In front of the stage couples rose to dance and he saw no prejudice in Mamma's. Thin, gangling aliens danced with short, squat ones, fat with lean, while one alien shaped like a walrus clapped its flippers while an Arcturian whirled around its rubbery body.

Don felt the urge to stand and get out there himself. "Too bad there's nothing human to dance with," he told Puddlefoot. He tapped his foot to the music.

Their drinks arrived. "Sorry for the delay folks," Manny apologized, "we're shorthanded at the bar tonight. Food's coming right up." She left three steaming flagons behind as she hurried off. Don picked up the small cup accompanying his flagon and filled it.

He took a sip.

Smoke did not really pour out of his ears, as Puddlefoot claimed later, nor did flame issue from his mouth. "Whew. They should sell this stuff for rocket fuel. You could fly to Mars the way it burns going down."

Puddlefoot took a cautious taste, and then a larger one. "'Tis not bad, Sire. Though perhaps, it could use a touch of lemon."

"Drunkard," Don muttered under his breath.

Frik returned along with their food. The Arcturian plopped down and gasped, "Whoa. Talk about your phone calls. I think I talked to half the planet." He poured himself a drink and downed it. "Ah-hoo. I'm Frik the terrible, and I feel like partying." He filled his cup again and settled down. "I talked to the Vegan, and he's collecting a crew to retrieve my ship."

"Did you have a chance to ask anyone about the Vas?" Don inquired.

"Yep, did that too. Took me a while, though. Checking around is what kept me so long. Fella lives in an observatory. He was busy photographing a star." Frik waved to the food. "Come on, boys, dig in." He was already doing so. "You're never gonna find eats like this again."

Don took a bite, chewed and swallowed. *Not bad,* he thought, roast lamb with a hint of mint.

Puddlefoot was of a different mind. The little brownie sniffed at the food, and pushed his plate way. "Nay, friend Frik, this I cannot eat. Order me a gammon of ham, and I shall be happy."

"Suit yourself," Frik replied. He divided the food between himself and Don. "I made us an appointment to see the stargazer fella tomorrow morning, at ten o'clock. Here," he scribbled on a napkin. "This is the address. Tell the cabbie the scenic road. It's on the campus of the Arcturus University. Tuck the directions away in your pocket."

Don accepted the napkin. "Aren't you coming back to the ship with us?"

"Nope. Have to see a couple of people tonight, business won't wait." Frik tried pouring another drink. His flagon was empty. "Hey, Manny. Over here. We've run dry." He held up the container. "Three more all around, will yah, sweet cheeks?"

He said to Don, "I'll meet you at the observatory. Which reminds me..." He produced a thick wad of silvery currency and held it low. "Here, take this. You'll need it for the cab and such." He peeled off several bills and slid them across the table. When Don protested, he shook his head. "Nah, take it, trading's been good."

Their drinks arrived and Frik entertained them by telling stories of the places he'd been. Each story invoked a, "As a matter-of-fact," from Puddlefoot. Frik ordered a third round, then a fourth.

"I tell thee, Master Frik, she was from Aldebaran, and she had a two-headed brother who..."

"I've been to Aldebaran," protested Frik, trying to focus all three of his eyes on Puddlefoot, "and they don't have two heads. They don't have heads at all." He succeeded in training all his eyes on the brownie.

"'Tis true. This is what makes the story so interesting." Puddlefoot finished his drink and reached for his flagon. It was empty.

"Time for another round," said Frik. He raised his tentacle, but Don stopped him.

"I think both of you have had enough for one night," he said. "We have a lot of work to do tomorrow."

"Ah, come on. One for the road," protested Frik.

Don frowned. "Well...I guess so, but make it a short one."

Frik laughed. "Hey Manny. Yo." He looked around. "Where did that girl go to?"

Don scanned the bar. He spotted their waitress on the dance floor, talking to a white gorilla-like alien with a woodpecker's crest. "Over there, Frik," he nodded. "She's with a customer. Give her a chance."

"Where?" Frik twisted around. "Gal sure knows how..." His words chopped off.

The alien had snatched two of Manny's tentacles in one of his huge paws. As they watched, he cracked the frightened waitress across her body with the other. Frik was out of his chair, charging down on the pair with Don and Puddlefoot hurrying in his wake.

Frik bellowed, "You, cowboy, what the heck are you trying to do? Get your paws offa the lady, *now.*"

The gorilla grunted, and inserted his foot between Frik and the floor. Kicking his leg up, he hurled the startled Arcturian into the crowd of dancers. He released Manny and started after Frik, producing a long, wicked knife from his shirt.

Without breaking stride, Don flung himself forward. He curled into a ball and crashed into the alien, knocking him backward. In a flash, Don sprang to his feet, and with a savage kick rid the gorilla of his weapon.

Frik was having trouble disengaging himself from the dancers. Two grabbed him bodily and sailed him back in the direction of the alien, by either luck or good aim, Frik slammed into the gorilla. The alien slumped again as he started to rise.

Other aliens entered the fight. The walrus swung its flippers at Don. The blow connected and he staggered back half senseless. The gorilla wrapped his arms around Don from behind, Frik, in turn, harassed the gorilla. In reflex, Don drove his elbows backward into the solar plexus's of the alien. The gorilla collapsed again, this time with a howl of pain. Don ducked as two Arcturians flew at his throat. While squatting, he felt a tug at his ankle. He glanced down and saw a small alien, protected by a shell, ready to take a bite. He leaped sideways and tripped over Frik.

"Ooo-eee. Ain't this some fun?" exclaimed the trader. "Nothing like some exercise to work off the booze."

"Yeah, fun," Don grunted. "Watch out, incoming."

A multi-armed alien held the kitchen's cutlery, and threw knives at anything moving. Four steak knives flashed over Frik's head forming a diamond in the wall behind the trader. The knife-throwing alien dropped beneath a concentrated rush from the kitchen crew. Meanwhile, the gorilla recovered. To make matter worse, the walrus, and several more aliens, temporarily join forces. Don and Frik backed into a corner, faced by a throng of menacing creatures.

"Whatever happened to Puddlefoot," grated Frik. "He bug out on us?"

"I don't know. He must be around someplace." Don wasn't sure though. He had a feeling Puddlefoot was long gone. Not that his presence would help, but Don had one recourse left. The pistol tucked in his boot.

The gorilla managed to snatch one of the steak knives. The other aliens surrounding them wielded similar weapons, except the walrus. With foot long tusks, he needed none. The aliens tightened their circle while Don and Frik waited for the onslaught.

"For God and country!"

The cry rang out above the aliens. Puddlefoot appeared astride the walrus, a club raised in his hands. He brought it crashing down on the head of the creature, and then jumped off as the walrus sank senseless to the floor.

"Sorry for the delay, my lords," Puddlefoot shouted to Don and Frik. "I had to fetch my shillelagh." He flailed with his weapon, knocking aliens down, but was outnumbered. Don punched Frik lightly and jumped back into the melee.

Frik vanished under the attack of three Arcturians, the trader bled from multiple stab wounds. Don didn't know where Puddlefoot was, but an alien would scream and disappear from view. Don decided it was time to use his pistol if any of them would escape alive from the bar.

From the back of their attackers, Don heard another scream. The aliens parted, rather, brushed aside. A creature the size of a transatlantic rocket wheel waddled into view carrying a baseball bat, sweeping everything from its path. The giant stopped before the pile of aliens underneath which Frik lay. It flung the creatures aside, exposed the trader, and bodily lifted him up in one tentacle. The other limb holding the baseball rose also, the club swung with menace back and forth.

Don clutched his pistol and advanced on the giant. Before he could shoot, Frik shouted, "Don't worry, Don, the cavalry came to the rescue." He smiled at the giant and patted the tentacle holding him. "Ya'll, I want you to meet the owner of this joint. This here is Mamma."

***

Outside the bar, it was dark and late, the streets nearly deserted. Frik issued a contented grunt. "Yeah, Bo. Some place, huh? I told yah, you gonna have some fun. Now, I have to get you boys home before you find yourselves in trouble."

Don flashed him a lopsided grin. "Gee thanks, Frik. I wouldn't want to get into a fight or something, going home alone."

"You're right, Bo," Frik agreed as he hailed a cab. "There's some mean hombres walking these streets at night."

Don grimaced and issued a groan as he climbed onto the cab. His side throbbed from the knife wound, and he had a headache. "I still can't understand what possessed that alien to hit Manny," he wondered aloud to the brownie as they zipped along.

"Us," replied Puddlefoot. "He was asking about us. The foul creature liked not the answers she told him."

"Where did you pick this up?" Don said, surprised.

"Why Sire, I asked Manny herself, 'afore we left the tavern."

"Probably wanted to know what system you guys came from," put in Frik. "You're pretty odd looking, you know."

The taxi landed at the port. "Ya'll remember," Frik reminded them as they slid off the cab, "I'll meet you at the observatory at ten sharp. Have you got your time pieces set on local time? Good. See ya'll later."

The cab sped off leaving Don and Puddlefoot behind. They walked up the concrete strip to their ship. Don glanced at the night sky and marveled how different the constellations appeared from

Arcturus, and he hadn't travelled far. He understood how Frik felt, he had so much to see and learn.

A shadow detached itself from the ship and strolled toward them. "About time, gentlemen. I was wondering when you'd arrive here."

Don went for his pistol, but the stranger said, "No, put it away. The time for fighting has passed. I came to issue a warning."

Off on the landing field a freighter landed. A stray beam from its lights illuminated the *Sparrowhawk* and the surrounding vicinity. For an instant, Don saw the stranger revealed in the light.

"Hey buddy, you're right. The fight's over. Why don't you let bygones be bygones, and we'll forget the whole think."

The gorilla advanced until he towered over them. "No fight," he said, "a warning. Stay away from Frik."

"What's Frik got to do with you?"

"Don't ask any questions. Do as you're told. Stay away from Frik." The gorilla lite a long cigar and blew a cloud of smoke. "He's bad news, and he'll bring you nothing but trouble. Take my advice and let him go. You will be much happier."

"You can't..." Don stopped. Their visitor had faded back into the darkness. He searched for the alien, but he had vanished.

"Sire, methinks we art falling into someone's schemes." Puddlefoot's eyes sought Don's. "Perhaps it is wise to follow this creature's advice."

"No, this is proving intriguing," replied Don, rubbing his chin. "I think tonight was a setup, but I don't know why. Let's play this hand out and see what happens. It's as far out as it was in."

"If thou hast the strength for it, Sire," the brownie replied darkly.

"Not tonight, Puddlefoot," Don sighed as he undid the hatch of the ship and entered, "but tomorrow is another day."

Chapter 9

Strange hoots and smells greeted them the next morning as they left for their rendezvous with Frik. Don and Puddlefoot were still arguing about last night's events when the taxi deposited them on the side of a mountain.

"All out, folks," the driver stated. "This is it."

"You've got to be kidding," Don exclaimed, looking around in dismay. Trees, rocks and bushes clustered all around them. "There's no observatory here?"

"Of course not, bub. The observatory's up there." The cabbie hooked a tentacle toward a faint dirt path winding its way to the top of the mountain. "It's about three miles. Take it easy, not much oxygen up on top.

Don stared from the trail to the cabbie. "Can't you drive us up?"

The Arcturian shook his head. "Nope. The law says we can't go over eight thousand feet. You're on your own." The taxi rose, hovered, and flew back down the mountainside.

"Well, Sire, what do we do now, walk?" The brownie was enjoying Don's plight.

"Yep." Don leveled a stare full of poison at the brownie and started trudging up the path. "It doesn't appear like we have much choice, do we."

Puddlefoot tried a hasty turnaround. "Sire. If thou wishes, I…"

"Forget it," Don cut him off with a snarl. "We don't have time for a lot of talk. We still have a long climb ahead of us."

An hour later, they rounded a curve. It brought them to a massive stone structure, the observatory, which dominated the surrounding landscape.

A piercing whistle shattered the stillness. "Hey, you guys, over here. Let's go. We're late." Frik waved to them from the verandah circling the building. "What happened, over-sleep?" he asked.

"Why didn't you tell me cabs weren't allowed up the mountain?" Don complained. "If I knew we'd have to walk halfway, I would'a left earlier."

Frik replied in a puzzled voice. "Why take a taxi halfway to the observatory? You take a taxi to the base of the mountain, and then the monorail from there to here. You boys must have given the driver the wrong instructions."

"I did not," Don exclaimed, red-faced. "I gave him the directions you gave us."

Puddlefoot interrupted. "Sire, didst thou not tell the driver to take the scenic route?"

"Yeah, but why should he…"

Frik nodded. "I think I understand. You told the cabbie the scenic route, not the scenic *road*. Did you like it?"

Don paused. "It wasn't bad, except for Puddlefoot. He started griping after the first mile."

"Nay, Sire, 'twas thou," the brownie countered. "Quotest I, 'My feet hurt…Where's the observatory…? How do they expect people to find this place?"

"Okay, folks, that's enough," Frik said. "We still have to see the head honcho in five minutes. Let's go."

The squat, balding director, Doctor Tocos, was busy examining photographs when they entered his office. He glared at them, and returned to his pictures. The three stood by, waiting. After five minutes, Tocos noticed them again. "Sorry for the delay." He scooped up the pictures and placed them in his desk. "Please, have a seat."

Frik introduced Don and Puddlefoot and came directly to the point. "Sir, you are known as the best astronomer in the galaxy. My friends are looking for a certain system and race. Can you help these two?"

The doctor purred at the compliment. "It's true I've studied all the solar systems of the Milky Way, and most of the nebulas beyond. Maybe *I* can help you. Which planet do you seek?"

Don spoke up. "These are transcripts of conversations with the race we're searching for." He handed over a thick package. "Plus the direction the aliens came from. There's also a brief description of their appearance. Can you identify them?"

The doctor accepted the package and opened it. Laying the pages on his desk, he stared at them, frowned, and shook his head. "This will take a while. Can you return this afternoon?"

"Why sure," Frik said, "but how late this afternoon? I have another appointment at three."

"Not too late, come back at one," the doctor replied, already engrossed in the transcript. He flipped a page, studied the conversion tables, and scurried off to a bookshelf lining the wall, pulling down a thick volume and thumbing pages while talking to himself.

Frik touched Don on the arm. "Let's leave," he said. "We might as well get a breath of air and stretch our legs. He's gonna be busy for a spell."

Outside, Puddlefoot remarked, "Methinks the man lives in a world of his own."

Frik nodded. "Yeah, I reckon so. I hope he doesn't stay there too long. I've got to see my mechanic by three-thirty."

"Who is he?" Don asked.

Frik grimaced and scuffed the dirt. "Aw, I'm gonna try the Vegan, Soo-pa again. When I called him last night to complain about the sloppy over-haul he gave my ship, he confessed he jobbed the contract out last time."

"Master Frik, ye still trust this Vegan?"

"It's not like it sounds, Puddlefoot," Frik hastened to explain. "Soo-pa's been my mechanic for going on twenty years. He really is the best. Last night he told me he had thrown work his nephew's way. One of Soo-pa's repair docks broke down and jobs were piling up. He promised me he would handle this overhaul himself." Frik chuckled. "In fact, Pa doesn't even talk to his nephew now, seems I wasn't the only unsatisfied customer."

***

While they waited for the director, they decided to walk the grounds. The observatory was a tourist attraction as well as a place of science. They stopped at an observation deck, overhanging a cliff. The monorail had arrived during their interview with the director, bringing visitors and sightseers. The deck was crowded with them. Don saw an opening through the bodies, with his larger bulk he pushed his way to the front, leading Puddlefoot and Frik to the guardrail. The crowd closed in behind.

The town spread out below, and beyond, the landing field. Past the city limits, cultivated fields of grain and vegetables stretched to the horizon.

"This is beautiful, Frik." Don gazed over the landscape. "You have one beautiful planet here."

Frik nodded in agreement. "Yeah, it's nice."

"Master Frik, where art all thy people? I seest no more than three score of buildings outside of yon town?" Puddlefoot asked, mystified.

"Oh, they're around. You don't see them, though. Most of the people live underground, and a few in space. We don't need lots of big buildings and industry. Our approach to life is simpler. Common folks, you know."

"How did your people... Ahhh." Don felt himself going over the edge of the deck, pushed from behind. He tried keeping his balance, but the low-slung guardrail tripped him. He grabbed for it and missed.

Puddlefoot felt a push too, but when he swung around, no one was there. He turned back as Don toppled over the rail, and leaped to help his friend, but quick as he was, Frik was faster. The trader jumped to the railing, wrapped two tentacles around it, and seized Don with the others.

"Puddlefoot," Frik yelped, "grab hold and pull."

The brownie sprang on the railing, snagged a handful of shirt and heaved. Between the two, they managed to drag Don back to safety.

"Sire, Sire. Thou art safe. Hast thou been hurt?"

Shudders ran through Don's body as the threat of impeding death left him. He took a deep breath. "No, I'm okay, shaken up. Who pushed me?"

"I knowest not, Sire. When I looked they wert gone."

"Frik, did you see anybody?"

The trader shook his head. "Nope. Someone shoved me and I darn near fell over the edge myself. Next thing I know, you're out in space, flapping your arms like a mamma bird teaching her chicks to fly."

"Nah, off balance. I'm like a cat." Don grinned feebly.

"Sire, truly, thou wert halfway down the brae 'afore we caught thee."

"Whatever," Don replied with hot, burning anger rising inside, "but someone is out to kill us. Frik, what do you know about the alien who was beating up on Manny last night?"

"Alien? Oh, you mean the guy from Spica." He shrugged. "Nothing much. I guess he had one too many. Spicians have a reputation for bending the elbow, if you know what I mean."

"He *was* asking about us," Don replied. He added to himself, *For some reason he told us to stay away from you.* Don shook the thought off. As far as he knew, Frik played straight with them. "Let's get out of here. It must be time to see the director." He noticed a group of curious onlookers. "Attention, folks, show's over. The next one starts at three, sharp. Don't miss it."

They hurried away and strode to the observatory. When they were ushered into the director's office, they found him once again deep in a trance. The papers Don brought scattered about in a mess, and the doctor had added sheets of his own. He sat, shaking his head, frowning, and muttering to himself.

After an extended wait, Don decided to start things moving. "Doctor Tocos? Sir? We had an appointment with you, remember?"

Startled, the doctor looked up in confusion, his eyes focusing on Don. His frown deepened. "Oh, so it's you. Please be seated." The director snapped, "All right, who put you up to this? Was it Bolu? Maybe Frigna? Or is this some first year astronomy student's idea of a joke. In any case, you three have wasted my whole afternoon with your inane pranks, and I demand an explanation."

"What?" Don exclaimed. "Really sir, there's no hoax. We asked a legitimate question about a solar system we know little about. Whatever gave you the idea we were playing a joke?"

Doctor Tocos still looked angry, but perplexed as well. "Maybe it was not a joke, but..." He flipped a toggle switch on his desk, "for the record. You want the system of Beta Bootis. However, the race you described does not live there." He added with emphasis, "In fact, the race you seek does not live anywhere. They do not exist."

"They do. I saw them," said Don, flabbergasted. "If not in the system we described, then in a different one. Maybe our scientists made a wrong calculation when they back-tracked the Vas, but the Vas themselves exist."

The director waved his tentacles. "Not in that system. The Federation conducted a survey there twenty years ago. Every race...every sun, planet, and moon were recorded and catalogued. The system designated in your transcript exists – the race does not."

Don nodded, relieved. "Oh, I see what you mean. They might live in another part of the galaxy."

"No," replied the director, "I said what I meant. They do not live on any known planet. In one respect, your astronomers were accurate. If such a race existed, they might well originated from a star such as this. Several planets fit their needs, but those worlds are uninhabited."

"Somewhere…"

Tocos shook his head. "No. I checked your description against every known race. The computers turned up nothing. I did not stop there, however, some reports never enter our records for one reason or another. Four clerks combed through unfiled data for two hours and still came up empty."

Frik said, "Say, I know what happened. My friend here says these critters are mighty fierce. The Federation discovered them and fudged the coordinates of their planet in the survey, or maybe, left the race out altogether."

Tocos paused thoughtfully then said, "I will tell you something…" He flipped off the recorder, "in the strictest confidence. My head computer programmer came to work for me five months ago from the Navy. He knows all the access codes in the Federation's computers, and especially their files on alien races. We checked every record they had and found nothing. We then used the federation computers to access secret information from other planetary computers throughout this region of space. Still nothing."

The director gathered up the papers on his desk and stuffed them in a large envelope. "Here, these are your papers, along with my findings, and the coordinates of the system in question. Go there and check for yourself if you don't believe me. You will see I am right. Now, good day."

The three left. They remained dumb during the ride down the mountain, until they reached the sky-car Frik rented for his stay on Arcturus. Once they were airborne, Frik said, "Well folks, what are ya'll gonna do now?"

"We still have to find the Vas and stop them." Don looked at Puddlefoot. "What do you say, little buddy?"

"Aye, Sire. They must be vanquished 'afore they destroy your planet, but thou hast gone to one who knowest all, and he can help thee not."

"Not quite," Don answered. "He supplied us with the name of a system, a place to start."

The brownie perked up. "Aye Sire, thou sayest right. We knowest not the who, but we knowest the where."

"Next stop," Don shook the envelope in his hand, "the planet of the Vas."

"Yeah, Bo. You know the way to do it." Frik slapped his side. "Damn the torpedoes. Geronimo. Attack." He nosed up the sky car and gained altitude. "First we're going back to the ship."

"Why?"

"Because the *Sparrowhawk* is where I told Soo-pa I would meet him." Frik checked the time. "If we don't step on it we're gonna be late." The Arcturian tromped on the accelerator. Don and Puddlefoot cringed in fright. "Hang on and hope there aren't any cops around."

***

The Vegan put down the schematic diagram of the *Sparrowhawk* and smiled when the three entered the ship. Soo-pa was tall and slender, covered in short, iridescent blue fur glowing in the light of the cabin.

"What the heck are you doing with those?" Don angrily demanded when he saw what the

Vegan had been studying, "and how did you find them?"

"Ahhh, fear not. I will not hurt your ship. I know her and she knows me." Soo-pa's expression didn't waver.

"Yeah, but the personal lock – how did you get in here?" Don demanded.

"Yes, the lock, designed to keep bad people out, people who would hurt the ship. Not me. This ship and I know each other," the Vegan repeat.

Frik said, "Don, Puddlefoot, this is Soo-pa. Soo-pa, these are my buddies."

"I know these two from the log," replied Soo-pa. He addressed Puddlefoot. "It is not often one meets a member of the little people. Joy fills my hearts."

"Master Soo-pa, I am pleased to meet you." Puddlefoot bowed from the waist.

The Vegan addressed Don. "You must be Captain Weiss. It is a joy to make your acquiesce, also. This is a beautiful craft."

Don felt his face shading pink. "Sorry about yelling. I thought you were about to hurt my ship. Call me Don." He stuck out his hand.

Soo-pa took it in a soft paw. "Never would I hurt this ship. My best friends call me Pa. Please, both of you call me that, too."

Frik said, "Okay Pa, everybody knows everybody else. Let's talk turkey." He scurried in front of the Vegan. "How much you gonna take off the cost of this overhaul? Don't forget, you did me no good on the last one."

Soo-pa looked stricken. "Please, do not remind me of this sad incident. My ungrateful nephew has brought me nothing but disgrace since my brother sent him here from Vega. Now, about the terms you seek. I will do the overhaul at cost, and further, I will make good any business loses you have incurred from the delay of your cargo. Does my proposal sound fair?"

Frik squatted on the deck while he calculated his profit and losses for his trip, plus guessing how high he could jack up Soo-pa. Finally, he gave a grudging nod. "I figure your offer is fair enough, subject to what the buyers have to say. Don't forget, I could'a died out there if Don and Puddlefoot hadn't come along."

Soo-pa started pacing, his eyes closed. When he looked at Frik again he said, "I will take your predicament into consideration on our future dealings. Tonight my crew will arrive at the *Hell-be-gone* to start work. If you can join me there the day after tomorrow, you can take her and will be free to go where you want. If your ship needs further repairs, we will bring it back to my docks."

Frik waved his tentacles in the air. "Agreed. That concludes business for today. How have you been Pa? What's the news?"

Soo-pa relaxed and squatted on the deck. "Nothing of interest. The Federation drafted me to construct a new battle cruiser for them and repair two others. The fighting in the Coal Stack has flared up again. My niece is coming to teach at the university this spring. I do not recall if I ever mentioned her to you. Her subject is intragalactic history from the time of Leo XI to the Civil War."

The Vegan drummed his fingers, thinking. "Oh, yes. I saw your business manager, Knos, yesterday. He said the time was right to trade in Spica weed. He will leave the information in your mail drop. Nothing much else. What is new with you?"

"Same old stuff, Pa, except I have these new chums." He put his tentacles on Don and Puddlefoot. "Did you check their ship out before we came aboard?" he asked with a broad grin. "Is she in good shape?"

"What goes on here?" Don asked, alert. It was bad enough Pa entered the ship, but with danger all around, the thought of him tampering with the inner working sent shivers up Don's spine. "I didn't authorize any inspection of the *Sparrowhawk.*"

Frik chuckled. "With Soo-pa you don't have to ask for an inspection. He can no more help investigating a strange ship than a dog can a fireplug."

Soo-pa put his paws up and replied soothingly, "Don, do not worry about your craft, she is in fine condition, and I touched nothing. Tell me, why make so little use of her power?"

Don strolled over to the controls and scanned the tell-tales. The instruments showed normal, but he didn't like Pa implying his she was not perfect. She was his baby. "You're kidding." He pointed to gauges. "This ship makes good use of its energy. The engines are one hundred percent efficient, all essential parts are non-moving, and she's able to leap parsecs in the blink of the eye."

The Vegan chuckled. "Your ship's wiring is only eighty-seven percent conductive," replied Soo-pa, shaking his head. "I see no defensive screens, and your offensive capability is close to nil." The Vegan clasped his paws together and swung around to Frik. "I will make a deal with you canceling out all obligations I own you. I will service this craft, replace the electrical system with super-chilled plasma, and install a new weapons and defensive system. My service will be free, call the work a labor of love. Is it a deal?"

"You've solved my problem, Soo-pa," Frik exclaimed. "You hit the nail on the head. I've been searching for some way to repay these guys for rescuing me, and this is it. Don, Puddlefoot, what do you say?"

When Don hesitated, Puddlefoot said, "Sire? 'Tis a generous offer."

Don thought it over. He saw the advantage of advanced technology, and if Pa wanted to sabotage his ship, he could have done it already. Don was afraid both Frik and Soo-pa would have to be disappointed. "No, I can't spare the time," he said, unhappy. "I would like to, but I have to find the planet of the Vas. You understand, Frik."

Soo-pa countered by saying, "It will not inconvenience you, Don. I shall start on the job tonight. By tomorrow afternoon, I will be done. When I am finished, you can field test the *Sparrowhawk* by dropping off Frik at his ship. Tonight you must stay at my home here in the city, I will leave word."

Don could think of no reason to argue. The offer was too good to pass up. He shoved his hand out. "Okay, Soo-pa, you've made yourself a deal."

"That's more like it," approved Frik. "Now Pa, I have to leave for a while. Take care of these guys, will yah? Don, Puddlefoot, I'll see you tomorrow. I've still have a lot of running around to do if I'm going off planet so soon."

Soo-pa produced a phone and began making calls. First, he ordered a work crew of his own men, for what he called, "A crash priority, number one job." Next, he called his senior wife and told her to expect company. "Excellent friends of mine, dear. They will be my honored guests."

A taxi arrived for them after Soo-pa called. As they flew off, they passed a crew of the Vegan's men hauling in the exotic equipment he'd called for. Once they reached Soo-pa's home, Don and Puddlefoot faced an endless round of introductions to cousins, second cousins, daughters, sons, and wives. They fell into their beds exhausted.

The noise of the bustling household woke them the next morning. Don and Puddlefoot dressed, thanked their hostess, and left.

"Sire," Puddlefoot said, "'Tis still early. Might we not go sightseeing? 'Twill be our last chance on this planet."

Don glanced at his palmputer, and then at the quiet town waking up. "Might as well, we've got plenty of time to kill."

They strolled down the main street, window-shopping. When the sun was high in the sky, and Don's feet had begun to hurt, he said to the brownie, "It's late, buddy. I think it's about time we returned to the ship."

"Aye, Sire, 'tis sad, but true." Puddlefoot hung his head down.

They turned away from a display of tools in a hardware store. Puddlefoot skidded to a stop. "Look Sire, yonder. Across the street! A clockmaker's shop. May we go hither? Pleassse?"

Don groaned but gave him an indulgent smile. Sometimes the brownie acted like a little kid. "I suppose so, Puddlefoot." He sighed, "Let's make it quick, it's getting late." He took the brownie's hand.

They started to cross the street. Midway there, a ground-car careened down the road. It swerved and headed straight towards them. Don and Puddlefoot stood frozen surprise.

"'Ware Sire, he is going to hit us."

Don tensed his muscles for a leap to safety. Before he could move, he heard a 'pop'. A spinning sensation washed over him, which made him dizzy and disorientated at the same time. The whirling stopped and he found himself thirty feet away from the road, standing on the sidewalk in front of the clockmaker's shop. The ground car flashed through the space he'd occupied only a second before. The driver swerved again around a corner and disappeared.

Don was still clutching Puddlefoot's hand. He looked down and said, "Our friends are still watching us, little buddy."

"Ye believe the accident was meant for us, Sire?" said the brownie in surprise.

"Well, it's strange a car drove by as we were crossing the road, but stranger things do happen." He gazed at the corner where the vehicle vanished. "Nevertheless, I'll feel safer once we're back in the ship with space around us. By the way," he added, "thanks for getting me out of there. You pulled off a neat trick. You have to show me how you pop in and out one of these days."

Puddlefoot smiled and scuffed the sidewalk. "'Twas nothing, Sire. I could teach thee the way of it in three score of years."

Don did the math in his head. "Yeah, well, maybe later. Right now, we don't have too much time. Let's find the ship."

Puddlefoot turned and gazed at the clear plastic window behind them. "Sire, thou forgetest the clockmaker's shop. After all, we art right here."

Don groaned. "You've have a one track mind, my friend, don't you. Let's get this over with. Someone might drop a bomb on us."

**

Don and Puddlefoot passed the last of Soo-pa's dirtside crew leaving the *Sparrowhawk* as they pulled up to the ship. The Vegan strolled to the head of the gangplank, his business suit replaced by a pair of coveralls.

"Blessings to you, my friends," he said, wiping his paws on a rag, "how was your day?

"Interesting," Don replied as he entered his craft. "Say, the old bird doesn't look any different." He poked into corners. "I thought you were going to make a super-ship out of her?"

"I was up all night rewiring this ship," Soo-pa retorted, indicating a garbage can full of used harnesses and wire with a nod of his head. "I finished installing the defensive screen and tied them into your main energy banks. I've checked the system three times and they work to perfection." He waved to the main control console. "Come see, I will demonstrate your super-ship."

Pa sauntered to the pilot's couch and motioned for Don to lie down. Don reclined and noticed the contour felt different, better somehow. He shot Soo-pa a questioning glance.

"Oh, I personalized you seat from your bio specs. I know you sleep here. Look at the left armrest." Don studied it and noticed a series of three lights recessed in a line along with the other controls. Soo-pa straddled the edge of the couch and explained them.

"Cover the first one," he indicated the lowest light, "and it switches on a matter repellent shield. Use it against meteorites or missiles, whatever you choose. The second is the same, only stronger. Use it in battle against all material weapons."

Don asked, "Why not have one light?"

"Wait," replied Soo-pa, "let me finish." He continued, "Cover the third light and the shield converts into a screen against all energy based weapons. When the second and the third lights are covered together, they form a screen no known weapon will penetrate. However," Soo-pa cautioned, "the first light uses the least energy, the second and third combination the most. On a larger ship, with bigger generators and more energy to use, this might not matter, but with the *Sparrowhawk* the drain could well impede the ship's ability to run and maneuver during attack."

"What do you mean?"

"Only this. Your ship does not have unlimited energy for all its needs. If the screen is soaking up all you power, the engines might falter. Worse yet, since the *Sparrowhawk* has a finite amount of energy which can be supplied, it is possible to overload you screen. When you strain the system to excess the generator tends to blow. Nasty business."

"I would guess so." Don inhaled deeply. "But it's logical, isn't it. What else?"

The Vegan smiled and nodded. "Your offensive capability. "I've kept the idea of an over-under arrangement. It's a good one for the *Sparrowhawk*. I won't forget that when I outfit small ships, but I got rid of the lasers. I have replaced them with a high-energy output unit, blasters in the vernacular, used by the Navy. What it does is channel all the energy of the ship in a microsecond discharge. When you use it, you will feel a rocking motion of the ship. This is caused by the power diversion from the engines." He frowned. "Like the screens, it has one drawback. Because of the power diversion you will be left without your defensive capabilities. You may use one or the other, but not both at the same time."

Soo-pa did not look happy with the solution he'd compiled using the ship's limited resources, but Don didn't mind. The ship was in better condition than when he left Earth, and he didn't plan to do any fighting. In fact, he was surprised at how much extra gear Soo-pa placed in his ship.

"You keep talking about power and energy," he asked, wondering. "Exactly where am I drawing all this extra energy from? Magic?"

Soo-pa smiled broadly at Don, but said nothing.

"Nay, Sire, if 'twas magic I wouldst know," Puddlefoot interjected, placing his hand on the control board. "He doth tease thee."

"Friend Don," Pa explained, "the energy was always there, but ill-used. If I had more time, I would install a bigger generator, but the measures I have taken will suffice your needs unless you attack, or are attacked by, a ship stronger than yourself."

"Say ya'll, anybody home?" Frik stood at the open air lock. "You're lucky I wasn't the enemy. I could have shot you all."

"Well, come in and shut the door," Don answered. "Are you all finished with your running around?"

"Sure 'nuff. When do we take off for the *Hell-be-gone?*"

"Not for a few more hours," Pa replied. He stood. "I have a few more details I must attend to in person. Then I am leaving for your ship. I'll meet you there in seventy-two hours, which allows you enough time for a short nap before blast-off." He unplugged a small computer screen jacked into the communication system of the ship and swung to leave.

"What's monitor for, Soo-pa?" Don quipped. "Watching soap operas?"

"Of course not." The Vegan looked tired. "How else can I supervise the work on Frik's ship? It is not easy being in two places at once."

Chapter 10

"We should be within sight of the *Hell-be-gone* in twenty minutes or so." Don called from the pilot's couch.

"Good," Frik replied from the deck of the control room. "I can't wait to see that ship of mine again." He turned his attention back to the game of chess he played with Puddlefoot. "Hey, what did you do, you weasel? The knight wasn't there before."

"Perhaps the cat bumped it," Puddlefoot suggested. "Here, I shall move thy rook back where it belongs. 'Tis your move, Master Frik."

Don had taught the Arcturian to play the game on their journey to Arcturus after rescuing the trader. Frik picked up the moves once he had the pieces explained to him. Puddlefoot was a past master of the game. Nevertheless, he had one fault. The brownie liked to cheat. Don watched the game out of the corner of his eyes. Puddlefoot was trying a fool's mate.

"Bear in mind, Master Frik, 'tis all in the pawns." Puddlefoot moved his bishop.

"Pawns? Why the heck are you shuffling a clergyman around the board?" Frik moved his other knight.

Don chuckled to himself when he saw Puddlefoot's expression. Checkmate in four was the first thing he'd taught Frik. The brownie was blocked. Returning to his radarscope, he saw a flashing white dot.

"Woops. There she is guys." Don picked up the radio mike and called, "Sparrowhawk *to the*

Hell-be-gone...Sparrowhawk *to the* Hell-be-gone...*Do you read me...? Over."*

A reply came back. *"Greetings to you and your comrades...Your ship is two thousand kilometers from us and closing. Match orbits and come aboard...Over."*

"This is the Sparrowhawk, Hell-be-gone...*It is good to hear your voice, Soo-pa...I am matching orbits and will see you in a few minutes...Out."*

"Say, I'd better get my spacesuit on, or you boys are gonna leave me behind." Frik hurried aft to get his gear.

"No rush, Frik," Don called after him. "It may take me a while to pinpoint your ship." He was being modest. After a few minor adjustments in the ship's speed and trajectory, they slowed, fell in behind the *Hell-be-gone,* and crept up on the other craft. By the time Frik returned, his ship was visible on the view scope.

"Well, dang me, I'm going to miss you boys." Frik looked from the 'scope to Don and Puddlefoot. "If you ever swing back to this part of the galaxy, stop by and look me up. You can leave word at Mamma's Place or call Soo-pa. He'll know where to find me."

"Standby Frik, we will be locked onto your ship in a jiffy. Don checked his radar. "What the...I've got an UFO tracking in fast on a collision course. Hang on, we're bugging out of here." He goosed his ship and she darted away. Don checked his radar again and watched the unidentified object approach the *Hell-be-gone.* "Do something, Soo-pa," he said under his breath. "Don't sit there."

The trading ship did nothing. The three sat frozen to their seats as the single blip of light closed the distance. Before the two lights merged, two smaller specks detached themselves from the intruder. The specks fused with the blip that was the *Hell-be*-gone, and for an instant there was but one large light, expanding. The glow faded, leaving nothing behind except the blip of the attacker.

"My dear God," cried Frik. "Those were rockets. They've killed Soo-pa and destroyed my ship."

Don didn't have time for emotion. His only comment was, "Yeah, and now they're coming after us." He covered the second light on Pa's defensive panel and banked the *Sparrowhawk* to starboard. The next instant they felt a violent explosion as rockets detonated against their screen. He cut back to port and threw the ship into a turn. The attacker flew past and he brought the ship in on the enemy's tail. "Two can play at this game," he rasped from between clenched teeth.

Flicking a switch, crosshairs appeared on the radar. Don zeroed them in and depressed a button, a heat-seeking rocket of his own wooshed toward their attacker. The ship performed a series of complicated maneuvers designed to rid itself of the heat-seeker and metal chaff scattered behind the craft. Its twisting tactics worked. The alien vessel banked and the rocket sped past. The ship turned back to the *Sparrowhawk*.

A faint, luminous glow enclosed their enemy. It was the same type emitted by the *Sparrowhawk's* screens. He decided the time arrived for a different mode of attack. "Well, we didn't win, did we? Let's see what the blaster does."

"S-S-ire," Puddlefoot chattered, "let us flee. Fighting boots us not."

"Maybe so," Don agreed, "To be sure, though, Soo-pa is going to take an honor guard with him."

The enemy ship loosed two more rockets. A death grin spread over Don's face as he switched to the blaster and aimed. Puddlefoot cried out, "No Sire, NO. The energy diversion, the shield."

Too late, Don realized what the brownie meant. His thumb convulsed and a blast of raw energy emitted from the main battery. The glow surrounding the ship dimmed and disappeared. At the same moment one of the alien's rockets slammed against their bow. A resounding *clank* echoed and the power snapped back on.

"Whew," Frik sighed. "Thank the Lawd for duds."

Don was glad the ship lost power when it did. If the rocket hit a split-second later, mid-ship, it would have ripped the *Sparrowhawk* apart, explosion or not. As it was, the rocket had merely ricocheted off the ship's nose.

"Sire, where hath the enemy gone?"

Don glanced at the radarscope. It was empty. "I don't know. Let me expand the range." He adjusted the controls. "Nope, nothing there. Space is clear."

"What happened?" Frik asked.

"Either we blew the craft out of space, or they ran like the devil. The former I think. We should have picked up the ship on the 'scope." Don stopped, thinking. *Why had the alien attack in the first place?*

"Poor Soo-pa."

"Don't feel sorry for him, Puddlefoot," the trader said. "He died like he lived. Pa never did want to go in bed. I'm sorry there's nothing left of him. He always wanted his bones to be sent back to Vega."

Don locked his board and turned to the others. "Well, it's time to move on," he stated with an immense sigh. "Frik, I'll take you back to Arcturus. You can tell the proper authorities what happened and notify Soo-pa's family."

Frik coughed, embarrassed. "Don, Puddlefoot, I can't rightly return home. You have to help me out."

"What dost thou need, Master Frik?"

"I have to get to Epsilon Bootis, Izar IV, in a hurry. I need you two and this ship to take me there."

"Hold on," Don said. "Can't you go back to Arcturus and buy another one? You must be covered by insurance."

"Well, I haven't been completely honest with ya'll." Frik stretched out a tentacle and scratched his head. "I'm only a trader part-time. Most of the time I work for the Federation's secret service. I'm a senior officer, in fact."

"What?"

Frik held their undivided attention. "Yeah, it's kind of strange to me, too. Anyway, I must get to Izar, and I need to get there fast. Will you give me a lift or not?"

Don rose slowly from the controls shaking his head. "Come on, Frik. You know as well as I do they have other people and ships to go there," he argued. "Tell them what happened, and let another agent do the job."

Frik sighed and sat on the deck. "Impossible to recruit anyone else, Don. Years ago, I saved the prince regent of Izar. Saved his life, I mean. They won't deal with anyone of a different race, but they deal with me. Call me friend, which is rare. They're a paranoid race. In fact, the mother-queen of the pack…"

Don looked sharply at him. "Wait. What did you say?"

"Why, I said, 'the mother-queen of the pack'" Frik replied, puzzled.

Don snapped his fingers. "Exactly. The Vas called their ruler by the same name. The mother-queen."

Frik waved his tentacles in denial. "Hey, hold on…you're way off base. They were the first race I thought of when you said the Vas lived in this sector. You described the varmints as little, though. The Izarians ain't nothing like little. At full growth they go about six feet in diameter and gross about three hundred pounds."

"Aye, master Frik," Puddlefoot agreed. "You do not describe the Vas. I saw the creatures." The brownie paused to think. "Mayhaps they be kinsmen?"

"I doubt it," Don said. "Frik, where is this Epsilon Bootis?"

"Izar," corrected the trader. "They call their system, Izar, and it's on your way. You can drop me off and go about your business, without anyone being the wiser."

Don thought it over. "Well," he said finally, "if you say it's on the way, okay. Remember, you owe me one."

Puddlefoot was bouncing up and down like a puppy. "Aye, Sire, let us go. I have not traveled to this system 'afor."

Don scowled and shook his head, hurrying back to his couch. "It's settled, then. Let's make tracks out of here before the enemy realizes we're still alive and kicking."

After Don programed the computer with the coordinates of Izar, he asked Frik, "Who is trying to kill us, and why? What are you doing so important people want to kill you?"

Frik was busy constructing a makeshift acceleration couch. Two of his eyes swiveled to Don. "Rebels I figure. As to whom *they* are, the Federation thinks they're Spicians, or at least backed by Spica."

"The guy at Mamma's, you said he was a Spician. He's one of the killers?"

"Exactly," Frik agreed, all three eyes trained on Don as the trader make himself comfortable. "Let me fill you in on a little history.

"The Federation is not a government. It's more of a mutual protection society. The individual planets contribute a specific amount of ships, men and material. In return, they look to the Federation to protect them from outside aggression.

"About twenty years ago, a bunch of miners started a rebellion in the Coal Stack spreading as far as Orion's Nebula. There rebels were comprised of Spicians, but enough other races joined to confuse the issue.

"Rigel lays claim to this portion of space. She moved against the miners and pushed the rebels back to the region of the Coal Stack where they started. Things looked good for Rigel, until the insurgents started receiving men and ships from an outside source. The fighting stared again, but this time the rebels tried for a takeover of Rigel itself.

"To make a long story short, Rigel called for Federation help. After some delay, the Federation intervened and crushed the rebellion. Everyone suspected Spica as the outside source who helped the rebels, but no one could prove anything, and of course, Spica denied the whole matter."

"I think I understand it," Don said. "The rebels were Spicians. As long as the fighting went their way, the mother system was glad to stay out of it. Once the rebels started losing, somebody called home and hollered, 'Rally around the flag, boys'. Spica did, but unofficially, of course." He looked puzzled. "I don't see what an old war has to do with the here and now, though. You said all this took place twenty years ago." Don flipped switches on his panel and checked their progress. Nodding, he relaxed and turned back to Frik. "Go on."

"This is where we come in," Frik continued. "The Federation discovered a plot to overthrow the mother-queen of Izar.

"Izar is not a member of the Federation. It never has been, and doesn't want to be. They cooperate with us only when they want to and have a big enough Navy so no one is tempted to bother them. In that respect, they are proud of their neutrality.

"That is under the present ruler. The Federation has evidence showing the plot to overthrow the mother-queen is backed by Spica. Now, Spica has a big Navy, too. Combine their military with the Izarian Navy, and you have a force able to rival the Federation's."

Don checked his board again, nodded in satisfaction, and unstrapped himself. Frik scurried over and squatted next to him. "When I was dirtside, I picked up details of the plot. Names, places, and times proving the conspiracy to the mother-queen. I also picked up one other important piece of information from Soo-pa."

"Soo-pa?" Don said, surprised. "What did he have to do with this?"

"He was my dirtside contact," Frik explained. "He supplied me the last piece of information bringing this whole thing together."

"Huh?"

"The renewed fighting in the Coal Stack. With the backing of a Spic-Izar alliance, the rebels will be able to defeat anything in the sector. Then the Spicians can draw a neat line from the Coal Stack through Spica to Izar and split the Federation in half!"

Puddlefoot unstrapped himself from the co-pilot's seat and looked from Frik to Don with a worried expression. "'Twould mean war throughout the whole galaxy," he exclaimed.

Don said, "Divide and conquer. With most of the Federation's forces busy in the Coal Stack, and the Federation itself divided in two, Spica can pick off the member worlds at leisure."

"Right, but it's worse than you can imagine," exclaimed Frik. "Once the planets realize the Federation is powerless to stop the Spician-Izarian forces, they're gonna become spooked. First thing you know, the members will start withdrawing their ships from the Federation to protect their own worlds. Pretty soon a stampede will start, and the only unified forces will be those of the Spicians."

"It could happen," Don said, rubbing his chin. "It's why you have to get to Izar. To stop fighting before war starts."

"Now you've got the picture." Frik's tentacles waved in the air. "I'm the only one the mother-queen and prince regent will listen to. They have the best spy system in the galaxy and know it. They don't trust any other information but their own."

***

The principle planet of Izar was a chaos of broken crags and snow covered valleys. The powers of nature had run amuck in the formation of this frozen world. From space, Don saw huge symmetrical impact craters where meteorites punched through the thin atmosphere, adding to the devastation of the landscape. The planet was desolated, lifeless, and dead. Don observed no trace of vegetation, nor did he see evidence of any liquid water.

"Intelligent life lives here?" Don asked, incredulous.

"Yep." Frik joined him by the viewer. "Not on the surface, of course. They retreated to the interior eons ago as the planet died. They live in caverns underneath the ground now. Pretty nice, too. They never have to worry about the weather."

"Master Frik," Puddlefoot asked the trader, "how do they see? Isn't it dark in these nether regions?"

Frik chuckled and rubbed the brownie's head. "No problem, Puddlefoot. Natural phosphorescence of the rock gives the people plenty of light, dim to our eyes, though, but don't forget, the Izarians are civilized. They have artificial lights and all the modern conveniences. Electricity, atomic power, taxes. If you want to insult an Izarian, indicate his culture is not up to the standards of the rest of the galaxy. Watch out, you do so at your own risk."

Underground living didn't bother Don. He spent more time in the tunnels of Luna Base than he had on Earth in the last ten years. He asked with a worried expression on his face, "Talking about civilization, where is this fleet of theirs? We've been in their space for three days, and we haven't been challenged once."

"Keep playing the code I gave you over the radio, and we won't see their Navy, I hope," advised Frick, "unless the coup had already taken place."

"In that case they would be swarming over us like an angry hive of bees." Don scanned his forward view scope. "Where is their spaceport, anyhow?"

Frik pointed to a low row of mountains rising on the landscape. "I've chosen a deserted field to land on. Part of the code lets the mother-queen know which one. It should be coming up soon on your port. I don't want anyone to see us arrive. Did I tell you it's an extinct volcano?"

Don glanced up from his 'scope in surprise. "No. You expect me to land in a volcano? Are you nuts?"

Frik waved him off. "Extinct volcano, I said. It hasn't erupted in fifty thousand years."

Don shook his head in denial. "Uh-uh. If it hasn't exploded in so many eons, it's due."

"Have it your own way, buddy." Frik gestured to the 'scope. "There it is, in front of you. We either land, or float around up here forever. Take your pick."

Don studied his port view scope and saw the outline of a ragged mountain, its sides corroded by countless lava flows, but Frik was right. The cone was quiet, dead somehow. It had not been active for ages. "Very well, Frik, you win," he conceded with his fingers crossed. "We're going in for a landing. Hang on to your seats. Puddlefoot," he said to the brownie, "do you know any prayers?"

The brownie bobbed his head. "Aye Sire, one. Why dost thou ask?"

Don smirked. "Curious, but if you know one, this is the time to say it, to be on the safe side, you know."

Puddlefoot appeared dubious, but said, "Aye Sire, if devotions be your wish." The little brownie clasped his hands and bowed his head. "Now I lay me down to sleep . . . ."

"Sheesh." Don gave him a sidelong glance. "I didn't think you'd take me literally."

Don eased the *Sparrowhawk* over the cone of the volcano, and started his decent into the guts of the ancient mountain. As the ship sank lower into the bowels of the volcano, he noticed the temperature of the atmosphere begin to rise. After they settled to the hardened lava plug, the temperature read seventy degrees Fahrenheit. Nor was it dark. As Frik mentioned, the rock issued a faint light. Don checked the atmosphere and found it breathable. Barely. He resolved to wear a respirator and oxygen pack. "Well, this must be the place." He unsnapped his safety web and said to Frik, "What next?"

Frik was busy staring at the view scope. He swiveled one eye at Don and said, "Next is, we wait. If you haven't realized the fact by now, we're been under constant surveillance since we entered this system. They're watching us now. Since we aren't vaporized by their Navy, being alive shows the mother-queen recognized my code and is honoring the signal. I told you, though, they're paranoid. Give the folks a few minutes to check us over. They'll send a courier to collect us before too long."

Don grunted and started hauling out survival gear he would need on the planet. Puddlefoot watched and shrugged with faint scorn. He didn't have to worry about low air pressure, or the lack of potable water.

Frik's reaction was more drastic. "What the heck do you think you're doing?" He grabbed a respirator and canteen from Don's hand and stuffed them back in the locker. "Yah want to insult them? I told you they're touchy. If you walk out wearing all that stuff they'll think you don't like their planet."

Don snatched his gear back, feeling on edge. "Well, I don't," he snapped. "There's not enough oxygen in the air to breathe, and not enough pressure to get what little oxygen there is into my lungs. Where do you think I was born, Tibet?"

A bang on the ship's bull interrupted them. Frik gave Don a dirty look. "Carry the oxygen and use it if you must. The rest of this stuff stays."

Don entered the airlock muttering to himself about what he'd do with the oxygen bottle if he suffocated. He did not mention the pistol tucked in his boot. He knew what Frik would say about *that.* He closed the hatch and set the controls to cycle, feeling the pressure change to Izarian normal, and hoping his nose wouldn't start bleeding. He didn't want to embarrass the trader.

Undogging the outer hatch, the three stepped onto the frozen magma. Don drew a labored breath and coughed. *Rotten eggs.* The air was loaded with sulfur on top of everything else. He quickly placed the oxygen mask to his face and inhaled deeply. Frik gave him another look, and swung to the two Izarians who'd come to greet them.

"Honorable Izar. I am Frik, known to your Prince and Mother-Queen as friend," the trader intoned, bowing low. "I have come bearing news and bringing others who are friends, also. We seek…"

"Can the chatter alien and get in the ground car."

Frik stopped short and gaped at the Izarian. "Huh? The mother-queen…I want to see her."

"Well, she doesn't want to see you." A snub-nosed laser appeared in the Izarian's claw, his spiderlike body tensed, ready to spring to the attack if he saw any sign of resistance. The other Izarian scurried closer, mandibles clicking.

Don meant to resist. With a sudden motion, he swung the oxygen tank over his head, smashing it against the alien's claw. He jumped high, planning to crush the life out of the Izarian, but he'd forgotten the lower air pressure. His leap carried him past his adversary, and he landed, sprawling, on the lava floor. Before he could recover, he felt an immense, hairy body fall on him. He struggled, but the lack of oxygen hampered, made his reactions slow and weak. The Izarian had no trouble subduing him.

They bound Don, arms and legs, with a sticky substance exuded from their bodies, and then tossed him in the back of the car. A second later, a heavy weight thumped against his back. He twisted his head and found himself staring into two of Frik's eyes. The third extended to full length studying their surroundings. The Izarians had bound him similar to Don, but left the trader ungagged. They'd given up trying to locate his mouth.

The two Izarians piled in the front seat of the vehicle and drove down a conduit leading away from the landing. Bumped, jostled around, and tossed high in the air when the car hit a pothole,

Don and Frik were in jeopardy of hurling from the car. A long claw reached back, pushing Don down to the backseat again.

Unfortunately, Frik occupied this particular spot. The two spent the rest of the trip gazing into each other's eyes.

Their ride ended before a dull granite wall. The driver blew his horn twice and settled back to wait, while the other twisted around and inspected them.

"Ivan," their guard addressed the driver, "comrade Bonsh will be well pleased with our catch. His agents have been chasing these two over half the galaxy."

"Quiet, Stephen. I don't need your senseless prattling. See to the Earthling. He is having trouble breathing."

Don was suffocating. His tortured lungs couldn't draw in enough air with the gag stuffed in his mouth. He thrashed about in panic as his vision went blurry. A claw fumbled at the back of his head, and the gag disappeared. He drew huge lungfuls of the thin air into his chest.

"There," said Stephen with a satisfied grunt, "he can breathe again. These Earthlings are such weak creatures," he commented to his companion, "I am surprised Comrade Bonsh was fearful of them."

The driver, Ivan, corrected the other in a soft voice. "He only wished to tie down lose ends in one sector of space. Now, silence. The door is opening." A portion of the wall dilated sideways. The ground car roared into life and sped through the aperture, following a tunnel, which continued on the other side.

The second portion of the journey was short. They entered a cavern pot-marked with the mouths of caves. The car screeched to a halt before one. This cave blocked by a large boulder plugging its entrance.

"Put these two in with the other," Ivan commanded. Stephen dragged Don and Frik from the car. They fell to the earth. "I am going to report to Comrade Bonsh," Ivan said as he scurried away. "Be sure you stand guard here. We don't need them getting free and causing problems at this stage of the game."

"Yes, Ivan," Stephen grumbled, "it shall be done."

The alien walked down the line of caves, disappearing into one at the extreme end of the cavern. Stephen watched him leave then scurried to the boulder. He put his back to it, and with eight claws straining, pushed the rock aside. "In you go, Earthling." He picked Don up by his bindings. "Tomorrow the mother-queen falls, and then you will be bait for the ziths." He tossed Don in.

Frik bounced in next. The boulder slammed back in place. They sat alone in semi-darkness.

The cave was still. The light-bearing rock prevailing elsewhere in this subterranean world was missing, except for a few, small patches scattered about.

"Frik, are you all right?" Don whispered through the blackness.

"Old buddy, I sure am sorry I brought you into the mess," the mournful reply came back, "I truly am."

Don listened, squirmed in the direction of the trader. "Don't worry about it Frik. You didn't know."

They rested in silence, each collecting his thoughts, when out of the darkness another voice spoke. "Frik…is that you?"

"Who's talking?" the trader exclaimed, startled. The timid voice held no threat in it. Frik peered into the black and said, "Wait a minute. Reggie, are you in here with us?"

The voice replied in relief, "Oh, yes. You remember me. Thank the mother-queen you're here."

"How did you get into this mess, Reggie?" Frik demanded. "Your mother doesn't let you out by yourself."

"Excuse me," Don said, butting in, "but will someone please tell me what's going on?"

"Huh? Oh. This here's the prince regent, Don." Frik said in a dramatic voice, "Reginald Nicholas Ramonof the Third, Emperor of all the suns under God, Protector of the weak, and Duke of, of, ahhh, I forget. Reggie, this is my buddy, Don."

"Don," the voice sounded stronger, "thank you for rushing here to save our royal person. When this crisis has passed, you may call upon me for your slightest want. You are now bestowed the title, 'Friend to the Crown', and may talk to me whenever you wish."

"Gee, thanks," Don said, awed. "This isn't getting us out of here, though. Frik, do you have any ideas?"

"Nope, I'm plum out." The shadowy outline of Frik's bound tentacles waved helplessly. "Maybe Puddlefoot will spring us. Whatever happened to the little critter anyway? He take off on us again?"

Don sighed and wiggled over. A sharp piece of rock was sticking him in the rump. "I don't know, but he must be around. I'm not going to wait on him, though. Don't worry he'll show up in his own good time."

Don's eyes adjusted to the lower light level in the cave and he could make out shapes. He squirmed the rest of the way to the Arcturian and stopped to catch his breath. "Frik, come closer, let me take a look at your bonds." The trader inched himself over and pushed his tentacles forward.

On closer inspection, Don saw the substance the Izarians used to bind them was composed of thick threads. He checked to see if they joined, but didn't find them knotted in any manner. He thought up, and dismissed, several schemes to rid Frik of his bonds. Finally, he hit upon an idea that might work. He sniffed the threads and resolved to gnaw his way through them.

Don opened his mouth, and stopped, his teeth a scant half-inch away from the bindings. He recalled how the Izarians produced the threadlike substance, and felt nauseated. "Reggie…what is this stuff?"

"Why it's a bodily fluid excreted during…"

"Enough," Don groaned. "After this, I think I'm gonna be sick." He gulped more air and applied his teeth to the threads.

Don gnawed at the bonds until his jaws ached, and then tried tugging on them with his teeth, but as much as he'd chewed, the threads would not part. In despair, he gave up and pulled his mouth away.

All this time Frik was flexing his tentacles, straining with all his strength, trying to assist Don's efforts to free him. Unexpectedly he exclaimed, "You did it. This gook is starting to break."

Don took a deep breath and exclaimed, "I didn't do anything. The threads…"

With a last effort Frik pulled. For a second nothing happened, and then the threads parted and he was free.

"Ah, that's better." The trader extended his tentacles to their full length and stretched. "Get back, Don. I can do the rest myself." He produced a small penknife from inside his pressure suit and sawed away. His best efforts, however, proved fruitless and he wound up staring in bafflement from knife to his bonds and back again.

Don was busy examining the broken ends of the threads. They were soft and mushy, as he watched they melted to jelly.

"Frik, swing your legs over here," he ordered with a smirk, "and I'll show you how it's done." Don chewed on the remaining threads, making sure he worked plenty of saliva into the ropes. "Wait two minutes and give them a tug. It won't take long. My mouth was dry the first time." Before Frik could demand an explanation, he was busy at his own bindings.

When they were both free, Frik studied Don. "How'd you gnaw through those ropes, boy? You got steel jaws or something?"

"Nay, something much better," Don scoffed, "Ptyalin. This stuff must have a starch base. My saliva dissolves it."

"Well, I'll be darned." guffawed the trader.

"Ahumph," came a sound out of the darkness. "It seems you gentlemen have forgotten something."

"Oh, sorry Prince." Don hurried to the regent working up more spit. "I'll have you free in a jiff."

Chapter 11

After releasing Reggie, the three huddled together, planning their next move. Through a crack between the cave mouth and the boulder, they observed the lone guard. Stephen lounged against the car, staring at colorful pictures in a magazine.

The prince motioned them away from the entrance and said in a whisper, "I know this one of old. He was a member of the Palace Guard until the Master of the Guard demoted him and sent him back to the ranks for sleeping. He is stupid. It won't be hard to trick him. Now…"

The prince searched the floor of the cave until he turned up two large stones. "Frik, take this rock and stand over here. Don," Reggie handed him the other stone, "you take this and stand over there. Here is what we're going to do…"

The prince regent approached the entrance again. He called out, "Stephen. Oh, Stephen – come quick. I fear the Earthling has hurt himself."

Stephen dropped his magazine and scurried close to the boulder. "Who is speaking?" he said, trying to peer into the crack. "What is happening in there?"

"You know me," Reggie called back. "This is your Prince, Prince Reginald."

"What do *you* want? You can't tell me what to do, Sire. You're on your way out."

Reggie frowned but replied, "It's not for me, Stephen. The poor Earthling gasps for air and trembles. I fear he is dying. My arms and legs are bound, and I can't help him. Please, come in here and see to him?"

Stephen shook his head. "Well, I'd like to, Sire, but Ivan would be vexed if he found me in there."

"Surely Ivan doesn't want the Earthling dead," Reggie said reasonably, "or he wouldn't be saving him. Now hurry. The Earthling dies."

Stephen scratched his head and looked woebegone. He glanced around for someone to advise him, then stared at the cave again and came to a decision. Putting his back to the boulder, he pushed, and when the rock rolled far enough to crawl past, stuck his head inside.

From either side of the opening stones crashed down, with a grunt the Izarian collapsed to the floor. Frik and Don grabbed the lifeless body and dragged it deeper into the cave, the prince binding him in the same fashion they had been, while Frik stuffed a gag in his mouth.

Don strode to the entrance of the cave and poked his head outside. Peering around, he checked for more rebels, but the cavern floor was deserted. "The coast is clear," he shouted back.

"Well," Frik said from behind, poking him in the rump, "move your skinny fanny out of the way so we can get out of here."

Don bit back a remark, wiggled out the rest of the way, and stood. He ran to the car and hopped into the driver's seat. "Come on," he shouted to the others. "Let's get." He stared at the array of pedals, switches, and dials. "I'm a pilot," he muttered, "I can do this." He flipped a toggle switch to see if the car would start.

The windshield wipers turned on.

"Don, scoot over and let me drive."

The prince regent leaned over the door, Frik fidgeting beside him. "Reggie, you know how to operate one of these things?"

"Do I? I told you, scoot over." Don did so. The prince jumped in the vacated seat while Frik piled in the back. "Now watch my dust." Reggie performed a complicated motion using six of his claws. The engine roared into life. He threw the vehicle in gear and peeled rubber. The car gained speed, bumped, and swerved around rocks, hitting a pothole on its way through the cavern.

A few curious Izarians poked their heads out from other caves as they drove by, but no alarm sounded. The car left the cavern behind, traveling down a featureless conduit. Don kept watch to the rear for signs of pursuit but relaxed when he saw none. A thought struck him. "Reggie, do you know where you're going?"

The prince was enjoying himself, wind blowing his hair back. "I think so," he said, swerving around a rock, "I remember my father taking me down these tunnels when I was a child. We are in the deserted section."

"Deserted?" Don asked, worried. "Why is it deserted?"

The prince chuckled. "According to legend, a thousand years ago an alien monster was said to have invaded these ways. Since then everyone is afraid to come here. Foolish, of course, but the peasants believe it."

"Fostered, no doubt, by the rebels," Don said, "but not for a thousand years?"

"You would be surprised," the prince retorted. "Someone is always trying to rebel on this world." Reggie paused in reflection. "What better place to hide then in the deserted section. That's why my father brought me here, he said. So I could find my way out if I were forced here."

"Your father was a good man," Frik agreed. "I remember him well from my first trip. He always tried to do the best for you."

"Yeah, Dad was good." Reggie nodded. He slammed on his brakes, swerved, and sped up again.

Frik leaned on the back of the front seat and shouted, "I recall a time, why, it was just before your mother, the mother-queen I mean, ate him he…"

"What did you say?" Don bolted upright in his seat and stared at his companions in disbelief.

"What's the matter, buddy?" Frik asked with concern.

Don stared at him, aghast. "Did you say the mother-queen ate her husband? Reggie, what is he babbling about?"

"How else, Earthling? The king fertilizes the queen. When they assure enough spawn, she eats the king to make way for the prince regent. I will marry and there will be a new mother-queen. The cycle continues." Reggie braked the car and cut down a different tunnel. "How else can we create room for the new?"

"Don't know. Retirement homes, maybe? I guess it makes some sort of sense. When do we get out of these tunnels?"

"Right," agreed Frik, looking at the featureless tunnel. "Are we any closer to the palace?"

Reggie laughed. "Of course. Didn't I tell you I know these ways? We're almost out. Our delivery won't be long now." He turned right and drove for a few more miles, until they came to a fork in the road. He slowed, hesitated, and halt as he studied the two branches. Gunning the engine, he drove up the right hand fork for a hundred yards, and stopped. He backed up to the junction.

"What's the matter," Frik asked the prince. "We take a wrong turn?"

Reggie scratched his chin. "This fork is familiar, but I don't know which tunnel is the right one."

Don examined the two roads, but didn't see any feature indicating one was better than the other. "We went down one and you didn't recognize anything. Let's try the other and see what happens," he suggested.

Reggie drove up the left fork for a short distance. He shook his head and halted the car. "It's no good. I don't see anything familiar here either."

"Then we countermarch," replied Don with determination. "When in doubt, go with your first guess." The prince regent dutifully backed the car around, and they shot off again.

The conduit meandered its way underground until it led to another cavern. This one was a hundred times the dimensions of any they had seen before.

Don tried to see the ceiling, but both walls and roof were lost in the dim light given off by the rocks.

The floor grew rougher and Reggie slowed the car to a crawl. When a hug slab of ancient lava blocked their path, he stopped altogether. The prince inched the car backward, seeking a route around the mammoth stone, when the engine died. Reggie checked the controls, tapped a gauge with his claw, and sighed, "Well, we can forget about the vehicle. We are out of gas. Wherever we're going, we will have to walk."

They piled out of the car. "Which way?" Frik asked Don, making a three hundred and sixty degree circle.

Don stared at Reggie, who shrugged and replied with a silly grin. "Do not ask me. I have been lost for the last hour."

Don frowned in anger. *You could've said something,* he thought. Aloud he snapped, "Fine, then," he said, "we're all in agreement. We go *thataway.*" He stalked off in the general direction they'd been traveling without looking around to see if the others followed.

Frik and Reggie hurried to catch up, and then fell in beside him. Frik searched Don's face to see if his anger had cooled. When Don smiled tightly and nodded, the trader relaxed.

"Reggie, the Federation dispatched me here to tell ya'll about this plot to overthrow your mother-queen." Frik explained his mission to the prince. "Once we get back to your palace, and I can lay tentacles on the evidence I brought in Don's ship, I'll show you documented proof the Spicians are behind this whole plot."

They were taking a short break. The prince regent stood and yawned. "Do not worry, Frik. Our spies have kept us fully aware of the connection between the rebels and the Spicians. Come, let us march on."

"Hey, wait a minute." Frik caught Reggie by one arm and spun him around. "You mean to tell me you knew all along about this conspiracy?"

Reggie shook his tentacle off. "Of course," he replied. "You know we have an excellent Criminal Investigation Bureau. The CIB boys infiltrated the rebel ranks years ago." The prince grinned and added, "Did your people also tell you the prime mover behind this plot?"

"Sure. I told you, the Spicians."

This brought a chorus of chuckles from Reggie. "No. They are dupes like foolish Stephen we left behind, mere pawns moved about by master players behind the scene."

Don asked, "If you knew what was happening all the time, how did you get into this mess? You must have had an armed guard around you."

Reggie stared at his legs and looked sheepish. "Well, we all make mistakes. I believed a young lady who said she wanted to get better acquainted. I told my guards to wait while I went into the hovel where she lived. Ahh, the next thing I knew, I woke up in that blasted cave where you rescued me."

Frik was still, wondering whom the prince was referring to as 'the prime mover'. He asked, "If your rebels aren't behind this coup, and the Spicians aren't. Who the heck is kicking up this ruckus?"

Reggie covered his mouth and yawned, bored with the conversation. "Oh, no one special." He waved a claw in dismissal. "They are a tiresome people. My great-great-grandmother chased them off this planet years ago, but from time to time, they try something like this. We squash them as necessary."

"Alright, but who *are* they?"

Reggie smirked. "Oh, a bastard race...mean, stunted, sly. They call themselves the Vas. The name means 'great' in our language."

"Vas." Don asked Reggie eagerly. "This is the planet of the Vas? Where are they? Where are they hiding?"

Reggie looked shocked at Don's outburst and replied, "Not on our world, certainly. I told you we ran the little mischiefmakers off. What's your interest in them anyway?"

Don told him of the attack on Earth. Reggie listened with interest. "It sounds like the Vas, but I do not know what they would be doing in your part of the galaxy. They like to stay at home and tend their own gardens, except for trying to conquer Izar, of course."

"I'll find out," Don said grimly. "When I do, you'll never have to worry about them again."

Reggie tut-tutted him. "Do not be so hard. The Vas are a mere nothing."

Don wagged a finger at him. "Maybe to you. Tell me, do you know where their home world is now?"

"Why it is, er." Reggie stopped and appeared puzzled. "I really do not know. Out around Epsilon or maybe Gamma Bootis somewhere. In one of those systems, I believe. When we return to the fortress I will have it looked up for you. The CIB must have their world on file."

Don slapped his hands together and started walking again faster. "Great. Let's start making some speed. Reggie, you're sure you don't know where we are? None of this looks familiar?"

The prince shook his head. "No. I am at a total loss. A major earthquake occurred here ten years ago. This must have been an area particularly hard hit. Everything has changed since I was here as a boy." He glanced toward the ceiling. "I remember a cavern," he continued, "but I do not recall it being so big. Maybe I wasn't paying attention."

"Well, let's head toward that boulder," Don pointed. "It's high enough to allow me a good view. I'll climb to the top and try to spot the exit. I think I can see the far wall."

They picked their way across the rock-strewn floor of the cavern to the boulder. Don surveyed it, searching for handholds on the slick surface, and started to climb. When he reached the top, he lay there panting, trying to catch his breath in the thin air.

"You see anything?" Frik called from below.

"Hold on, will yah," Don gasped back, struggling to his feet. "I just made it up here."

"Well, what do you see?" the trader demanded.

Don turned in a wide circle, his mouth dropping. "What the...*Oh damn.* Wait a minute, I'm climbing back down." Don made the weary climb in reverse, this time dropping the last five feet in exhaustion. Reggie and Frik helped him to his feet, dusting off ash and cinders from his clothes.

"Did you see the exit?" Reggie asked hopefully.

Don grimaced. "No, but I saw something else that might amuse you guys. Follow me, I'll show you." He strode around the side of the boulder and continued for another hundred yards, stopped, waved. "Ta-da."

Frik attempted to say something then stood mute. The prince looked and groaned. "Impossible...it can't be."

They stood in front of the abandoned ground car.

"Yeah," Don answered their unspoken question. "We've been walking around in circles all this time."

The prince muttered under his breath and glared at Don.

"Hey, don't give me a nasty look. I never claimed to be an expert in tracking. All my navigation is done with a computer."

The prince regent flopped on the hood of the car and shook his head. "We are never going to leave this place. Someday they will discover our bones here, picked clean by cave rats."

"Don't lose hope yet," Don patted one of his claws. "Don't forget, we still live."

"Yes, but for how long?" Reggie whined. "My stomach is growling. I am dirty, sore, and tired. I do not think I can survive like this much longer."

Frik clasped the prince on the back. "Why don't you lay down in the backseat and take a nap," he suggested. "It will make you feel better. Don and I will figure out what to do."

A feeble smile of relief played across Reggie's face. "Yes, I think I will. Do not run off and leave me."

"Don't worry," Frik replied. "Everything's going to be fine."

The prince climbed in the car and curled himself into a small ball. Soon he was snoring. Frik moved off a few paces, and made himself comfortable in the dirt.

"Well Don, what do you think?" The trader glanced at Reggie. "I ain't in much better shape than the prince here. Should we stick around and hope someone finds us, or try for the exit again?"

Don dropped down beside him and leaned against a piece of lava shaking his head. "I don't know. The mother-queen must have search parties out looking for Reggie. Knowing there's rebel activity afoot, these corridors are one of the first places they'll look. The rebels are bound to be out here too in force. In fact, I'm surprised they haven't caught up with us already."

Frik winced and shifted uncomfortably. "So you think we should stay here and wait?"

"I guess so," Don said with a sigh. "I don't know what else we *can* do, and we aren't getting anywhere fast. I suppose it's better to be captured again than to wander around in this cavern forever." He brushed back a lock of hair hanging in his face, leaving a dirty smudge of volcanic ash behind. He stood. "I'm going to scale the boulder again and watch for a while. Maybe I can spot a search party looking for us. Who knows, the queen's men might come along."

Frik struggled to his feet. "You want me to go too and keep you company?"

Don looked at Frik's flat, circular body and grinned. "No. You'd better stay here with the prince and guard him. If he wakes up and finds us both missing, he'll wet his pants."

The ascent up the monolith was more trying this time. Twice Don missed handholds, managing to save himself from sliding down the rocky face at the last instant. After he reached the summit, he was half-dead from exhaustion. He peered down the way he'd come. It was a long drop, and the last thing he need was a broken leg. *Why didn't these things come equipped with elevators?* he thought with a sigh.

Don moved back from the edge and gazed out across the cavern floor, trying to detect movement showing help was on its way. Frik waved from the car and he waved back. Besides the two down below, not a creature stirred. The mammoth cave held the stillness of a tomb. He cupped his hands and shouted, "Hello. Anybody there?"

His words disappeared in the faraway darkness and only faint echoes returned. He finally stopped for fear of waking Reggie.

Don shrugged. *Might as well get comfortable,* he thought. *Looks like we're going to be here for a while.* Sprawling out on his stomach, he pillowed his head on his arms ready to keep a lone vigil. He searched for movement below.

His body ached from bruises. A dull pain throbbed in his overtaxed chest. Don tried to still his breathing and relax, making himself as quiet as possible. His mind wandered as the lifeless scene of ash, rocks and boulders began to bore him. He thought of Sam, and his mind drifted to Puddlefoot. Somewhere he could hear the brownie saying, "Aye Sire, 'twill be a short time, then we'll be off." The words kept repeating in his mind.

With a start, he bolted upright. *Damn, I fell asleep.* He looked around, annoyed with himself. He didn't know for how long he'd dozed off. His shatterproof palmputer broke in a fall, and the Izarian world held no day or night.

Don stood and stretched. He felt better after his nap. The pain in his body left him, and the fist squeezing his chest had relinquished its grip. He stretched again and glanced in the direction of the car for his companions.

They weren't there.

Don scanned the landscape, widening his search to include all sides of the boulder. When he still saw no sign of them, he tried yelling. "Frik, Reggie. *Where are you?"*

He made one more scan of the area before descending the boulder. Wherever they were, he was convinced they were not within sight or hearing of his voice.

The signs of a struggle were obvious once he drew near the deserted car. Burn marks from laser fire grazed a fender, and a green sticky substance covered the backseat. Reggie's blood. Don started a search pattern rewarding him with tracks of an all-terrain vehicle etched in the volcanic ash. He marked the spot, continued his search, but located nothing else. Returning to the tracks, Don studied the direction from which they derived.

Don picked out twin pinnacles in the distance. The tracks came and went between them. After checking the laser pistol in his boot, he set off.

The ATV picked out the easiest route among the boulders, easiest for the ATV, not Don. After fifteen minutes of hiking, he panted for air. When Don reached the stone peaks, he collapsed and rested. When he got his breath back, he rose with a grunt and set off again.

Don kept this up for hours, sometimes stumbling, and once falling down a small ravine. He picked himself up and dully inspected a cut on his forearm oozing blood. He felt around in his pocket for something to make a bandage with, but outside of some lint came up empty. "It figures," he muttered as he put the wound in his mouth.

At one point, the ATV ran up a small hill of cinders and rock. Don glared at the mound and doggedly began to climb. Before he was halfway to the summit, he slipped and tumbled to the base. He staggered to his feet and tried again. When he fell a second time and came to rest, he did not stir for a time. Finally, he rolled on his back and sat up, glaring at the hill in resignation. "You win. I'll take the long way around."

Don circled the hill and picked up the tracks on the other side. Soon after, the terrain changed.

The ash and rock vanished, replaced by stalactites hanging from the roof of the cavern. It dawned on him he'd passed through the cavern and found his exit.

The marks of the ATV faded as the ash disappeared. Don wasn't worried, he was again in a tunnel. As long as the passage ran true, he saw no chance of missing his friends. He walked on with confidence until he came to another, smaller cavern. This one was pot-marked with openings.

Which way had the ATV gone? Don studied the possible paths and sat to catch his breath before going on. The pain in his chest returned, multiplied by numerous bruises he'd picked up along the way. Time had no meaning in this world. He didn't know if he'd been walking for hours or days. He decided to sleep before attempting to discover the correct route of the phantom vehicle.

Don stretched out on the side of the tunnel and felt himself drifting off. In his dreams, hoof beats approached. A huge spider, astride a horse with eight legs, rode around him in circles. The spider kept prodding him with its hardened claw, demanding to know who he was. He decided not to answer. No spider would disturb *his* sleep. The spider was insistent. The prodding became stronger, hurting his side.

He woke up.

An eerie figure atop a horse stood before him, both man and animal were translucent. They radiated a faint emerald glow hurting Don's eyes. The horseman held a lance in one arm and a small bloodhound in the other. The tip of the lance had awakened him.

"Who are you, man? What do you do in these ways?" The rider's armor creaked with age as the horse shifted, but the lance did not waver.

"P-p-please…I'm lost. Don't hurt me," Don stuttered. Action would come later.

"What is your name, mortal man?" This time the lance bit deep into Don's side.

"Weiss. Don Weiss."

The ghost figure was quiet. Don estimated the distance between himself and the rider. If he could knock the lance to one side, maybe, he stood a chance. Easing to a squat, he prepared to jump.

"Come with me, you are expected." The lance jerked away and an armored hand reached out. Don hesitated then grasped it; the rider pulled him up into the saddle behind him. The hound sniffed at him. The beast's teeth bared in a snarl. With a kick of his spurs and a flick of the reins, the specter set his horse in motion.

The ride was like no other Don had ever experienced. The horse didn't walk. It flowed. Time and distance merged into uncertainty as stone melted before the steed's headlong rush. Their pace slowed and the horse galloped down another tunnel. It lost speed and approached the mouth of a cave.

Don tumbled to the ground. He picked himself up and approached the entrance. Inside, a small fire burn in one corner, rushes covered the floor, and the scent of cloves filled the air. To one side of the fire a deep backed stone chair stood. A figure stirred in the seat, disturbing the rushes. Don entered and stood uncertain, not knowing what to expect next.

"Lord, I have brought the mortal to thee as you asked," the horseman spoke in a hollow voice.

Don glanced at the ghost rider. He glowed more brightly, the gaunt eyes and stern face fixed on the chair. The shape stirred again, and a small figure rose to face them.

"Sire, I have found thee at last!"

Arms and legs wrapped around Don as Puddlefoot engulfed him a bear hug. The little brownie pounded Don's back with joy.

"Puddlefoot, you scared the life out of me!" Don disengaged himself from his friend's embrace. "What took you so long?"

Chapter 12

"Ah, sire...truly I am sorry at my delay." Don reclined in the chair before the fire. Puddlefoot crouched beside him, stirring a small pot bubbling in the glowing coals. He tasted the contents and smacked his lips. "Just right, Sire. Here, drink this."

Don took a bowlful. It wasn't bad...the boy had a talent as a chef. He shot Puddlefoot an inquiring glance.

"Scotch broth, Sire. An old recipe taught to me by my mother."

"It's good," commented Don. "Oh. Ummm...." He looked over the rim of the bowl at the brownie. "What happened to you back there?"

"At thy ship? When the fighting started, I ran to get my shillelagh. This knave..." Puddlefoot hooked his thumb in the direction of the silent rider, still astride his horse, "waylaid me. By the time I was free of him, you had already been captured and escaped."

Don raised his gaze to the grim specter. The ghost stared back. The shade's cold, green eyes bore into Don's, demanding something. With a shutter, he looked away.

"Who is he?" Don whispered.

A damned spirit, Sire. King Herla by name. He is doomed to ride forever on his steed until the hound he carries leaps to the earth."

Don raised his brows in faint surprise. "So? Who damned him, you?"

Puddlefoot sampled the broth again, nodded, and sat tailor fashion facing Don. The little man's eyes sparkled. "Nay, Sire a relative of mine. My great-grandsire, in truth. Herla is being punished for stealing a bauble when he was a guest at a wedding feast."

The little brownie stopped as if thinking of something and continued. "When this knave sensed my presence he hurried to my side, and beseeched me to release the spell binding him." Puddlefoot grinned at the wraith. "My grandsire will be much pleased you have been located, for 'twas many years and naught hast been heard of thee. Pray tell, where is the rest of thy company?"

King Herla's hollow voice rang out, "Thou knowest well, gone, all gone, from despair of never knowing death, until only his hound and I remain. Release me now, and keep thy promise. My punishment has been fulfilled many times over."

How many years had this thing, who had once been a man, wandered through the universe? Don wondered. The rider invaded the deserted section a thousand years ago, but he must have traveled for ages seeking liberation from his bondage, before settling in these tunnels. A pang of sorrow gripped Don's throat.

"Do it, Puddlefoot. Release him. Put the dumb bastard out of his misery."

Puddlefoot stood, wiped his hands on his pants, and squeezed Don warmly. "Oh, I intend to, Sire. His final death was part of our agreement. He awaits me now to break the spell."

Don swung in the direction of Herla and gazed at the spirit once more. *"Do it,"* he rasped.

"Aye, Sire." Puddlefoot approached the rider. Dog, horse, and ghost watched as the little brownie drew near. Puddlefoot patted the ground before him and issued a piercing whistle. Immediately, the bloodhound leaped to the earth. A sudden draft of air stirred the cave, turning rapidly into a gale, and as quick died away again, leaving Don breathless. Both rider and horse glimmered bright, sighed, and started turning to dust. King Herla raised his lance in a salute, seemed about to say something, maybe thank Puddlefoot for his release. No word uttered, not a whisper came forth as he passed away. In an instant nothing remained.

The hound took longer. It whined, looked around as if searching for his lost master, and started to fade. Puddlefoot picked up the dog and patted its head. "Return to my grandsire and tell him of what transpired here." The bloodhound licked his face and stopped whining. It melted from view in his arms.

"Is that better, Sire?" Puddlefoot asked.

"'All go to the same place. All come from dust, and to dust all return'," quoted Don. He took a sip of broth.

It was cold.

"Yeah, fine." He handed the bowl back to Puddlefoot. The brownie emptied it into the pot, refilled the container with more broth. "We still have to find Frik and the prince regent."

Puddlefoot filled a bowl of his own. He raised a hand, swallowed, and told Don. "Nay, Sire. 'Tis already done."

"What?" Don straightened in his chair. "Why didn't you tell me? Where are they?"

Puddlefoot glanced up from his bowl. This time he sighed and placed it on the floor next to him. Obviously, Don wasn't going to allow him eat in peace. "Not far from here, Sire. I have them stashed in a small cavern."

"How did you find them?"

"'Twas part of my bargain with Herla. He would locate thee and Master Frik. In return, I would release him," replied the brownie with a happy grin.

"Oh." Don said disconcerted. "You don't have the prince regent?"

"Oh, aye, Sire," Puddlefoot hasten to assure Don, "Master Frik, the prince regent, and the rebels who captured them are all together." Puddlefoot gazed at his broth. "I guided their vehicle into a cavern with no exit, after which, I sealed the entrance with a spell."

Don swallowed his broth in one gulp, wiped his mouth with the back of his hand, and gave the brownie a jaded smile. "Well, you've been a busy boy, haven't you? Let's get going."

"Sire, Don…" Puddlefoot said with concern, "is venturing out wise so soon? You are hungry and tired. At least sit by the hearth and finish this fine broth."

Don shook his head and stood. "No can do, amigo. I think the regent is hurt. If I delay, he could bleed to death. No rest for me, buddy."

Puddlefoot rose on his tiptoes and tried pushing Don back down. "Hold Sire, I beg thee. I have thought of that very thing. Over the whole of the cavern, I placed a spell, while it last, time within changes not. Ye could sleep for a year and a day, but not a second would pass for Master Frik or the prince."

Don laughed, delighted, and sat. "You're kidding me. You're sure? Since you're possitive, break out the fattened calf, afterwards it's forty winks." He stretched out in the chair with a sigh.

Puddlefoot hurried away and then returned with a can of beer. Don took a sip. The liquid was icy cold. "You're amazing, Puddlefoot. By any chance could you…"

"Right away, Sire." The little brownie scurried off again.

The strains of a Wagner opera filled the air.

***

Don and Puddlefoot materialized in a long straight tunnel. Even though Don knew time wasn't a pressing matter, still he was eager to liberate Reggie and Frik. More important, he had yet to find the Vas and complete his mission. He scanned the tunnel and exclaimed, "Where's the entrance? I don't see it."

Puddlefoot closed his eyes and frowned. "Did I tell thee not, Sire, I have cast a spell over it."

"Yeah, well, send it away," Don snapped, "or make it disappear or something."

Puddlefoot shot him a look, but pulled up the sleeves of his shirt. "Right away, Sire. Boss. Stand back. When I release the spell, time in the cavern will start again. It gets a little tricky at the interface."

Don paused and grinned. "Interface? Where did you learn the word?"

"Picked it up out of the ship's computer manual, Sire," chuckled the brownie, "now stand back."

Puddlefoot raised his arms and posed with a dramatic flair. He held the stance, clapped his hands together three times. Then, with the sound of thunder and tinkling glass, the mouth of the cave materialized before them.

Puddlefoot beamed and took off his cap, making a sweeping bow.

Pretty tricky," Don remarked with a smirk. "What do you do for an encore?"

Puddlefoot's mouth dropped and his brow knitted with anger.

"Hey, only kidding, buddy," Don protested when he saw the expression on the brownie's face. "Can't you take a joke?"

"Aye, sire. Can thee?"

Don's head spun. He felt himself lifted and came to rest hanging upside down, suspended in midair by an unknown force. "What the heck do you think you're doing?" He waved his arms frantically. "LET ME DOWN."

"How is that for an encore, Sire?" Puddlefoot snickered with glee.

"I should have known better," Don muttered to himself. He counted to ten, and for good measure, did it once more, backward, in Spanish. "Okay, Puddlefoot, I can take a joke, too. Please, let me down."

Don settled to the floor until his chest rested firmly, and then with a plop, fell the rest of the way. He tucked and rolled to his feet, grinning. "All set, buddy?"

"All set, Sire. Do you have all the equipment you want?" Puddlefoot had returned to the ship and retrieved a respirator and oxygen tank.

Don took a calming breath, strapping the gear on. "Yep, let's go."

The moved off into the cavern searching for the ATV. Before they'd gone a hundred feet, Don heard vices arguing from behind a granite outcropping.

"...you fool. We have been lost here for ten minutes. Don't you remember the way you drove in?" The voice was Ivan's. Even at this distance, Don recognized the arrogance in the tone.

"Ivan, I told you, it was right here. All I did was swerve off the path into this cavern when you thought you saw the Earthling. I backed up and the entrance was vanished." Stephen as well, it seemed like homecoming week.

"Worm. If you had not let them escape in the first place, none of this would have happened."

"I told you, Ivan, they tricked me. The prince regent said…"

"Yes, fool, you informed me of all this before. Drive around the rock again, maybe you will remember where you are."

Don crouched low behind a boulder and motioned for Puddlefoot to do the same on the other side of the entrance. He drew his pistol, checked the charge, and whispered to the brownie, "Get ready, Puddlefoot. They're coming this way."

"Ready, Sire." Puddlefoot grasped his shillelagh in his hands. He poised on his toes, eager to leap.

The ATV sped around the outcropping. "You see, Ivan," Stephen exclaimed, pointing at the cave mouth. "There is the exit. I was not wrong after all. It was merely hidden from view."

"Thank goodness for small favors, fool. Drive on, let us be out of here."

Stephen complied, and the ATV promptly sped up. He ignored rocks, potholes and other obstacles, making a beeline for the exit. When they were abreast of Don, he jumped out from concealment, covered the oncoming vehicle with his pistol, and shouted, "NOW." A glow of red appeared on the front grill and it burst into flames.

The ATV skidded to an abrupt halt, and from inside, fire spewed. Either Ivan or Stephen was quick-witted enough to take offensive action. A spark sprang to life between Dons' legs seeking his groin. He leaped sideways, avoiding the bean and sought refuge.

Puddlefoot appeared in the backseat. He swung his club and knocked Stephen out of the car. On its return arc, the shillelagh gained speed and crashed against Ivan. The rebel cried of pain and fell to his side. His pistol dropped into the dirt outside the ATV.

Don approached the vehicle with caution, laser outstretched, alert to a possible trick. With a deft boot, he kicked the gun away, aiming his own pistol at the two stunned rebels. In the front seat, Ivan twitched.

"Do not move or I will shoot." Don fell into the old cadence drilled into him during his Academy days. He motioned with his pistol. "All right, Ivan, get over there by your buddy."

The Izarian crept out of the car and hobbled next to Stephen on six of his eight legs.

"Puddlefoot, guard these guys." The brownie assumed Don's place, club held high in the air.

Don strode to the vehicle and peered into the rear. Three eyes held aloft on short stalks stared back at him banefully. Frik. Don gulped and removed the gag – it was the wrong thing to do.

"...Those slimy fiends, those cowards. Those pieces of..."

Don put his hand over Frik's mouth and the rest of the words were lost in a gargle. "Be nice," he told the Arcturian sweetly, "or I'll leave you here to rot forever."

The Trader nodded. Don took his hand away and undertook the task of dissolving Frik's bonds.

Puddlefoot appeared next to Don. "There is no need, Sire."

Don glanced in the direction of Ivan and Stephen, and then back at the brownie. "Who's watching the prisoners?"

"Puddlefoot, *you idiot*, get back there and guard those guys!" Frik said, scowling hard. "I don't want to go through this again."

"They sleep," the brownie said simply. He looked at Frik's bonds. They fell away.

Puddlefoot moved to the prince. Reggie was lying on the floor, thrown there by the vehicles sudden stop. His claws twitched helplessly as he squirmed upside down. Once Puddlefoot released him, Don hauled the shaken regent to his feet.

"Oh, Don, thank you," gushed Reggie. "I felt for sure no one was going to rescue me."

"Don't worry about it, Prince." Don helped him from the vehicle. "Let me take a look at your shoulder."

Reggie waved a claw, shrugged. "It's all right...a chip of rock hit me."

Don examined the wound anyway. After studying the gash he remarked, "Hmmm, you'll live, but we'd better bring you to a doctor. I think it's becoming infected."

"Infected?" Reggie turned pale. He craned his head to look at the cut. "Those beasts. They tried to kill me." He stalked to the two rebels and kicked Stephen. "Fiends, assassins, *BUTCHERS*. You try to kill your prince?"

Don ran after him. "Reggie, cool it They're unconscious for Christ sakes. Besides, it's only a scratch."

Reggie studied the cut again. "You are sure?"

"Yes, I'm sure." Don gave him a pat. "Let's check the ATV and see if we can start it running."

Frik beat them there. The Arcturian had the hood up and was buried in the engine compartment, poking around inside. Puddlefoot stood next to him and offered advice, which Frik ignored. When Don and Reggie strolled up Frik was saying, "...looks like Don nicked this wire here. Puddlefoot, hand me those pliers." He reached up a tentacle blindly and waited.

"Yes, Master Frik, pliers." The brownie studied a screwdriver, adjustable wrench, and pliers Frik had lain out from the vehicle's tool kit. He promptly grabbed the screwdriver and handed it to Frik.

Screwdriver and tentacle disappeared back into the engine compartment. A moment later, Frik shouted, "Not a screwdriver, you nitwit. The pliers." The unwanted tool flew out.

Puddlefoot went for the adjustable. Don stopped him and handed Frik the pliers.

"Lot's better, Puddlefoot," came Frik's voice. "You're getting the knack of mechanics now." He stripped the blackened insulation from the wire, twisted the two ends together. "There, that will do her. Let's try it." Frik straightened, glanced around, and saw the two latecomers. "Don, Reggie, it's about time. I'm glad my buddy here stuck around to lend me a hand." He patted Puddlefoot on the back.

Puddlefoot beamed. Don fought to hide his smile and said with a straight face, "try firing the engine up so we can bring the prince back to his mother."

Frik cranked the motor over, it caught on the first try. He gave the accelerator a few experimental taps, and declared, "Sound good. All aboard."

Puddlefoot woke the two rebels and made them climb into the backseat. The prince insisted he drive and took the driver's spot. Don, Puddlefoot, and Frik scrambled for places in the vehicle before Reggie left them behind. Frik was a bit faster than his friends were. Don and Puddlefoot found themselves guarding the rebels, while Frik perched in the passenger's seat. Don placed his pistol to Ivan's head.

"Now listen, you're going to be the navigator for the prince, and we're driving to the royal fortress. If we become lost in here, we'll leave your body to mark the spot for others. You understand me?"

Ivan stared back with a defiant look until he read Don's face. His resolution faded and he slumped. "I think so, but remember I'm not totally familiar with these passageways. I could get lost."

"If so, we have Stephen," Don gave him a wicked smile, "but for your sake, let's hope not. Reggie, better start moving."

Ivan proved to be a good navigator. Within an hour, they left the deserted section and swung onto a public road. Soon afterward, a CIB vehicle zipped in behind them with blue and red lights flashing. The ATV waited on the shoulder while the agents called for reinforcements.

In a short while more flashing lights, many Investigation Bureau Personnel, and twenty curious onlookers who appeared from nowhere surrounded them. A brief debate arose between Reggie and the officer of the day.

"I will not ride with you, Captain!" Reggie punctuated each word with a sharp claw to the officer's chest, "and that is final."

The official cowered and replied, "But, Sire your safety. The mother-queen said…"

Reggie ignored his plea. "I am safe with my friends. Now, return to your car and escort me to the fortress, or I will have you frayed and boiled in oil." The prince stormed back to the ATV and they started again.

"Reggie, don't you think the captain was right?" Frik spoke up after they rode for a mile in silence. "You would be safer with them."

"Not really," the prince said as he glanced in the rearview mirror. "They are behind me, on either side, and in front. I do not think they will lose me again. Besides, when I lead this caravan into Mom's fortress, after capturing two rebels, it will make great public relations."

A look of bewilderment passed over Puddlefoot's face. "But, Master Reggie, you did not..."

"Shhh," Don waved a hand at the brownie. "You're right, Reggie, it *is* great PR and your mother will be proud of you, too."

The prince nodded his head with enthusiasm. "Geee, you're right."

The motorcade entered the outskirts of the capital. The townspeople watched the vehicles zoom past. Someone recognized Reggie and shouted, "The prince." The cry flew ahead, and the inhabitants streamed from their homes to line the avenue. In the distance, church bells tolled. Reggie slowed to a crawl, clasped two claws together, and raised them in a victory salute. The crowd roared.

Reggie was happy with his melodramatics. Don wasn't. With mounting apprehension, he kept a careful eye on the multitude, waiting for an assassin's shot to cut the prince down.

"Reggie," he muttered in the prince's ear. "Quit the playacting and let's get rolling. This crowd is making me nervous."

"Nonsense, Don," Reggie was smiling and waving, "they love it, watch this." He stopped the ATV altogether and hauled the two rebels up where the townspeople could see them.

"These are the vermin who would destroy the mother-queen," he yelled to the crowd. "Should we suffer such creatures to live?"

"NO," the cry came back.

Reggie watched the city folk, waiting for silence. A hush fell over the people and he shouted, "These would-be cutthroats tried to steal your God appointed caretaker. The punishment for which is death. However, it is you they have wronged. You they have stolen from. You they have sinned against and tried to damn forever. What should be done with these two?"

"KILL THEM."

"Kill them?"

"Kill them. Kill them. KILL THEM." The chant rose to a scream.

Reggie raised his claws again for quiet. It was a long time coming. "I am taking them to the fortress. Justice will be done. Tomorrow, at noon – watch the parapets." The crowd went crazy at the unspoken sentence passed on the rebels.

While the regent whipped the crowd into a frenzy, Don tried to watch in four directions at once. So it wasn't luck when he spotted the barrel of a rifle protrude from a second story window across the street.

"Down, Reggie, get down!"

"What?"

Don tackled the prince and jerked him to the floorboards. A bolt of lightning passed through the spot Reggie had occupied, cutting a neat hole in the side panel of their vehicle. The CIB men, busy holding the crowd back, drew pistols and returned fire. The rifle barrel disappeared. It reappeared seconds later from a high window and spoke again. Shouts of panic, then screams, rose from the crowd as shots flashed back and forth. One of the bureau men crumbled. The rest dove for cover. The screams faded, disappeared as if by magic, as the avenue cleared.

"Are you happy now, Reggie?" Don rasped with deep sarcasm. "Let's vamoose before the guy finds his target."

Shaking, the prince crawled back into the driver's seat. Keeping as low as possible, he slipped the vehicle into gear and fed it gas. As they made their departure, the few remaining Izarians who found refuge beneath cars, cheered.

They approached the castle, slowed at the checkpoint, but didn't stop. The guards saluted and waved the motorcade on. News of their approach traveled ahead, and a sizeable throng gathered at the palace steps when they arrived. Reggie jumped from The ATV to the sounds of cheers from the nobles, military, and palace staff. They crowded around, asking questions to the delight of the prince.

Don watched the Izarians fawn all over the regent. He nudged Puddlefoot and winked as Reggie touched his shoulder. "He's milking this for all it's worth, but you'd think he'd have learned by now."

Puddlefoot nodded. "The prince hath found something to brag about and he speakest well."

Don sat back and folded his arms. "I guess being a monarch isn't the most exciting job in the world, especially when your mother runs the show. Hey wait." He sat forward again. "I think someone important has arrived."

A portly Izarian female waddled down the palace steps. In her wake, a dozen attendants followed. As she crawled forward, the crowd fell silent and parted.

"Reggie. REG-IN-ALD," she called. "Come here at once. Come to your mother." She stood waiting.

"Mom." Reggie hurried to the mother-queen and embraced her. "Oh Mom, I missed you so. Come, come see what I did." He took her claw, dragging the queen to the prisoners. "Rebels. I captured them."

His mother startled, glanced around, her eyes landing on the ATV. Don, Frik, and Puddlefoot sat there quietly, watching the empress and her son.

"Who are *they?*" she asked, stretching out a claw.

"Oh." Reggie gestured for the three to step out and meet the Empress of Izar. His mother. "These are my friends, Mom," he explained in a rush. "They helped me capture the rebels. You know the trader, Frik."

"Ah, yes, Frik." The queen peered at him. "I remember you well. Thank you for helping my son in his hour of need." She offered her claw to him. He took it and made a deep bow. "Who are these other two, my son?"

Reggie looked embarrassed. "Uh…this is Don, and this is Puddlefoot. The both saved my life," Reggie ended lamely. He decided to make the best of it and added with a flourish, "I now call them Friends of the Crown."

The mother-queen looked dubious but recovered and said, "Don, Puddlefoot, thank you for saving my son." She gave each a claw in turn. They replied with their deepest bows. "Now, let us be off," she commanded. "Reginald, Frik, you will accompany me, I have matters to discuss."

She swung around and beckoned to two of her waiting attendants. "Take Masters Don and Puddlefoot to the guestrooms. Make them comfortable and see to their needs. She said to Don and Puddlefoot, "Go with these servants. We will talk later." The mother-queen scurried off trailed by Reggie, Frik, and her retinue.

Don and Puddlefoot followed the servants by a circular route leading up rickety wooden stairs, through rubble-filled courtyards, and an unused stillroom, until they'd passed through the castle twice.

"What are we, poor relations?" Don bitched, as they climbed another flight of stairs.

"Oh, no sir," exclaimed one of the servants. "It's, uh, a lot of construction in the palace."

"Yeah?" It sounded plausible, but . . . .

Don's pique continued to build until he could take it no more. "I'm not budging from this spot until you find us a place to sleep," he declared, making as if to sit in the corridor they wandered through.

"Your rooms, sirs."

"Then why didn't we…oh, never mind!"

The attendants swung double doors open. Puddlefoot and he walked through into a lavish apartment decorated in purple tapestries, the color of Imperial Izar. The spokesman for the two servants asked, "Are these satisfactory?"

Don nodded in amazement. The other servant spoke for the first time, addressing Puddlefoot, "Sir?"

"Who, me?"

"Yes, sir. If you'll come this way?" He led Puddlefoot off to an adjoining suite.

The servant asked, "Sir? Will there be anything else?"

Don looked around. "No." His stomach growled. "Hey, wait. Any chance of getting something to eat?"

"Coming right up, sir." The attendant left.

His meal arrived shortly, covered in gold. As if on cue, Puddlefoot wandered in from his suite. The brownie sniffed the air, saw the dishes, and exclaimed, "Food." Before Don could sit, the brownie attacked the food as if he'd not eaten for a week. As the platters of food disappeared before Don's eyes, he stuffed his mouth before the brownie licked the plates clean. When the two could eat no more, Don stood.

"I think I'll take a walk," he said, patting his stomach. "Work off this meal." He strolled to the door, turned the latch. The portal refused to budge. "So that's the way it is," he said, rubbing his chin.

The little brownie glanced up from a morsel of sausage he was chasing. "Huh?"

"They locked us in, Puddlefoot."

"So what of it, Sire?" Puddlefoot swallowed the sausage and disappeared. As suddenly, he reappeared, saying, "Nay, Sire, it doth not seem locked to me."

Don glanced from the brownie back to the door. "Maybe not to you, but it's strange."

Puddlefoot nodded in agreement. "So it does, Sire. Shall we leave?"

"No. Let's play this hand out and see what happens."

Puddlefoot yawned. "If you desire so, Sire. 'Tis time for a nap."

"You're right," Don replied, still furious inside. "It's been a long day."

"Sire?" Puddlefoot was looking at Don's pockets.

"Yeah?"

"The knives, forks, and spoons?"

"Oh." Don shaded a faint pink and put the gold cutlery back on the table. "It was just…"

"Yes, Sire," Puddlefoot sighed. "You cannot stand wealth not yours."

"Right."

***

Sometime later, a knock on the door awakened Don. He rolled over and shouted, "Come on in."

The doors parted and Frik strolled into the room accompanied by a guard. "Hey, Bo," he greeted Don. Scanning the room, he whistled, "Pretty nice digs."

"Frik." Don glanced at the guard, ignored him. "What's going on? Why were we locked in?"

The Arcturian sat at the table and picked at the scant remains of their meal. "There's nothing to worry about. The mother-queen wanted to run a check on you before letting you have free run of the palace."

Don sat also, not mollified at all by this explanation. "Then why weren't you locked up, too?"

"You forget I've been here before. They trust me some. Once they know you, it will be fine. I told you, they're on the skittish side."

Don shelved his anger. It was too late to complain. Still, it wasn't good manners. "Who…what have you been doing?"

Frik leaned forward. "Oh. That's what I came here to tell you. The queen requests your presence at a council of war."

"WHAT?"

"Yeah," Frik said and nodded. "Well it seems when Reggie was hijacked, the royal forces whipped out the rebels, but they still have a Spician-Vas fleet somewhere in their system."

Don's eyes narrowed, he shook his head. "Frik, why do they want me?" He was smelling the trap. He wasn't here to fight. Not now, anyway, and he didn't like the direction the situation was heading.

"Well, Don, Reggie told the empress about what the Vas did to Earth. She thought you might want in on the fun. What do you think?"

Don gulped. "If I have a choice, I'll watch from the sidelines."

Frik chuckled. "Don't tell me you're chicken?"

"Always."

Chapter 13

Don swore he'd never ride in an Izarian spaceship again. "How am I supposed to make myself comfortable on these things?" he asked Puddlefoot, kicking his acceleration couch. It was comprised of three parallel poles, padded with a soft sponge-like substance, meant for an Izarian to drape over. The problem, he didn't fit.

"I knowest not, Sire," replied Puddlefoot from the deck. "Perhaps thou wouldst be better off next to me." Upon boarding the queen's flagship, the *Archangel,* and seeing the control room, the brownie disappeared. When he returned, he carried an armful of plush, silk-covered pillows. He spread these about in an out of the way corner and sat. When a bell rang the acceleration warning, he still reclined there, smiling.

Don gave up his attempt to straddle the poles. With a groan, he sat next to Puddlefoot. "At least those guys look comfy." the five Izarians officers who comprised the crew of the control room draped over their seats, waiting for blast-off. These were the cream of the Izarian Navy, each a seasoned veteran of the frequent battles with the Vas. Along with the *Archangel*, nineteen other vessels of the Izarian fleet waited, the pride of the Navy, every officer, each crewmember, handpicked by the admiralty because of their past performance.

Don sighed again and hoped the information was correct. For all his years in space, he had never fought in a battle before. For the first time in a long while, he was glad someone else was in the pilot's seat, happy to leave the command decisions to the professionals. He had only agreed to come along because the mother-queen expected it. Other than that, he could think of no reason for his presence.

Don relaxed and let the blinking lights of the control consoles hypnotize him. When acceleration hit, he sunk deep into the cushions. The pressure was not as great as he expected, a kiss instead of a kick. In moments, the increased weight lifted and he was able to stand.

"Wow the take-off was a rough one," one of the officers exclaimed, climbing down off his poles.

"Well, if you can't take the pressure, you shouldn't be in the Navy," another retorted.

"The equalizer *was* a bit slow to phase in," temporized a third. He was the pilot. The Izarian addressed Don and Puddlefoot. "You guys, okay?"

"Yeah," Don replied. "Was that it?"

"Sure was," replied the pilot, rubbing his back. "Pretty rough, too. I think, maybe we have a gyro going bad. Want to look in the 'scope?"

"Sure." Don peeked in the viewer. Izar IV was shrinking rapidly, and soon became no more than a pinpoint of light lost among the stars. The officer who commented on the takeoff pulled out a bottle of clear liquid and proposed a toast for the occasion. "Salute, my friends. Let the coming battle with the Vas be a short and merry one."

Cups materialized and each became filled with a finger full of the liquor. Don and Puddlefoot received glasses and raised them with the other members of the crew.

Don took a sip and gagged.

"Hey, what's this?" The pilot strolled over and patted Don on the back.

"Nothing," Don wheezed, "went down the wrong way."

"Have another then." A second officer joined them. He withdrew a silver flask from a pouch and refilled Don's glass. "Here, drink this. My hooch will go down smooth." He tipped the flask to his own mouth and swallowed. "Ahhh...much better than the cheap booze you pick up, Izzy. This cost twelve ninety-five a fifth."

"You buy the liquor cheaper because you have better connections on the black market, Gunney," joked the pilot.

"You're sooo right. I haven't waited in a line since the mother-queen made me her Chief Gunnery Officer." The Izarian swaggered off to talk with his companions.

The pilot disappeared also. Don stood by himself holding the half-filled glass. He took a cautious taste and felt the alcohol claw its way down his throat and land in his stomach. His eyes started to water and sweat beaded on his forehead. He finished the rest and declared, "That's enough for me. One more of those and you won't see me till next Wednesday."

No one heard him. More flasks appeared, and another bottle circulated from an open case on the deck. One of the officers brought a player recorder. Music flooded the control room, making it impossible to hear conversations. Don received the impression a party was going on, and the queen's commanders were trying to get drunk as soon as possible.

"Hey, pilot." Don cornered the officer as he wobbled past. "Don't you think you guys are drinking a bit heavy? You *are* going into battle."

"Izzy...call me Izzy. What did you say?"

"I said," Don screamed, "aren't you guys drinking too much? *There's a battle.*"

"Oh. Nah, done it a hundred times before," Izzy boasted as he tried to focus on Don. "As soon as the Vas detect our ships they take off. Maybe we have to shoot the big blaster a couple of times."

Don clenched his teeth. "What about the Spicians?"

"Never fought them before," admitted the pilot, "but if they're allied with the Vas, they must be chicken shit, too."

The music grew louder. The door to the bridge opened and a crewman entered, wheeling a cart loaded with trays of appetizers. He picked one up and circulated around the room, offering tidbits to the officers. Don took this in with disbelief and growing wonder.

Someone bumped him from behind. He turned and discovered the gunnery officer swaying gently. "Hey buddy, you look bored," he giggled. "You wait, in a couple of minutes they send out the girls."

Before the officer wandered off, Don grated, "If we're fired on, what do we do?"

The gunnery officer seized him by the shoulder. "Come along, Earthie, I'll show you." Gunney took him to the main weapon's board. "We fire the big blasters. Lookie here..." he flipped a switch and a viewer lit up. "Everything in white is our ships. Zero in and depress this key."

"You only carry one weapon onboard?" Don persisted.

The Izarian waved a claw and took a sip from his flask. "Nah, we got rockets, torpedoes, and a bunch of other stuff below, but those jugheads down there never learned how to fire them."

Don rubbed his forehead. "Great. You have plenty of weapons, but no one knows how to use them."

Gunney released a loud sigh. "Don't need anything else. Hmmm…I can switch control of everything up here, I think." The gunnery officer paused while studying his console. He depressed two buttons and flicked a switch. "There, that does it." He staggered off searching for the waiter.

Don realized he had not seen Puddlefoot since blastoff. Where had the brownie gone? It would be like him to disappear again, leaving him to cope with a bunch of drunken Izarians by himself. Don scanned the room and spotted his friend performing an Izarian folk dance with Izzy and another officer. Puddlefoot accepted a bottle from the pilot and took a swallow.

"Hold up there, buddy." Don snatched the fifth from Puddlefoot and put it down. "If you go drinking too much of this, I'll be the only one left sober."

Puddlefoot's lips drooped. "Ah Sire, 'twas but a wee drop."

Don smiled tightly. "Good, then you've wet your whistle for the night."

Puddlefoot's face clouded up and he looked indignant, then he slowly nodded. "'Tis true, Sire, you have the right of it." He surveyed the officers. "They drink too much 'afore going to battle. When the time comes, they'll be deep in their cups."

"We should be getting there pretty soon," Don observed. He watched the naval officers. Some were already too drunk to stand, the rest had not far to go. Off in the corner their pilot, Izzy, was sitting, singing to himself. "Puddlefoot, what kind of shape do you think the rest of the fleet is in?"

"I fear to look or ask, Sire."

"Me too. Say…" Don had an unpleasant thought.

"What, Sire?"

"If everybody's drunk, who's going to fight the Vas? For that matter, who'll pilot this ship?"

Puddlefoot looked confused and jabbed a stubby finger at Izzy.

"I don't think so," Don said, holding his growing fear in check. "He's been drinking since blastoff, right?"

"Right Sire, but have they not an automatic helmsman such as thy ship?"

"Probably," Don agreed, "but it has to be programed, and no matter how good your programs are, you can't use them for maneuvering during battle. What the heck is happening in this ship anyway?"

Don strode to the pilot, yanked him to his feet. "Hey you, who's flying this can?"

"Hic...hic...ahhh. Nobody. She steers herself."

"I didn't see you program anything!"

The officer smiled weakly. "How do you like my hair? Is it Saturday?"

Don's face clouded up and shaded from red to purple. "The computer, you ninny. *Did you program it?*"

The Izarian waved his claw vaguely in the air. "All preprogramed. We, uh, go out, stay a couple of hours, and then, ah, come back for a quick nap."

"Aren't you going to fight once you get there?"

"Where?" asked the inebriated officer.

"To the battle." Don's expression hardened into frustration. "We're flying into space to fight the Vas, remember now?"

"Oh yeah. You're right. We must be there, too." Izzy glanced foggily around and shouted,

"Someone wake up Gunney so he can push the button."

Don threw his hands up in the air. "Enough." He dragged the Izarian to the pilot's couch. "Show me how to switch this bird to manual if I have to."

The pilot stared at his board. "These." He touched a shaky claw to a series of colored light set in parallel.

"Can you switch the weaponry circuits over here?"

The pilot nodded, sobering some. "Press this button and everything on Gunney's board comes over."

Don studied the panel the Izarian pointed to, memorizing the function of each control. "How do you activate the screens?"

The pilot did not answer. Don looked up to see why. Izzy had passed out and fallen across the acceleration poles. He snored.

"PERFECT." Don snorted in disgust and shook his head. He said to Puddlefoot, "Time to throw out the drunks, starting with this one. Find a place to park him."

"Aye Sire." The brownie stared at the pilot. Izzy disappeared. He reappeared ten feet away where he'd been sitting before. "Far enough, Sire?"

"Fine," Don replied absentmindedly. He studied the controls on the console. Some were familiar, most weren't. He saw a yoke-like device used for steering under manual control he decided, three lights set in a line, which activated the screens. He already knew how to switch the autopilot on and off. He was clueless about the rest. By trial and error, he explored the majority of keys, knobs, and lights strange to his experience.

Before Don was through with his orientation, he felt the *Archangel* decelerate and drop to cruising speed. He checked the viewer and saw star glowing brightly. "Now to find the Vas," he told Puddlefoot.

"Sire, have no fear. Methinks they shall find us if we cannot find them."

"I was afraid you'd say something like that." Don tried laying across the acceleration plies in a last futile attempt to get used to them. He lasted thirty seconds before falling onto the deck. He gave a grunt and scrambled to his feet.

"Darn things...how do they expect a man to work?" Don kicked the poles loose and heaved them out of his way. Gathering Puddlefoot's pillows, he built a platform the right height for him to operate. After a vigorous wiggle and a shrug of his shoulders, he returned to his 'scopes.

Red dots appeared, flashing on and off menacingly as they approached the white ones. They were the Vas-Spician fleet. Out of the corner of his eye, Don spotted the weapon's officer stagger to his feet. Gunney lunged toward his board and stood there, swaying.

"Time to press the button," Gunney called aloud. The officer's unsteady claw hovered over the controls and then made a stab at the firing key.

From the flagship, a burst of energy leaped toward the enemy ships. As if on cue, other bolts sprang from the Izarian flotilla, striking at the heart of the hostile formation. Nearby space transformed into a blazing inferno, as the might of the mother-queen was unleashed.

"GREAT GOD ALMIGHTY," Don breathed to Puddlefoot. "Nothing could live in the hellhole we created."

The blasters stopped their discharge. To Don's dismay, the enemy fleet survived unscathed and was changing formation. "We're in for it now," he said to Puddlefoot.

From the weapon's board they heard a chuckle. "Watch." Gunney nodded to the radar. "Watch and see."

Some thirty of the hostile ships broke away from the fleet and formed a globe. Like a flock of frightened birds, they retreated from the Izarian fleet and disappeared off the 'scope.

Gunney swaggered up beside them. "You see, Earthie, the blasters work every time. The Vas never did like anything close to a fair fight." He laughed and drew another fifth of liquor from the case. "I'm going to take a nap. Wake me in thirty minutes and we'll shoot off the artillery again." He swaggered away.

"Hey, wait," Don called the Izarian back. "Did you see this?"

"Huh?"

Come back here, quick." Don stared at the radar. Fifteen of the red dots hadn't broken formation and run. Don, Puddlefoot, and Gunney gazed at the 'scope and watched as the remaining ships moved and regrouped. The maneuver took some time to accomplish. When the ships finished, they stared at a cone, its mouth facing the Izarian fleet.

When Gunney comprehended what the ships were doing, he took a few gulps from his bottle, gave a low growl, and cursed under his breath. "Those pipsqueaks think they can pull a fast one, do they? Well, old Gunney will show them a thing or two."

The officer crisscrossed his way back to his console and snatched up a mike. "This is her Majesty's Chief Gunnery Officer, Omar Ipnish, to all ships," he yelled into the microphone. "The enemy force is still attacking. On my command we will fire." Gunney was breathing hard. He glanced at his own 'scope and turned white. "Fire," he screamed, "...quick. Fire the blasters."

Gunney depressed his own key. Energy released from the guns of the *Archangel* and drove toward the enemy. Seven of the other Izarian ships fired also. The rest either did not receive his message, or were too drunk to respond. Even so, a spectacular display of power filled nearby space. The bolts of energy licked over the ships at the rim of the cone and spread among them. Defensive shields flared bright, but held. Here and there, a minor outage occurred, but the blasts of the Izarian's weren't concentrated enough, or long enough, to disable the enemy. None suffered serious damage. The mouth of the cone sped forward and engulfed the fleet, and stopped.

Don watched the battle, spellbound. When he saw the enemy fleet complete its movement, he quickly activated his own defensive screens. He was none too soon. The inside of the cone erupted in fire. A blanket of raw energy spread over the *Archangel's* shield, pushing them to their limits as they flared white and climbed the spectrum. On his board needles sung dangerously into the red, through the fiber of the ship, generators changed pitch. The moan built until a loud whine filled the air. Don cringed and waited for the screens to collapse.

As suddenly as the attack started, it stopped. The static filling the radarscope disappeared, replaced by red and white dots. The red dots still engulfed the white ones, but something had changed. Instead of nineteen white blips, only ten remained.

"We're bugging out of here!" Don exclaimed. He snapped to Gunney, "Tell what remains of the fleet to follow me." Without waiting to see if the officer complied, he covered lights and took control of the ship. The first of six lights were set in tandem on the right hand side of the panel, he touched one. The flagship slowly picked up speed.

"Bingo," Don yelped. "We're in business now." He skipped over the second light, instead blanking out the third in the series. Acceleration shoved him back as the ship surged forward. He twisted the yoke and aimed the ship toward the apex of the cone. On the 'scope other blips, the remains of the Izarian flotilla, banked and followed.

"Gunny, tell the rest of the ships to cluster around me. I want to make a cone of my own." The now sobered officer nodded, picked up his mike and relayed Don's instructions to the rest of the ships. With much guidance, and the loss of precious seconds, he managed the formation he wanted.

"Puddlefoot, see what you can do about getting those drunks strapped down," Don ordered. "Then come back here and strap down yourself. I'm taking us for a ride." He said to the Izarian, "Gunney, why aren't we being fired on?"

"Takes time to build up power again after a burst like that," said the Izarian. He added thoughtfully, "They could use rockets on us, though."

"Don't want to take a chance on missing us and hitting one of their ships by mistake," guessed Don, "but you gives me an idea. Tell the formation to prepare for acceleration, and to loose rockets at the point ship on my count." As best he could, he braced himself against the pillows. Ready? One. Two. Three. Accelerate."

He blocked out the sixth and final light. The ship rushed ahead and Don hurled backward from the burst of speed. He was brought to a halt by a bulkhead, managed to pick himself up when the equalizer kicked in. He shook his head, checked for broken bones, and was surprised to find none. Don made his way back to the controls.

"Prepare to launch rockets, Gunney." They were rapidly approaching the apex of the enemy cone. Don counted to three again and ordered, "Launch rockets."

A flick of missiles flashed from the Izarian formation toward the lone enemy ship. Three missed their mark. The rest struck the defensive screen of the ship and exploded in a crescendo of detonations. The screen flared wildly, flickered, and disappeared in a burst of light.

"We did it," whooped Don, grinning at Gunney. "We overloaded her. Fire at will." More rockets sprang from the fleet. The enemy vessel took four direct hits and disintegrated in a shower of spark, burning metal, and flaming gas.

The enemy cone responded with another burst of fire from its blasters, but the Izarians were almost out of the trap. Before the fleet was injured, it had passed through the end of the cone into empty space.

"Sire, thou hast done it. We can escape," Puddlefoot shouted with relief.

"Escape, hell." Don growled back. "Gunney, let's swing this fleet around."

The officer stared at him without blinking, hesitation plain on his face. "Are you sure? I don't know what's gotten into those Vas, but they've never fought like this before. Maybe we should take Puddlefoot's advice and escape while we can."

Don locked eyes with him. "Those aren't Vas, those are Spicians. I'm going back to give them a piece of my mind."

"Sire…" Puddlefoot started to protest.

"No, buts." Don cut him off. He issued instructions to Gunney who broadcasted them to the rest of the fleet. The ships slowed, broke off one by one from the main group, and turned in a graceful arc. Next, he ordered the Izarian to determine the battle damage aboard the other ships, and the status of the *Archangel*. While the officer got busy, Don started preparing a plan of attack with Puddlefoot.

"Can you make us appear to be still traveling away from the Spicians?" he asked.

"Aye, Sire, on their view scopes, but their other equipment 'twill not be fooled," replied the confused brownie.

"Perfect," Don replied. "We'll be coming and going at the same time. I want to slow them up some, anyhow. Okay, get to it. Gunney, any word on how the rest of the fleet made out?"

"Yeah, pretty bad, actually," the officer grumbled. "It seems most of the booze that was supposed to go the fleet was mixed up with a shipment of sparkling mineral water. Those boys are boiling mad."

Don stared at the ceiling and recited the books of the Old Testament. By the time he reached Ezekiel, he managed to say, "Pretty good you mean, but what about damage?"

"Oh. The ships surviving the first attack are in good shape. No major damage to report."

Don nodded. "How about the *Archangel?*"

The Izarian shrugged. "We still got, maybe, two cases of Vegan rum left."

"Daniel…Hosea…Joel…Will you stop with the liquor already. *Damage,* I want damage reports."

Gunney hurried and said, "No damage to the ship. We have about half the crew down below sober enough to fight."

"Well, tell the cooks to start coffee or something brewing to sober up the other half," Don replied. "How about these guys here?" He jerked his thumb in the direction of the four sleeping officers.

"Don't even bother." Gunney waved a claw in dismissal and shook his head. "Once they're out, they're good for a couple of hours, at least."

Don looked at the Izarian officers Puddlefoot had lashed to their acceleration poles. "I won't depend on them, then, but if they wake up we'll put them to work. Now here's what I want to do…"

Don plan was simple. The Spicians still flew in a conical formation, uncertain about the whereabouts of the Izarian fleet, thanks to Puddlefoot. Don meant to sail up one side of the cone with the fleet and catch the Spicians individually, before they could regroup.

"It's the only way," Don concluded. "The vessels are too evenly matched to make it a ship against ship fight. Besides, they outnumber us."

"It might work," hazarded Gunney.

"Then contact the fleet and let's get going."

The Izarian ships had been coasting, preparing themselves for the fight. Don snapped orders and the fleet moved with purpose. "Remind them to keep a tight formation," Don advised Gunney. "If they lose us the Spicians will eat them for breakfast. Puddlefoot, you can stop the razzle-dazzle now. In a minute the enemy fleet will know exactly where we are." He checked his 'scopes. They would be within blaster range of their first opponent within seconds. "All right, gang, this is where we tell the sailors from the weekend warriors."

Once the Spicians were certain of the location of the Izarian fleet, their formation changed once more, but by then it was too late. With the *Archangel* at the apex, the Izarian cone swallowed one of the enemy ships. A surge of energy engulfed the vessel as the cone discharged fire into its maw. The Spician's defensive screens ran through the spectrum and vanished. The next instant so did the ship.

Don swung the fleet and bore down on another vessel. The Spician fired two rockets at the approaching cone and tried to flee. Don ordered the Izarians to return fire and a score of rockets hurled at the retreating vessel. It tried to dodge but failed. In so failing the ship died, as the advancing rockets first destroyed its field then, literally, blew it into cosmic dust.

No more ships roamed the area for the moment. The fleet coasted on, waiting for other prey. Don took this opportunity to check nearby space, searching for the rest of the Spician ships.

"Ya-hoo!" cried Gunney, slapping Don on the back. "We're two for two, and nothing can stop us now."

"I hope not," Don replied. He was worried. The Spician Admiral managed to gather six vessels in a loose vee speeding to the rescue of their sister ships. He wasn't concerned about possible attack, but rather, the breakup of his formation. He had a deep, dark suspicion the Izarians couldn't possibly win a fight, unless the odds were in their favor. In anything like an equal battle, the mother-queen's ships would lose.

Don thought hard and fast. Suddenly a crazy idea popped into his mind. If this trick would work, however he must act now or not at all. It would only work once.

"Puddlefoot, do something to the Spician flagship."

"What, Sire?"

Don watched his 'scope. "I don't care. Just keep him busy for a couple of minutes. Gunney, ring up the fleet. This is what I want done..." He barked tense directions to the Izarian, who transferred them as tautly to the rest of the ships.

"All set? Implement," Don commanded.

The mouth of the cone widened, spread, and dispersed. So did the rest of the cone. Within thirty seconds of his order, the ship stood alone to face the oncoming Spician vessels.

"Puddlefoot, how'd you do?"

"Fine Sire." The brownie wore a merry grin on his face.

"*What* did you do?"

"Nothing much, Sire. I merely activated their damage control systems. All of them. It worked so well I did the other ships also."

"Wonderful." Don grinned too. "Remind me to double your ration of milk when we get out of this."

The enemy squad continued to bore down on the *Archangel*. Don hoped the confusion caused by Puddlefoot distracted their attention long enough so they did not realize what the rest of the fleet was doing. If the timing was right, he would emerge the hero. If any of a thousand things went wrong…He stopped speculating and got down to business. "Gunney, you said you had torpedoes aboard? How do they work?"

The Izarian nodded eagerly. "Oh, yeah. We run them out on wire. Guide each anywhere, stop them, or explode whichever one we want to at will. What do you have in mind?"

"Run a bunch of them out as far as they'll go and leave them there. What happens to the wire when I use the blasters?"

"Nothing. It's a special alloy."

"Good, let 'em rip." Don took a quick peek at the radar. "We're all set here, Gunney, now shoot off the rockets, continuous feed." The launchers spit out missiles, six at a shot.

"We can't do this for long," cautioned the gunnery officer.

"Hopefully we won't have to," replied Don. "They're in blaster range. Fire."

The middle of the enemy line took the brunt of the attack. The lead ship shivered as rockets detonated on its shield, while the energy of the blasters clawed at the tasty morsel beyond, but the line did not waver. In fact, it changed course to face the *Archangel* squarely. The Spicians launched rockets of their own, and then their blasters spoke.

Don tried dodging but was only partly successful. The majority of the rockets missed the ship but the blaster fire caught them fully. Needles in meters jumped as the shield generators took up the load. "All right, Gunney. They're directly over the torpedoes now. Blow 'em."

The enemy line heaved upward and sideward by the force of the explosions. One ship, less fortunate than the others, sat surrounded by four torpedoes when they detonated. Its shield vanished and a jagged piece of shrapnel tore through the bulkhead. Secondary explosions shattered the inside of the ship, transforming it into a flaming ball of fire.

So far, so good, thought Don. He kicked the engines into high, and the *Archangel* past the line of enemy ships. He slowed the flagship and threw her into the tightest turn he could manage. "This is part two," he advised the gunnery officer. "Let's see what happens. Bring our ships back in."

Gunney got busy on the microphone. As if rehearsed, the Izarian cone overtook the flagship and engulfed her. Don matched speed and was once again rode at the apex.

His plan worked to perfection. The fleet managed to disperse, turn, and come back together again, without loss of ships or configuration. "Phase three," Don said aloud. "Let's push it to maximum boost." The cone surged forward.

The Spician Admiral was in the process of swinging his line about. Another ship managed to regroup with the squad, but it added to, rather than lessened, the confusion when it tried to mesh with its mates. In a frenzy, the enemy line tried to straighten itself out as the cone swallowed it. Don nodded to Gunney. "Fire."

Energy spewed from the cone again. Like some giant worm, it commenced to digest what was in its guts. Spician screens flared, and then exploded, as the fire inside the cone rose to a fevered pitch. Within seconds, four of the trapped enemy disappeared. When the basters spent their power, nothing remained inside the Izarian formation, except for molten drops of glowing, red metal.

Gunney gazed intently at his 'scope. "My Lord, will you look at that."

Don checked his own 'scope. Somehow, a lifeboat launched from one of the Spician vessels and survived the inferno of the cone. It scurried on the edge of the fleet seeking desperately to escape.

Gunney asked Don, "Do we blast him?"

"Yes…no…shoot across his bow and send a raiding party over to capture them alive," decided Don. "Don't bring the lifeboat aboard, though. The ship may be booby-trapped."

Puddlefoot tugged on his arm. "Sire, 'twould be easier for me to fetch them hither."

"You're right, Puddlefoot," Don agreed. "Do it. Find the brig and pop them in."

Puddlefoot stared off into space. "'Tis done, Sire. What now?"

"Now we locate the rest of the Spicians. Gunney, can you spot anything on the radar?"

The officer glanced up from the 'scope and grinned. "Yeah, I saw them. After their flagship got wiped out they left so fast they must be halfway back to Spica by now."

"We're finished, then," Don said with a sigh and lounged back.

"No, it's not." Gunney scurried to the corner of the control room. He hurried back carrying three fifths of unopened Vegan rum.

"The guys are waking up, and we still have two cases of booze," he whooped, passing the rum to Don and Puddlefoot. "It's party time."

Chapter 14

"Well, Frik, that about wraps it up." Don, Puddlefoot, and the trader sat in the control room of the *Sparrowhawk*. Don added, "You're positive you don't want to come along with us?"

"I sure would like to," Frik replied, "but the mother-queen wants me to stay here a few more days. We have loose ends to tidy up. Besides, the Vas we captured on the escape pod is supplying us with all the plans of the Spicians."

"I take it the interrogation is going well," Don asked.

"Great. It's going great." Frik rubbed his tentacles together. "When the little rascal saw what the queen's High Executioner planned for him, he started babbling like a Capellain eating happy weed. I told you he was a nobleman, didn't I?"

Don nodded and made an adjustment on his control board. "Yeah. Count somebody or another. I still don't understand why he was on a Spician ship instead of a Vas."

"Count Bonsh is his name. He was there as an observer and advisor to the rebels. This morning he told us why the Vas are interested in Earth."

Don bolted upright in his chair and gave Frik his full attention. "What did he say?" His eyes sparkled.

"The Spicians found one of your space probes in an area where there wasn't supposed to be any intelligent life. The sent the Vas to locate the planet because the Vas are unknown in that part of the galaxy. The Spicians didn't want it nosed around they were interested in your sector."

"I still don't understand their concern in the first place, though." Don protested. "We haven't done anything."

"Oh. The Spicians didn't like the idea of a spacefaring race sitting on their flank when the fighting started," explained the trader. "They wanted to be sure they had no opposition to their takeover, and scare away any possible allies the Federation might make out your way."

Don issued a low whistle. "Well, I'll be. A bit premature weren't they? That's what I call blasting-off before you're fueled up."

Frik nodded. His expression changed and he gravely addressed Don. "Are you sure you still want to go to the planet of the Vas by yourself?"

Don frowned. "I didn't fly all this way to turn back, and now I know their system and home world. The human race still has a score to settle, remember. Besides..." he scratched his chin "...with the rebellion broken here, and the Spician fleet in this area destroyed, the Vas are going to look for someone to take out their anger on. I want to guarantee that someone isn't Earth."

Frik sighed. "I guess you're right. Have you said goodbye to Reggie yet?"

Don put his hands behind his head, leaned back, and chuckled. "Sort of. He sent a message this morning, along with a work crew. Here..." he reached into his pants pocket and produced a slip of paper. He handed it to Frik, "...read it."

Frik unfolded the note and read it aloud.

" 'Don old boy:
  We did them good. I cannot come to see
you off, so I am sending a present instead.
I am supplying you with our new blockbuster

*rockets, which I want you to know, will come
in handy when you encounter the Vas.
"'Mother sends her love, and she has
elevated you and Puddlefoot to the rank of
Rear Admirals in the Izarian Navy. I can do
nothing more than repeat, both of you are my
friends, and Friends of the Crown, forever.
I will not say goodbye, but rather, bid you
good luck on your quest. Till we meet again...
Your friend,
Reggie'"*

"Gol-ly," exclaimed Frik, handing the letter
back. "Rear Admirals no less. Your promotion sort
of puts a damper on what I was going to present you
guys."

Puddlefoot asked eagerly, "What gift, Master
Frik?"

"Captaincies in the Federation Secret Service."
Frik withdrew two wallet size folders from his
spacesuit and handed them over. "It ain't much, but
anywhere in Federation territory these credentials
will grant you help from the local authorities, food,
or transportation. Don't lose 'em."

"Thanks," Don said simply, gazing at the
shiny, six-pointed star on his.

Frik checked his timepiece. "Well, got to go.
You guys are blasting off in twenty minutes, and the
mother-queen expects me at the palace in thirty. If
you're ever in this part of the galaxy again, ring me
up."

Puddlefoot took Frik's tentacle. "Master Frik,
thou art a prince among beings."

Frik clasped him on the back. "Yeah, you too,
Bo. One day we gotta get together and count the
heads on an Aldebaranian. Don..." the Arcturian

started to get misty-eyed. He choked up and grabbed Don's hand, pumping it vigorously. "You take care of yourself, yah hear. Don't let those Vas sneak up on you." He hurried away.

"Well, Puddlefoot," Don said, watching the trader leave, "it's you and me again."

Puddlefoot looked up at him and asked, "Aye, Sire. Shall I make preparations for departure?"

"Yep, might as well. It's time." Don secured the airlock. "Let's give the place a fast look over. Make sure everything is battened down. I want to check the computer." He shot a fast grin at the brownie. "It wouldn't do to program the wrong location of the Vas's planet at this stage of the game."

They attended to their tasks. When Don was satisfied with his program, he asked Puddlefoot, "All set?"

"All set, Sire."

"Good. Let's strap down." Don called the control tower. *"Sparrowhawk to tower...permission to depart?"*

"Permission granted Sparrowhawk, *good luck."*

"Thank you, tower," Don replied. He started the countdown in his mind, timing it exactly to the ship's internal clock, and readied himself for acceleration. When he reached the five second mark he counted aloud. "Five...four...three...two...one...BLAST-OFF."

The ship burst into life, fire blazing from her jets. She pushed up and out of the volcano into the thin atmosphere of Izar IV. Don guided the ship into orbit around the planet, circled once, gained speed, and flung it at stars.

"All finished, we're off." Don unstrapped, sat up, and flexed his cramped arms. "Nothing to do until we arrive at Beta Bootis. Want to play a game of chess?"

"Nay sire." Puddlefoot surveyed the floor of the control room in disgust. "It has been too long since the ship hath been cleaned. Let me put my mop and broom at it for an hour, and then will I show thee how to play the game."

Don chuckled. "Suit yourself. I have to check the vectors, anyhow. We'll play when you're done."

***

One day blended into the next. Nothing happened, that is, nothing until the third day out.

It was Don's rest and recreation time. Puddlefoot hurried to the refrigeration unit, as usual, to fetch him a beer. Don lay back, listening to the strains of the *Grand Canyon Suite,* and saw the sun rise over the canyon. When it finally shone, he reached out to take a swallow of his favorite beverage.

His hand clutched air.

"Puddlefoot? Darn it, where's my beer?" He bolted upright, scowling. "I don't ask much, but a couple of beers when I'm trying to relax isn't a lot to do."

The brownie was nowhere around.

"Puddlefoot? Where the heck are you?" Don put his earphones aside and went in search of his sidekick.

Puddlefoot stood before the ship's refrigeration unit, busily pushing things aside and muttering to himself. When Don drew within earshot, the brownie was cursing softly, "By the Sons of Satan, where did he put it?"

Don peered over his shoulder. "What's the matter?"

Puddlefoot shook his head and looked sad. "I cannot find thy beer, Sire. "Twas here yesterday, I am sure of it, but now 'tis gone."

Don brushed him aside. "You're kidding. Puddlefoot, I put three six packs in there three days ago. I drink two beers a day. There should two more six packs left." He investigated for himself. "Say, you're right, they're gone."

"Aye Sire, as I feared. So is the Virginia ham, and the cheddar cheese, and the, ugh, Izarian lox you brought aboard."

"It can't be," Don protested. "I haven't touched my lox yet. Say..." he eyed Puddlefoot accusingly, "have you been raiding the icebox for midnight snacks?"

"Please Sire." Puddlefoot looked nauseated. "Ham and lox?"

"Well, if you didn't eat it, and I didn't eat it, then who..."

"We have a stowaway, Sire."

Don drummed his fingers on the refrigerator. "So I surmise, Sherlock. Let's take a look around."

They made a careful search of the ship, but didn't turn up a trace of anything alien. After Don searched the utility closet three times and found nothing, he declared, "It's no use. Whatever is aboard has discovered a good hiding place. I can't find a thing."

"Nor can I," agreed Puddlefoot. "'Tis most strange, too. I had thought I knew every corner of thy ship."

"Well, whatever is hiding will turn up eventually. It's only a matter of time. I guess we'll have to wait."

***

Food and beer continued to disappear from the galley at an alarming rate. Don set traps, and once, Puddlefoot waited all 'night', but the results were nil. Don began to suspect the only way they could find the stowaway would be to decompress the whole ship.

On the fifth day, Don awoke from a nap by a series of crashes in the galley. He yanked on his boots and went to see what all the commotion was about. When he arrived, Peter the cat had something trapped inside the refrigerator. The door stood ajar with the cat crouched down before it. Peter's fur stood on end. She emitted a series of low yowls.

"Begone, foul and vile creature, or I shall tie a knot in your tail," a voice from inside the refrigerator said.

The cat crouched lower and growled back.

"Hey, Peter, what'd you catch there?" Sliding his pistol out, Don approached cautiously and swung the door open, looking within.

Staring back at him was a miniature version of an Izarian, an empty beer can clutched in its claw. Underneath it, on a plate, was the remains of what was to be Don's supper. The creature threw the can at Don, missed, and started to reach for the plate.

"Hold on you. Get out of there." Don waved the laser in its face.

"Not until you remove your vile beast," the creature retorted.

Don glanced at Peter and swung his leg in her direction. "Scat cat." Peter retreated a few steps, and assumed her stance again by the galley hatch.

"Now out," ordered Don. "Make it quick."

The spider creature climbed down of the refrigerator and stood before him. Don noticed the panel at the base of the unit hung askew. *So that's where he was hiding,* he thought.

"Who are you and what are you doing here?" Don grated, keeping the alien covered with his pistol.

The Vas glared at him and said in an arrogant tone, "Count Bonsh, of the mother-queen's Navy, Earthling."

"Wait a minute." Don thought hard. "I've heard that name before." He remembered. "Hey, you're the Vas we captured in the battle. You can't be here. You're locked up in the palace dungeon."

Don heard a *pop* behind him. The next thing he knew, Puddlefoot stood beside him with his shillelagh raised high over his head. "Vas," he yelled and started bringing his club crashing on Bonsh.

The count scurried underneath the refrigerator.

Don grabbed the shillelagh on the down swing, bruising his hand in the process. "Ouch. Hey, you hurt me. Put the heavy artillery away, Puddlefoot. The time for fighting has passed."

Puddlefoot cocked his head. "Aye, Sire? He is Vas."

Don nodded quickly trying to calm the little brownie. "I know. I know." He released the club and shouted to the alien, "All right, you, come back out." When Bonsh did not respond, he knelt and placed his pistol at deck level. "NOW."

Two eyes peered cautiously out at him. Slowly, the count inched his way from under the unit. When he was fully exposed, he spoke. "Curb thy servant, Earthling, or I will see to it the mother-queen has you torn to bits."

Puddlefoot tightened the grip on his club. "Curb thy tongue, Vas, or I shall splatter thee on the deck." He raised the shillelagh again.

"Hold."

"Both of you cut it out and be civil," Don ordered. "One more crack and I'll space you both, understand? Now, Bonsh, how did you get here and why?"

The count and Puddlefoot glared at each other, and then Bonsh addressed Don. "I escaped," he said. "The Vas still have friends on our ancestral home. As to why…" he paused, "this is the only ship traveling to my world. I need this vessel to take me there."

Don laughed at the little monster in amazement. "You've got a screw loose. I'm turning this ship around. The Izarians still have questions to ask you."

"No Earthling," Bonsh replied smugly, "you will not. Without my help you will never find our mother-queen."

Don started to protest. The count hurried on, "Of course you know our sun, sure you know our planet, but can you locate our colony when no one else has been able to?" He snapped his claws deridingly. "I think not. You could search our world for a year and still be no closer to the mother-queen than you are now. Only I know the landing places, only I know the secret locks, only I know the passageways."

Damn, he has a point, Don thought. If the Vas lived underground like their bigger cousins, he's never find them, but... "What guarantee do I have you won't turn us in once we've brought you home?"

"Why, my word as a nobleman!" Bonsh said, indignantly. "If my pledge is not good enough for you, you still have me as a prisoner. What can I do when I am in your power?"

Don weighed the pros and cons in his mind. On impulse, he shoved out his hand. "It's a deal."

"Thou ravest, Sire," Puddlefoot said, aghast. "Dost thou knowest what you do? He is Vas."

"I know Puddlefoot, but he's right." Don grimaced and looked sideways at the count, who smirked back at the brownie. "He knows how to get in and we don't. It's as simple as that."

Puddlefoot made a scowl of his own. "As you say, Sire, but I shall watch this creature. I trust him not."

"Nor do I," agreed Don. "Keep your eyes on him."

The journey continued. A truce of sorts developed between Count Bonsh on one side, Puddlefoot and Peter on the other, with Don stuck in the middle as peacekeeper.

They entered the system of Beta Bootis, and Count Bonsh directed them to the fourth planet from the sun and had them take up orbit there.

"We will planet at a landing field not far from the colony," he advised. "From there we can walk to the main tunnels."

Don finished testing the atmosphere. He asked, "It looks like I'm going to have to bring spare oxy bottles too. The stuff you breathe is mostly methane. How can you guys inhale and not choke to death?"

"Forget the oxygen, Earthling," the Vas sneered. "There will be plenty of it for you once we reach the tunnels. We do not breathe the planet's air. We keep our atmosphere and pressure contained against the outer world, as we do our presence."

They landed in an old crater. Don couldn't guess its age, but the sides were worn smooth by countless eons of erosion. Off to his right Don made out the cone of a smoking volcano. It belched poisonous fumes into the already deadly fog enveloping the planet. He climbed into his pressure suit and instructed Puddlefoot, "I want you to stay here and guard the ship."

"Leave thee at the mercy of this rascal, Sire?" the brownie protested. "Nay. How could thou ask such a request of me?"

"I need you to protect the ship," Don whispered to the brownie after making sure Bonsh couldn't hear them. "She's our only means of escaping this planet. If something happens to her, she's captured or destroyed, say, we'll die here."

"Sire," the brownie objected, "Canst thou not put thy lock on her?"

"Yes, but any personal lock can be broken, given enough time. In case this little bugger is lying, I want to know the *Sparrowhawk* is safe." Don led him to the controls. "If I'm captured I want you to press this button. It will send the ship into orbit."

"Aye, Sire." Puddlefoot's lips turned down. "I shall try and watch thee, nevertheless."

"I know you will, buddy, and I appreciate it."

"Are you two done sniveling at each other?" Bonsh was dressed in his spacesuit. He glared at them, and said with faint scorn in his voice, "let us go, and leave thy servant behind if you will. He would only get on my nerves with his continual whining."

"Yeah, Bonsh, let's go." Don said out of the side of his mouth, "Puddlefoot, remember the button."

They entered the airlock and Don cycled it. Outside the ship, Bonsh took the lead crossing the floor of the crater until they reached its wall. There, he waved Don close to him.

"Stand next to me, Earthling, and be prepared to move when the door opens."

Bonsh reached as high as he could and pushed a small outcropping of stone. Thirty seconds passed, and then another thirty. When Don started to think the Vas picked the wrong location, a portion of the wall slid back.

"Now Earthling. Move."

Bonsh was already scurrying through the opening. Don jumped after him with just enough time to squeeze in before the door shut behind. The tunnel was pitch black, but ahead he heard a soft noise scurrying away. "Bonsh," he whispered.

He heard nothing.

"Bonsh? Where are you?"

From down the tunnel a faint reply echoed back. "Foolish Earthling, the mother-queen will eat your flesh for breakfast! The pack will track you down in theses tunnels and crush your bones to dust. Goodbye, foolish Earthling – goodbye.

"Damn." Don flicked on his suit's headlamp, found it didn't work, and sprinted after the retreating voice without thought of where he was going. He took fifteen steps and crashed into a bend in the tunnel. He fell backward, half-stunned, and scrambled back to his feet. Arms outstretched, he groped for the walls. By sliding along, Don found the tunnel bent to the right and ran true for another twenty paces. He crept on, but slower, feeling his way as he went.

The tunnel twisted to the left and started to widen. Soon his arms extended to their limits as he slipped along. After a short time, he couldn't touch the walls at all, but contented himself with keeping his right hand on one side while the other was held out in front. Several times, he met other openings, but these he passed up, keeping to the main tunnel.

His anger cooled. It was foolish to try to locate Bonsh in these dark, subterranean passageways. The Vas could be anywhere. Right next to him, or ten miles away, and he'd never know it. In any case, Bonsh was gone, that was certain. The count probably had an army out searching theses tunnels right now.

Don stumbled upon another side passage and slowed his pace. Fumbling ahead, he kept slapping the darkness ahead of him, seeking to feel the side of the corridor. He maintained as straight a course as possible, while counting his paces. He did not want to wander into the side corridor by mistake. After forty paces, he still hadn't touched the wall. He stopped and contemplated his position.

The wall of the tunnel might not resume. For all he knew this could be a cave. Before he ventured any farther and became hopelessly lost, his best bet was to turn around. Better yet, good sense dictated he backtrack all the way to the crater wall to the ship. Upon reaching a decision, he did an about-face and retraced his steps.

Forty out. Forty back. Don counted as he walked. When he reached the magic number, he started sidestepping to his right, hoping to catch the wall as he went. When this didn't produce the results he wanted, and it became ridiculous to move any farther in that direction, he stepped double the number of paces to the left. This gave the same results. He returned to center again, advanced ten paces, and repeated the operation.

After performing this a number of times, Don conceded he'd somehow got lost. *Probably wandered into a cavern and turned,* he thought, with chagrin. He'd walk straight ahead until he struck a wall, swing right or left, and pray he hit the right passageway. He moved off again, and after a few more steps, touched stone with his extended hand. Don scooted left and fell into the mouth of a tunnel.

Relieved, he crept down the passage. The tunnel twisted right, but memory told him it should bend to the left. He reviewed the tunnel's curls and turns prior to becoming lost and concluded it was the wrong passageway. He went back the way he had come and searched the cavern wall for another exit. He was still trying to find his way out when a Vas patrol entered the cave and placed him in irons.

***

"Give me a break, fellas," Don protested as four of the Vas tried manhandling him along a tunnel. "Isn't this the way to the museum? No? I swear, I'll never book a vacation with this travel agency again. This is the third time they've put me down in the wrong place. The last time it was a…"

"Quiet worm," A Vas sergeant, who was in charge of the patrol, cut him off. The noncom held an electric torch in one claw, and a pistol trained on

Don's chest in the other. "Quit your prattling. We are taking you to the mother-queen, so move lively now. She does not like to be kept waiting," A soldier pushed him from behind.

Don stumbled forward, tripping. "Hey, cut it out. I can take a hint. Next year I'm staying at home." They lead him away, down a side passage, and soon reached a series of light panels at the intersection of two tunnels. The Vas sergeant called a halt.

"You." He picked out one of his men by eye. "Run ahead and advise Count Bonsh the Earthling has been captured. Tell him we are going to the castle Danque and deliver the prisoner into the hands of the mother-queen."

The soldier hurried off along one tunnel. The squad, with Don in the middle and the sergeant in the lead, turned and marched down the other. They traveled for a half an hour, going deeper and deeper into the bowels of the Vas world. As time passed, Don noticed cut marks on the tunnels to enlarge them. He wondered who did all the chopping. The Vas didn't look the type to do manual labor.

The passageway leveled off, becoming wider and higher as their party entered into a manmade cavern. After seeing the tunnel and the cave, his curiosity got the better of him. He said to the chief Vas, "Hey, Sarge, who dug all this stuff, imported labor?"

A gruff laugh issued from the soldiers. The sergeant responded with, "Silence, worm." A moment later he replied, "You will learn soon enough who made these tunnels. First, however, the mother-queen wishes to inspect you. Yonder, in the castle Danque, you will meet your doom."

An aperture swelled in the distance, the wall of the cavern chiseled away around two stalactites. Projecting upward, two stalagmites rose to greet them. To Don they looked like the features of a wolf, its face bared in a snarl. The squad marched him through the mouth and into the castle.

Inside, Don received a quick briefing. "Listen, Earthling," the Vas sergeant said, "when you are brought before the mother-queen you are to kneel. Do not look up. To do so will mean your death. When the audience concludes, you will hear a clap. Touch your head to the floor, and we will take you away. You will not speak unless she speaks to you. Understand?"

Don understood. The Vas hustled him upstairs to a hall. At ten-foot intervals, guardsmen stood at the ready. The Vas dragged him before a portal in front of two more guards. The sergeant walked up to them and held a brief conversation. One of the guards nodded and entered the chamber. The sergeant returned, inspected his men, and warned Don, "He has gone to announce us, Earthling. Don't forget what I said."

In a short while, the guard returned. He swung the doors open wide and the squad entered. A multitude of Vas stood inside, dressed in gem-encrusted harnesses and ribbons. They watched Don, dirty and bleeding, who glared back before stopping in front of a grotesque Female Vas lying on a throne. After a fleeting glance, he looked away and knelt.

The queen took no notice of him and the squad of soldiers. This was fine with Don. The longer she waited the longer he lived. He made himself comfortable on the marble floor and listened to the conversations of the Vas nobility around him.

"...The queen is wroth about the loss of the fleet..."

"...is he an Earthling? Look at him, what an ugly creature..."

"...is said to be in grave trouble with the queen. The rebellion was his responsibility."

Don zeroed in on this conversation and listened further.

"He brought back the Earthling. He promised a new uprising in six months' time."

"Count Bonsh has promised this before. The queen grows tired of his failures."

"Then perhaps the count's tunnels will soon be vacant. I must talk to the duke about this."

"Possibly, but I think the duke has designs on them himself."

So, Don thought, *Bonsh has been the bad boy all along. Well, he'll get his soon enough, if I have a chance. Maybe I can help things along.*

As if cut by a switch, the voices fell still, a hush spread through the hall until not a sound echoed. Don resisted the urge to glance up and waited for what was about to happen.

A thin, wavering voice spoke. "Who are these things that would approach me?" When no one answered, the voice went on, "Well, come hither, don't stand about." Claws jerked Don to his feet and dragged him nearer the dais. When they were close, a rough claw pushed him down again.

"Sergeant, what have you brought to me?" the queen asked.

"An Earthling, your Majesty."

"How odd he appears. Who told you to bring him here?"

"Count Bonsh, your Majesty."

"Ahhh, yes, my precious count." The queen addressed the audience at large. "Where is Count Bonsh now? If he is present, let him stand before me and explain why he sends an Earthling to my throne instead of delivering Izar."

The hush deepened. From behind, Don heard a shuffling. It stopped and Count Bonsh knelt beside him.

"Well, Count, we see you are here. What have you to say for yourself?"

"Your Majesty, due to no fault of my own, our cause on Izar was set back a few months. I have brought the cause of this delay to you so he may have a fitting punishment."

"Through no fault of your own, you say?" the mother-queen sneered. "What were you doing while this creature destroyed all our carefully laid plans, sleeping?"

"Your Majesty," the count blustered, "I was busy…"

"Silence. I would hear from the Earthling. Tell me creature," the queen addressed Don, "how is it a worm like yourself could stop the plans of the Vas?"

"Your Majesty," Don started, keeping to the format of address, "it is not my place to speak unkindly about the subjects of the mother-queen, but the whole affair was conducted very sloppily, very sloppily, indeed."

The queen laughed. "You see, Count, even this dumb animal, from a backward planet, knows stupidity when he sees it. Maybe a few weeks with a hammer and chisel in the tunnels will make you smarter. The Earthling can accompany you as a tutor until Gaea arrives. Dismissed."

"Your Majesty. A word please?" Don stood fast before the throne and shook off guards.

The mother-queen glared at Don with more astonishment than anger. "What? You dare speak to me without being addressed first? How impertinent."

"Please, your Majesty, I am a stranger in your land. Even on my own planet, though, you are known for your grace, charm, and tolerance toward visitors."

The monarch snorted in surprise. "Really? I would not think it likely. However, you are correct. You may have your say."

Don composed his words mentally before speaking. This was his sole chance to plea Earth's cause before the Vas, to complete his mission in a peaceful manner without further fighting.

"Your Majesty, a grave misunderstanding has arisen between our people. My world wishes to be friends with the Vas, to exchange ambassadors, set up trade, and develop a give and take of ideas and views.

"I have been sent here to initiate these first steps, which will lead to a better understanding between our two races. I offer you the chance to heal the wound of contention that has developed. I entreat you to deal with us in this manner, so we may know the Vas are a fair people. Your Majesty, I extend to you the hand of friendship." Saying this, he reached out his right hand to the queen.

Don couldn't read her expression. The queen contemplated his hand gravely, at last spoke, "Your misshaped claw would look better with a pickaxe in it. Guards, take this vermin away."

Chapter 15

Don found himself in a cell carved into the side of one of the lower tunnels, chained to a wall by the sergeant who conducted him there. Before closing the cell door behind him, the Vas chuckled, "You are lucky to be alive, Earthling. The mother-queen must have liked the reply you gave her."

"Yeah, and for that she housed me in the deluxe suite," Don retorted. He glanced at a pile of dried bones pushed in the corner. "Someone else the queen liked?"

"Hope you do not end up like him, Earthling." The sergeant slammed the door and left.

In the silence, Don started to puzzle over the whereabouts of Puddlefoot. Now would be the perfect time for him to appear, but the brownie had the knack of materializing only when he wanted to. Don knew he would show up eventually. He wished it would not be too much later. He looked again at the bones and shuddered.

He hadn't eaten since leaving the ship many hours before. His stomach growled at him demanding food. Don decided to do something about it.

"Hey. Yo. Anybody here?" he shouted and banged on the bars of his cell. "Don to Vas, Don to Vas. Come in Vas." He kept the racket going until he received a snarl from down the tunnel.

"Silence scum. Don't you know better than to disturb me while I sleep? I'll haul you out of there and give you a taste of the lash."

A Vas crawled up to the cell, its sparse hairs grey and missing one leg. The others moved stiffly as the creature approached, stopped, and banged the hilt of a whip against the bars of the door.

Don backed up quickly. "Hey mate, don't get angry. I just want to know when dinner is served."

The guard peered into the cell. "Why, I could have sworn you had two heads and four legs the last time I looked in here," he exclaimed. "What happened?"

A chill ran down Don's spine. "You're thinking of the fellow over there." He gestured to the pile of dried bones. "I'm the new tenant. When do we eat?"

"Amazing," the Vas mumbled and shook his head. "They change them too fast for old Charlie." He stopped talking and crept away.

"Hey, wait." Don hung on the bars and rattled them. "When do we eat? Come back."

"Don't bother," a voice close by said. "He's already forgotten about you."

Startled, Don asked, "Who's there? who are you?"

"Next cell. I'm a prisoner like yourself. Call me Nicholas."

"Hey, Nick, when do they feed us around here?"

A hollow laugh came back. "Feed us? Tomorrow we'll be taken to extend the tunnels. If you're lucky you can steal food leaving, or returning. If you're not..."

"If I'm not," Don finished the sentence, "I'll wind up as a little pile of bones swept in the corner?"

"Exactly."

Don sighed and sat back against the wall. The chain holding him clamped to the rock with three pins and to his leg by a clasp and lock. He picked up the chain and examined it. The links were old and rusty. He gave it a few experimental tugs, but the shackles remained firmly together. It was not *that* old.

Next, Don investigated the lock. The metal was as old and worn as the chain. He hunted in his pockets for something to pick it with, but came up empty.

Don looked around his cell. "Come on," he muttered, "there must be something in here I can use to escape." Outside of the pile of bones, and a few loose rocks, the hole was empty. He stared from the rocks to the chain, shrugged, and picked one up. "Well, it works in the movies."

Don scrutinized the chain, this time checking each link, searching to see how worn they were. He found one particularly decayed, rusted halfway through. He placed the link before him and commenced pounding away. Slowly, and with methodical beats of the rock, he kept hammering until he fell asleep, exhausted.

***

A beautiful woman knelt beside him. She held a silver platter on which a roast turkey lay. Placing it beside him, she filled a goblet full of sparkling rose wine.

Don pulled off a turkey leg and accepted the glass. The woman, a blonde, sat on her heels waiting to do his bidding. He started to take a bite of turkey, but before he could do so, the woman spoke. "You must get up."

Don shook his head and murmured, "Uh-uh, I'm staying right here."

"UP." A hot sting flashed across his belly. Don bolted upright and rolled as a whip bit the spot where he'd slept. Before he could stand, the whip caught him across the shoulder, bringing a scream of pain from his lips.

"Up, I said. Old Charlie has no time to waste on a sluggard like you." The whip spoke again over Don's head.

He scrambled to his feet. "Yes sir. I'm up. I'm up."

"That's better. Come here, I want to unlock you." His jailer produced a key and fiddled with the lock. "Too much for old Charlie to do," the Vas said to him. "Prisoners come in, but none go out. There." He stepped back and flicked his whip. "Now, don't go getting any ideas. Quick march outside and let me hook you up again."

Don did so. Once outside four other prisoners waited. Don noticed Count Bonsh at once. He stood at the head of the chain gang. The count was dirty, tired, and scared. His legs slumped, and from time to time, he trembled. Two other aliens waited behind him, both of the same species. They looked like Vas, but had only six legs instead of eight. Upon closer inspection, Don saw their bodies segmented into three parts.

Charlie pushed Don beside the last prisoner in line. Don knew the other's race. He was a Spician. The apeman failed to take notice of him as Charlie shacked them together, but once they marched off the Spician spoke.

"You kept me awake yesterday with you infernal banging. That's fine with me, and old Charlie is half deaf, but others can hear. You'd best figure out a way to tone it down."

Don recognized him by his voice. Nicholas. The same prisoner who'd spoken to him after he'd been jailed. The thought of his conversation reawaken hunger. Don's stomach growled, saying, *Feed Me,* in no uncertain terms.

"Thanks for the advice," Don replied. "I'll remember. What did you mean yesterday about eating when they took us out?"

The Spician gave a low chuckle. "Watch me, and do what I do. In a few minutes, we'll approach an open air market. If fortune smiles on us you will have your breakfast."

The tunnel they marched along broadened, turned into a small, brightly lit cavern. Scattered about, selling food and dry goods, stood booths. The chain gang wormed its way between the stalls, sometimes swerving out of the way of small vans conveying produce. The Vas weren't big on streets.

The prisoners approached one stand dealing in meat pies and cooked vegetables. As they drew abreast of it, the Spician moaned and thumped his hands together.

"Uhhh…uhhh…uhhh." Nicholas rocked rhythmically back and forth. Don mimicked his fellow prisoner, not knowing why.

The proprietor of the stall rushed out shouting at Charlie, "Stop. Please, stop. This is the fourth time this week you have brought him past my store, and now he's has another one doing it."

Old Charlie stopped and cocked his head. "Eh? What'd you say?"

"No, go. He's starting." The storekeeper waved his claws at them.

The Spician's moans grew louder. He threw himself into the stall. The sides split and pies, vegetables, and proprietor went flying. Don had no choice, Together with the rest of the prisoners he landed in the middle of the mess.

A feast lay all around Don. The Spician whispered in his ear, "Quick, take something." Don saw a smashed meat pie and some fresh vegetables that looked like carrots. He scooped them up and stuffed the treasure inside his pressure suit. Right after this, the storekeeper pulled him roughly to his feet.

"See! See what you've done." The Vas gestured to his ruined shop. He shook a claw at old Charlie, "It's the government's fault. They're your prisoners. I'll sue, that's what I'll do."

"Eh?" said Charlie. "Problems, problems, problems, that's all old Charlie gets. Stand up, you." He tugged on the chains. "It's off to work. You..." He addressed the Spician, "no more of your pranks. You hear."

Nicholas winked at Don and stood, strolling out of the wreckage of the booth. Don and the other prisoners did the same, with the exception of Count Bonsh. Bewildered by the Spician's actions, the count curled himself into a tight ball. Their guard flicked his whip over the nobleman. "Didn't you hear me? Time to go to work." Bonsh uncurled slowly and peered about. The chain gang marched away, dragging the count as they left.

Old Charlie led them to the end of the tunnel. Sledgehammers, chisels, and pickaxes scattered about the ground, dropped from the previous day's labor. From long habit, the two aliens and Nicholas picked up the tools and fell to hacking away at the rock. After a moment's hesitation, Don and Bonsh did the same. Old Charlie settled back and watched as they labored, once and a while snapping the whip in their direction and ordering them to work faster.

After fifteen minutes, Don could contain himself no longer. He dropped the chisel he held and withdrew the battered meat pie from his suit.

"Psst, put the food away." Nicholas placed his sledgehammer down and flexed his tired muscles, covering Don as he hid his food again. The Spician waited for him to pick up the chisel and resumed hitting it. Between blows he whispered, "Charlie will be asleep in a few minutes, wait until he is quiet, then we can eat."

Don followed his advice. In another quarter hour, old Charlie's head nodded. A short time after, he snored gently. The prisoners continued hammering at the wall for a few more minutes. Then, as their guard's snores grew louder, they stopped.

The twin aliens sat and produced loaves of bread, filled with hunks of dark, fatty meat, pilfered from the food stall. Nicholas squatted on his haunches and pulled out three meat pies from beneath his tunic. The Spician indicated a spot in the dust next to him where Don could sit.

"Better hurry up, old Charlie doesn't nap very long."

He didn't have to tell Don. As soon as the aliens sat, Don hauled out his own plunder and started cramming bits into his mouth. After the apeman's invitation, he squatted next to the Spician, never stopping the process of chewing and swallowing.

"Hey, where did you fellows get the food?" Bonsh gawked at them in wide-eyed astonishment, saliva dripping from his chelicera. "I didn't see anyone pass out breakfast."

The aliens tittered in high squeaks and continued to gobble their bread. The Spician did not even do that. He stuffed another meat pie into his mouth.

"Aren't you going to share? Please? We're all in the same predicament. I'm hungry."

The three ignored Bonsh and finished eating. Don licked sauce from his fingers, withdrew the carrots from his suit, and glared at the count.

"Here," he growled, splitting the vegetables in two, "This will have to hold you." Don tossed the vegetables in the general direction of the Vas.

The prisoners reclined, relaxing. Presently, the twin aliens stood and started work on the tunnel again. Nicholas sighed and got to his feet. "Well, I guess it's time. Old Charlie will be waking up from his nap soon."

Don tucked the remainder of the carrots away and picked up his chisel. "Do you want me to hammer for a while?"

The Spician grinned and shook his head. "Uh-uh. I was born with two hands, and I want to keep them."

Don took the sledge from him. "So now you're going to learn what the term shaker really means."

Count Bonsh didn't resume working when the others did. He crouched in the dust and make comments.

"You creatures are foolish," the count remarked with some of his old arrogance. "The doddering fool will sleep all day. Why wear yourselves out?"

"Doddering fool, am I?" The whip slashed across the count's body. He sprang erect, stared around in panic. "Back to work you lazy bum." The whip spoke again.

Bonsh rolled away from the lash and pulled himself to his full three foot height. "I am Count Borris Bonsh. How dare you treat me like *this?*"

Charlie snapped the whip. This time Bonsh flew off his feet. "I don't care if you're the mother-queen herself. You're here to cut this tunnel. Now work."

The count scrambled to his feet and hobbled back to the wall. Charlie gave him one more slash, nodded in satisfaction, and settled back. Don continued to hammer away mutely, content he'd eaten, and trying to hatch a plan of escape.

As they cut deeper into the wall Don felt the rock grow warmer. He'd discovered talking was permissible, if kept in quiet tones so not to disturb Charlie. He asked the Spician, "How come this rock is getting so hot?"

"A volcanic conduit on the other side," remarked Nicholas, wiping sweat from his face. "The Vas run their tunnels parallel to them when they can for heating. In fact, this whole colony rest on a lake of molten lava."

"What?" Don said, incredulous. "You gotta be kidding, they're nuts."

"I know it sounds crazy," added the Spician, "but their engineers say everything is under control."

Ten hours later Charlie halted the work. Don dropped his sledgehammer and their group marched away. He cursed the blisters on his hands, and limping where he'd slipped and hit himself in the foot. Don planned to steal a chisel and take it with him, but Nicholas warned against it. "They keep a count of the tools," he cautioned when Don stated his idea.

Shuffling to their cells, old Charlie led them along a different route through the market. Nicholas again had a sudden bout with insanity, this time in front of a booth selling smoked fish. Don learned from his previous experience. He packed his suit to the rim before the irate storeowner hurried them on their way.

Locked away, Don spread out his plunder and ate ravenously. He regretted his choice of victuals at once. Old Charlie had allowed the prisoners only one drink during the day, brought by a Vas water bearer, who doled out a cupful of brackish liquid to each member of the chain gang. Don was thirsty, and the fish didn't help. He resigned himself to wait for the next work period when he could steal a drink.

After finishing his repast, Don resumed his attack on the chain. He heeded Nicholas's warning and covered the link with a piece of cloth ripped from his shirt. It wasn't perfect, but it did change the clinking of the hammering to a dull, thumbing noise. He worked for hours, afterwards laying the rock aside in disgust. Exhausted, he stretched out and tried to fall asleep.

The rest he needed wouldn't come. His body ached, but his mind refused to settle down. He worried about Puddlefoot. The brownie should've arrived by now. That he hadn't made an appearance meant something was amiss at the *Sparrowhawk.*

After endlessly tossing and turning, Don nodded. In the curious state between wakefulness and slumber, he discerned movement in the cell with him. Fear gripped his throat as the thing drew near, and red beady eyes glowed from an evil face. Frantically he struggled back to consciousness and sat up with a start.

A small animal crouched before him. It was light pink, about two feet long including the tail, and hairless. The creature bared its sharp, pointed teeth in a snarl when Don moved. The worst thing about it was the smell. A rancid odor of decay and rotting flesh emanated from the pink skin and filled the cell.

Don gagged and drew back in horror as the animal closed on him and sniffed his boot. Clutching at the rock he used as a hammer, he hurled it at the creature. The thing emitted a squeal, twisted around, and fled. Afterwards, Don stayed awake and maintained a careful vigil.

When the time came to leave for the wall again, Don staggered to his feet, bleary and spent, presenting the perfect picture of a man on the verge of a nervous breakdown. During the morning foray, he opted for three cans of a sweet, sticky beverage he drank in quick gulps when Charlie fell asleep. During the day, he felt the taste of the whip twice for slacking off, and by the time old Charlie rounded them up and marched them off, he could hardly stand. Tottering along beside Nicholas, he stole only two pieces of unappetizing fruit on the way home. After his jailer locked him in his cell, Don sank spent to the floor.

He wanted desperately to sleep, but feared of what lucked in the shadows. Instead, he lay on his stomach with a sharp piece of stone under his throat. He jabbed himself several times as his head bobbed, and in disgust, threw the rock aside. Tomorrow would bring another day of hard physical labor, if he didn't sleep now, old Charlie would rip him apart with his whip. Don closed his eyes and nodded off.

Before sleep could overtake Don, movement again startled him. This time the shadow stood silently in the semi-darkness watching him.

"Get away, blast you," he moaned. Don pushed himself into the corner of his cell and grasped the thighbone of the cell's former occupant. Still groggy, he swung it over his head.

"Hold sire. 'Tis I, Puddlefoot."

Don dropped the ancient bone. It fell to the floor and shattered into a dozen pieces. He blinked hard, shook himself awake, and gaped at his friend.

Puddlefoot's coat had burn marks at the edges. His hat was sooty, and black smudges streaked his cheeks. One of his eyes was swollen shut, but the brownie gave Don a merry smile, until he saw Don's wretched condition.

"Art thou well, Sire? Ye look like the cat's play toy."

Don could barely contain himself with joy as he replied, "Yeah, tired, old buddy, that's all. What happened to you?"

Puddlefoot crossed his arms and said, "Oh, nothing Sire, but you were right in having me stay with the ship. Shortly after you left with the knave, Bonsh, his friends arrived." He glanced at his clothes. "They took me by surprise."

"Did you manage to do like I asked?"

Puddlefoot chuckled softly, "Oh, aye, Sire. I pressed the button, and the *Sparrowhawk* flew into space. She is up there now, circling the planet, waiting for thee."

Don felt relief flood through him like a spring rain. "Swell, all we gotta do now is snap these chains off me, and we can get the heck out of here."

Puddlefoot inspected Don's shackles and shook his head. "Nay, Sire, have I not told thee 'afore I possess no power over iron? I can do nothing to free thee."

Don's face dropped. "You've got to be kidding me. Nothing?"

Puddlefoot stared at the chains and said, unhappy, "Not with iron, Sire. We must ponder upon the question."

They sat on the floor and thought about the spell of iron. Finally, Don exclaimed, "Puddlefoot – I have cutting tools aboard the ship. Bring them back here, and I can break this chain myself."

Puddlefoot winced. "Nay Sire, I hath thought of that. All thy tools are steel, which is made from iron."

Don cursed. "Next time remind me to bring a titanium hacksaw blade along."

"What Sire?"

"Titanium," Don replied, "a very strong metal…harder than steel, in fact. If I had a saw like that you could transport it, and I could cut this chain…" He stopped and repeated his words. A glimmer of an idea formed. "Puddlefoot, I don't have anything other than steel, but I bet the Vas do, especially with the outer atmosphere of this place. If not titanium then maybe bronze. You know what bronze is, don't you?"

"Aye Sire."

Don's eyes locked onto Puddlefoot's. "Great. This is what you to do. Search factories, tool and die makers, and machine shops. You'll find something we can use not made from iron. When you do, bring it back here, and I can free myself."

"Sire, it will take time." Puddlefoot appeared doubtful. "When I came searching for thee I found these tunnels extend for many miles."

"Don't worry," Don said, grinning. "I'm not going anywhere. Now scoot. The faster you start moving, the quicker I get out of this mess."

Puddlefoot nodded. With a *POP,* he was gone.

"Hey, Puddlefoot, wait."

Don heard another pop. Puddlefoot stood next to him again. "Aye, Sire?"

"As long as you're here anyway, do you think you could...?"

"Oh. Right away, Sire. I'll be back in a flash." This time Don heard a triple pop like the sound of a cap gun shooting. By his side, he found two cans of beer.

"The boy is going to make a great wife for someone," Don said as he grabbed one can and opened it. He added to himself, *Thank goodness for aluminum.*

Chapter 16

A month passed. After the first week, Don lost hope Puddlefoot would return. By the end of the second, he felt sure something happened to the brownie. Days passed with little change in his routine.

At the conclusion of the second week, Count Bonsh's release came. Don didn't see him leave but missed him on the chain gang. Not that his presence lightened the workload. Nevertheless, some of the drudgery disappeared as, time after time, he watched the count find himself in trouble because of his arrogance.

The following day Bonsh returned with another Vas. While the prisoners waited outside their cells, the two talked with old Charlie. The three argued briefly until Charlie threw up his claws and agreed to whatever they demanded. From that day on, the chain gang marched to the wall by a longer route. One not including the market.

Things became rougher after the tunnel change. Nicholas accepted this with outward indifference, as he took all problems. During the course of the workday, he told Don why.

"We Spicians have two stomachs," he grunted, swinging his sledgehammer. "The first digests food quick, for extra energy. The second takes about a month. I keep that one filled for emergencies like this."

Don envied him and wished his stomach were as full. Unfortunately, he needed food every once and a while, otherwise his belly said the rudest things.

He survived. Don found his nighttime visitors quite tasty after starving for three days. He didn't mind the smell, or the taste of raw meat. What was even better, the animal had brothers and sisters Lots of them. Whereas before he quailed at the thought of falling asleep, now he sprawled out eagerly and pretended slumber, until his supper arrived.

The twin aliens were not so resourceful. By the end of the third week they could barely walk. A few days later, they failed to appear on the chain gang. Instead, the horrid smell of rotting flesh gradually filled the tunnel.

More aliens from different worlds arrived to swell the ranks of the work crew. The point came where it took Old Charlie half the day to beat his wards out of their cells, shackled together, and to the wall. He would march them home after only an hour's work.

During this time, the Vas never fed their prisoners. This didn't worry Don until he noticed the population of his food supply take a dramatic downturn. Apparently, some of the new captives possessed the same need to eat as he.

During a work 'day', Don asked Nicholas, "Nick, hand me the straight dope. Why are the Vas treating us this way? If they want us to work, shouldn't we be fed?" The Spician contained a wealth of information about the Vas. If anyone knew what was happening, he would.

Nicholas chipped away at the wall before stopping to find a new grip on his hammer. "You really don't know?"

"If I knew I wouldn't ask." Don moved his chisel to a different spot. "They don't feed us, they've been marching us round in circles. Why? They don't need us to do their work at all." Don glanced at Old Charlie. The Vas snored away. "I've seen their work crew bore a tunnel and finish it in two hours, using high speed drilling equipment. Why don't they let us sit in our cells and rot? Or kill us off?"

The Spician took a few experimental swings at the chisel. "You didn't realize this is a holding pen? No, of course not..." he corrected himself, "how could you. You said you've never heard of this planet before."

"A holding pen? What are they holding us for?"

Nicholas grunted as he swung his hammer. "Their feast of Gaea. The day after tomorrow is the anniversary of the Vas flight from Izar, and the day when, hopefully, they will return." He stopped swinging and said, "The highlight of the holiday is the battle in the arena, where the forces of the galaxy are pitted against the Vas."

"Huh?"

"We represent the bad guys. The forces of the galaxy," Nicholas explained, "different races brought together. The Vas herd us into their national stadium, and bring in a bunch of carnivores. The Vas import the beasts for that very reason. The meat-eaters represent the Vas. There's a battle and the Vas win. It's supposed to be symbolic of what they'll do when they regain Izar."

Don said in a hushed voice, "How can you stand there and say we're going to die so calmly? You're talking about us. We're going to be killed."

Old Charlie grunted and opened one eye. Don moved his chisel and Nicholas swung at it. The Spician continued in lower tones, "What would you have me do? Tear my hair out and scream? We will die, and we can do nothing about it. That's why the

Vas do not feed us. From their point of view it would be wasteful."

"So why this runaround?" Don persisted.

"Who knows?" The Spician shrugged. "Maybe to keep us occupied so we don't riot in our cells. Maybe they figure one hour's work is better than none at all."

Don and Nicholas changed tools and Don swung the sledgehammer. "You talk as if you've seen this battle in the arena before. Have you?"

Nicholas glanced at Charlie and nodded. "Yes, once, five years ago. I was a cultural liaison attach to the Spician Embassy. I only remained a few months, but I stayed long enough to see that."

"Were they armed? The prisoners I mean?"

Nicholas issued a booming laugh causing Charlie to scowl their way. "Well, if you call spears, clubs and swords weapons, then, yes. It didn't help them any. What a bloody spectacle the slaughter was. You should have seen it."

"Don't worry," Don replied darkly, "from what you told me, in two day I'll have a front row seat."

"You two, shut up." The whip snapped over their heads. "Time to leave anyway," grumbled Charlie, getting to his feet. "Back to your cells."

Locked away in his prison, a scuffling in the corridor disturbed Don's bleak thoughts. *New Prisoner. They always put up a fight before they're thrown in here.*

He lay down and feinted sleep. It was time to catch his dinner. Indeed, one of the small creatures did slink along. It approached, sniffed cautiously at his out-flung arm, and snarled as it scurried forward.

The animal paused in its attack. The creature looked in the direction of the cell door, and with a squeak, disappeared. The door banged open and old Charlie crept in, pushing a new captive ahead of him.

"In with you now, march, before I break your skull."

The prisoner stumbled forward. Charlie ordered the new inmate to sit while he chained the man to the wall. After securing the manacles, he said with some concern, "Too many for old Charlie to watch. If this continues, I must ask the duke for extra men." He shook his head and left.

"Weiss, this is starting to become a habit. One of us is a jinx."

Don took a good look at the new prisoner. "Captain Sims?"

"In the flesh, buddy." The Captain stretched his legs out and massaged his thighs. "Ahhh. That feels good."

Don stared at him in disbelief, speechless. "Captain Sims," he asked, "how did you find me? For that matter, how did you get here?"

The provost marshal held up a hand. "Whoa, slow down, Weiss. Let me work the cramps out of my legs. Those critters paraded me through these tunnels all day, and my legs aren't use to all the walking."

Don waited a decent interval and repeated, "How did you locate me?"

The captain sighed. "We had the *Sparrowhawk* wired."

"Huh?"

Sims scratched his chin with a wry smile and said, "Yeah, your ship is bugged. We have a tracer in her. Every movement from the time you left

Earth, until the time you planeted here, has been monitored."

Don felt violated. What were they thinking back on Earth? Was Doctor Thomas preparing a room where he could live out the rest of his life with brownie delusions?

"How come no one told me?" Don shouted.

The captain pursed his lips and wiggled into a comfortable position. "Well, you'll remember times were pretty hectic, the last few days before your departure," explained Sims. "I guess no one thought to tell you. It's an experimental device…sends off a beep that's transmitted instantaneously back to the receiver. The Navy decided to place one in at the last minute."

"Oh, a beep." Don was relieved. "Well, I'll be. What will they think of next." He added, "How did you get here?"

"Flew in the *Dragonfly*. The navy had her outfitted with the same gear your ship received." Captain Sims shook his head and glanced ruefully around the cell. "I wish I'd arrived in a battle cruiser instead."

"Me too," agreed Don. "Two or three companies of Space Marines with lasers would be a welcome sight right about now. How come they sent you instead?"

The captain shrugged. "I had to test flight the *Dragonfly,* and Spaceways wanted someone to check up on you? Your ship hasn't moved in a while, and Hershey was fretting. So here I am."

Don shook a finger at him and snapped, "You shouldn't have landed. What did you think that would accomplish?"

Captain Sims grinned sheepishly. "I didn't exactly want to land. They forced me down. There's a lot of activity up there. It looks like the Vas are searching for something."

Don nodded. They must still be hunting for his ship. He was surprised the Vas hadn't captured her yet, but that was fine by him. It meant he still had a possible escape route if he ever broke out of this jail.

"Well, that's about it for me," concluded Sims. "Man, I'm starved. I haven't eaten since I left the *Dragonfly.*" He shuffled to the cell door and tried peering down the tunnel between the bars. "When do they feed us?"

Don laughed. It was the first time he'd done so in a month, and it felt so good he couldn't stop. A torrent of mirth bubbled out of him like thunder on a summer's night. His giggles grew loud, but he didn't care.

Sims gawked with building concern, finally seizing him by the shoulder. "Weiss, Don, what's the matter? What's wrong?"

"I'm all right, Captain," Don said as tears dripped down his cheeks. He hiccupped and gained control over his emotions until his laughter subsided to an occasional chuckle. It would break out anew when he repeated the words, "When do we eat?"

"Don't worry about chow," Don replied at last. "Besides, you frightened it off."

"Eh?"

"Forget it. We have more important things to worry about. In two days the Vas are going to kill us." Don related Nicholas's story.

"Mmmm…sounds interesting," Sims commented. "Swords, spears, and clubs you say. Well," he scratched behind his ear, "I was fleet champion for two years running with the saber. How about you?"

"I studied them all in the Academy," Don admitted, "foil, epee, and saber. I was captain of the fencing team my senior year."

The older man smiled. "If nothing else, we'll provide them a celebration they won't forget for a while."

Don commenced to get an idea. "You know…when I was in the Academy, my fencing instructor said a sword was more dangerous than a laser. I always wondered what he meant by that."

"Not necessarily," corrected Sims. "It depends on the man behind the weapon. What brings that up?"

"Well, I had a thought," Don said. "If we survive the arena, we can hand these monsters something more than a memory."

The captain grinned. "I like the way you're thinking, boy. You have any details?"

"Maybe. What if we…" Don went into great pains describing his idea to Sims, and they spent considerable time working out particulars.

***

Old Charlie never returned to take them to the wall. Instead, when it approached the time their jailer usually arrived, a different Vas appeared pushing a cart. He banged on their door, counted bodies, and ladled out two bowlfuls of a thin gruel.

"Come and get it while it's still hot," the Vas shouted, thrusting the dishes into their cell. He passed along the tunnel to the next hole in the rock and repeated the operation.

Don erupted from a sound sleep to stare at the cereal. Before it vanished, he scooped up one of the bowls and greedily slurped its contents.

Captain Sims was more hesitant. He picked up the remaining vessel and sniffed it doubtfully. "They don't feed you guys too well, do they?"

"Don't be silly," Don replied as he licked his bowl clean. "Finest cuisine in the world."

The unexpected nourishment wasn't the only break in the daily routine. As time wore on more Vas appeared, roaming up and down the prison tunnel, and peering within the cells. At first, they gathered in ones and twos, but as the day progressed, a carnival atmosphere spread throughout the passageway as scores of the spidermen descended upon the tunnel.

A short, grey Vas, accompanied by a younger version of himself, approached the hole where Don and Sims were quartered. Both aliens dressed in gaudy harnesses studded with gems of different shades. The older Vas studied the two Earthlings and singled out Don. "Fifty credits says that one on the right will last twenty minutes in the arena."

The younger one snickered. "Him? You've must be kidding, Arthur. That one looks like voulp meat inside of ten, but you're on."

The length of time the prisoners would survive in the arena was not the only thing the Vas wagered upon, the captives strength, stamina, and general prowess, were also favorite topics. Don even overheard three of the spidermen arguing among themselves over which prisoner would scream the loudest when ripped apart.

Much later, they had another visitor to their cell. Count Bonsh. He was dressed in a red leather harness and highly agitated. He scurried near the cell bars and examined Don.

"Earthling, I am glad you are looking fit. You will do well tomorrow."

Don made a lunge for the nobleman, but the Vas skipped nimbly back. He replied between clenched teeth, "No thanks to you, fink."

The count shook his head and said in a placating voice, "Gentle, Earthling…I have honored you and now you will help me. It is not good that you take this attitude."

Don's natural curiosity got the better of him. "Yeah? How am I going to help you this time?"

The Vas approached the bars again, but not too close. "I have suffered financial reverses due to your meddling, Earthling. Now comes the time to recoup these losses. I have wagered the last of my fortune you will be the last standing on the stadium field tomorrow. Make sure you are."

Don broke out in a smile. "I'll do my darnest," he replied sincerely.

"Good." Bonsh glanced around, crept closer to the cell, and passed a small bundle inside. "Eat it all," he whispered. "It will provide you the strength needed for the fight." He back peddled and vanished down the tunnel.

Brown, butcher's paper covered the package. Don picked it up and turned the parcel end over end. "Well open it," urged Sims. "You'll never know what's inside until you do."

Don unwrapped the bundle. Nestled in the paper, still warm, were two steaks cooked rare with the juices oozing from them. "I'll be," he exclaimed, staring at the captain in surprise. "The little rat is making sure we have enough energy to die tomorrow."

Sims eased one of the steaks from the package. "Don't complain, Weiss." He took a bite and chewed. "This is more like it. Nice friends you've made here."

Don worked on the other steak. "Yeah," he said, "one big, happy family."

After eating, Don laid down. His eyes barely closed when old Charlie swept through banging the hilt of his lash on the cell's grating. "Let's go. Wake up. Shake a claw."

Don and Sims scrambled to their feet. Charlie entered, unlocked their fetters, and motioned them to step outside their cell. "Come on now. Step lively, I don't have all day," he bellowed, gesturing with his whip. "Fall in line and let's move."

They scrambled to the rear of shackled prisoners where a second Vas snapped leg irons on the two. When all the captives had assembled, old Charlie flicked his whip and marched them off. They entered a tunnel new to Don, the passageway rising until he thought it must lead to the surface of the planet, but it leveled off, ran straight without interruption, and intersected another corridor. This one was larger and filled with traffic.

"At least they could have provided a bus to transport us," Don commented. "I feel like the monkey at the zoo." Vas of all ages gawked at them as they marched along.

"Pretend it's Unification Day, and you've been selected for the parade," advised Sims. He strode along, swinging his arms back and forth, staring straight ahead. Out of the corner of his mouth he joked, "This isn't bad. At least we don't have horses or elephants in front of us."

They reached the stadium, turned into a tunnel that ran along the perimeter, and stopped when they hit a gate marked, 'Authorized Personnel Only'. A security guard ushered them through. After some delay, another guard led them to a locker-room with benches.

A Vas clad in a diamond-covered harness strolled in. Old Charlie whispered to the other guards, "Hey guys, the Duke." He snapped to attention followed by the others.

"At ease," the duke ordered. He nodded to the guards and addressed the prisoners. "You have been brought here for a glorious event," he intoned. "Today is the feast of Gaea, a day of remembrance and hope. Soon you will take part in a duel to the death, a saga that will one day come true. The recounting is up to you to make it believable, and we ask each one of you to do your best so you will be thought of well." The duke paused to let the gravity of their task sink in.

Don whispered to Sims, "He makes it sound patriotic to die for old Gaea."

The nobleman added something, but Don missed his words. The prisoners rose, were herded from the room, led through an archway, and emerged onto the floor of the amphitheater. Old Charlie and the other guards unlocked the irons that bound them.

"You're free," Charlie told Don as the chains fell away. "Go fetch a weapon, and we'll see what you can do. Listen here…" he gave Don a significant look, "the duke wants this to be impressive. Stay alive for a few minutes."

Don nodded. He planned to stay alive longer than that. He pushed his way through the other prisoners to a section of the arena where swords, pikes, clubs were thrown on the baked dirt. He passed over the pikes and clubs, and studied the cutting weapons with care. One sword caught his eyes. The blade was four feet in length, double-edged, and as keen looking as a razor. The weapon reminded him of an old highlander's claymore he'd once seen in a museum. When he hefted the sword he found the blade surprisingly light, and the balance perfect. Don gave it a few experimental, two-handed swings, and then more cautiously, tried again one-handed. The sword performed like the saber he was more familiar with, and he knew he held the kind of blade legends grew from.

If Puddlefoot were here, he reflected, the little guy would make up a song, or know one, and he would know if magic was in this blade. He needed to name the weapon. All swords of legend had names. What would be a good one? Magic sword? No. Puddlefoot's blade? Not quite, it sounded confusing. Elves' Magic? That rang better. Yes, it would do.

On impulse, Don scooped up a hunting knife and tucked it under his belt, and then pushed out of the crowd and searched for Captain Sims. Overhead a loudspeaker blared a martial song, while near the middle of the stadium, a Vas read a speech. He couldn't hear what the alien said, nor did he care. He was eager for the battle to start.

"You look like something out of the thirteenth century."

Don swung about. Sims leaned on a javelin, a saber pushed through a makeshift scabbard around his waist.

"Yeah, me in my pressure suit," Don retorted, grinning.

"Well, make it the twentieth century then," responded Sims. "That was still a savage age."

"Okay." Don studied the older man. "You look barbaric yourself." He shifted his gaze to include the rest of the combatants, the gate they had entered from, and the high stone wall encircling the amphitheater. He asked Sims, "Did you check the entrance yet?"

"Yep. As soon as they unchained us. The gate's locked and barred from the outside, we can't escape that way."

"Well, you know what we planned." Don pointed. "I see a low spot in the wall over there. We'll make for it and try to climb over. After that, we have to play it by ear."

Sims nodded in the opposite direction. "Don, we'd better head for that spot quick, or we may not get there at all. Do you see what's coming?"

A gate opened on the other side of the arena. From within, Vas drivers herded a fantastic collection of giant scorpions and other arachnids into the amphitheater. The creatures milled about the opening, and then they spread out across the floor, urged on by the Vas behind.

A ten-foot scorpion was the first to sight the captives. With a bellow of rage, it rushed forward, the rest of the herd trailing in its wake. Cries of anticipation sprouted from the mob of spectators in the stands as they watched a few of the prisoners form a battle line.

"Hurry," Don shouted to Sims. "Let's bug out of here." Without waiting to see if the captain heard, he sprinted across the open floor. Immediately, one of the monstrous scorpions veered from the pack to stalk him.

Don halted as the monster dashed between him and the wall. The scorpion poised, snapped its pincers, issued a hiss from its mouth, and charged. Don steadied himself and took a firm, two-handed grip on Elves' Magic. When the beast drew near, he beat at a claw, slicing off a section of the pincer.

The scorpion jerked back in alarm, not expecting resistance, and bellowed in pain.

Taking the offensive, Don jumped and lunged at one of the creature's eyes. The blade sank deep, and he retreated to prevent the wounded arachnid from ripping the sword from his grip as it threshed about.

"Very good, Weiss. Your Balestra was superb!"

Captain Sims stood there, a lopsided smile lighting up his face. "Thanks Captain, but I could use help."

"Why? You did fine." Sims gestured to the scorpion with the point of his javelin. The monster rolled on its back, the eight legs curled in death. "Let's climb that wall before his friends decide to eat us," he added.

Don wasn't listening. He watched past the captain toward the middle of the arena. A towering daddy longlegs chased one of the aliens. Every time the beast came close, the fleeing alien whirled, and swung a massive club at it. When the creature stopped, the prisoner dashed off again. As the two combatants drew near, Don recognized the features of the alien.

It was Nicholas.

He tripped and fell. The daddy longlegs strolled over the Spician and halted.

Without hesitation, Don sprinted off. The captain yelled, "Hey, where are you going, Weiss? You're gonna get yourself killed."

Don paid no attention.

The gigantic limbs of the monster rose before him like gray pillars of stone. Don grasped Elves' Magic and swung with all his might. The impact stunned him to his elbows. The creature paused in mid-bite, its leg bouncing away. Nicholas rolled and swept another limb from beneath the longlegs as Don leaped back in and hacked away at a third, giving the Spician time to make his escape. The arachnid retreated, grumbling from the assault and investigated its wounds.

"Thank you, Don," Nicholas called to him, bowing, "but I fear you have saved me for nothing, look."

A giant scorpion approached. To make matters worse, the daddy longlegs finished its examination and prepared itself for attack. The monster stomped its six remaining legs until the earth shook, roared, tensed its body, and scurried at the two.

Don leaped sideward to avoid the first rush. As the creature passed, his sword struck. By chance, he hit the same leg already cut in two. The longlegs teetered and stumbled on top of the scorpion, which was about to spring on Nicholas. The scorpion twisted its head, startled by the assault. The jaws gaped. A javelin flew past Don's ear to embed itself in the target. The mouth closed abruptly, splintering the shaft, and drove the head deeper into the gullet.

Captain Sims ran up. "What do you think you're doing Weiss? This ain't no time to play with animals."

"Sorry," Don replied. "Stopped to help someone." He said to Nicholas, "Come with us, we're breaking out of here."

"Can the chatter and let's move," Sims interjected in a worried voice. "Those bugs are getting themselves untangled."

The two creatures had separated and stood facing each other. The scorpion advanced on the longlegs and seized one leg in its pincers. Before the restrained animal could break loose, the scorpion's tail flashed, jamming the needlelike stinger deep into the longlegs' body.

"Let's go." Don sprinted for the wall flanked by Sims and Nicholas. They covered the rest of the distance unmolested, stopping before the low point in the stadium. Don took a running jump and sprang for the lip.

He fell short by three feet.

The crowd peered over the edge and jeered as he sprawled in the dirt. Don picked himself up, grabbed a stone, and threw it at one of the more obnoxious spectators. The crowd booed and responded by pelting him with empty bottles, but their attention became diverted to another portion of the arena. They began to cheer.

Farther down the wall, five prisoners made a last desperate stand against eight of the scorpions and two of the longlegs. As Don watched, three of the aliens crumbled before the concentrated rush of the monsters. The other two fought, and then they too disappeared beneath the churning legs. One scorpion lifted a broken body and commenced feeding. The other arachnids stormed away seeking new prey.

A longlegs discovered Don, Nicholas and Sims. The creature scurried toward the three in short bursts. The rest spread out, fanwise, and followed his example.

"Well," Sims said to Nicholas to Don, "school's out. What do we do now?"

"Nicholas," Don estimated the height of the barrier, "Do you think you can leap to the top of the wall?"

The Spician sized up the obstacle. "Perhaps," he said, "but how will that help you?"

Don kept one eye on the monster bugs and replied, "When you get up there, toss down the longest thing you see. We'll climb up somehow."

The apeman backed off a dozen paces. He ran, leaped high in the air, and kicked the wall. Then he was over the edge, scattering the crowd left and right in landing.

Sims cupped his hands and called, "Hey, throw something down, these critters are getting close."

The monsters gathered in a loose circle around Don and Sims. The ring filled in and tightened by the second, each beast gaining courage by the addition of a mate.

Above, Nicholas searched for something to use as a ladder. He shrugged off a security guard who tried to put handcuffs on him and approached a row of bleachers. Grasping the steel beam the seats attached to, he heaved, and wrenched it loose from its bolts.

"Watch out below," the Spician yelled. He dropped the seats over the edge making a series of steps from the ground to the lip of the wall. He swung around and faced three more security officers.

Don glanced from the makeshift ladder to Sims. "You first," he ordered. "I'll stand by until you can help Nicholas."

"Not on your life, buddy, you go."

"Don't quibble," Don snapped back, "move it. I think these things have made up their minds to attack."

Sims bit back a remark, face blank. He scrambled up the bleachers. After verifying the captain was on his way, Don faced the semicircle of beasts, prepared to defend their line of retreat to the death. One longlegs, bolder than the rest, drew close and hissed. Don whirled Elves' Magic over his head and severed one leg. The creature hobbled back in panic, replaced by a scorpion.

Don took a chance and glanced over his shoulder. Captain Sims was halfway to the top, but managed to tangle himself in the seats. The captain cursed aloud as he tried to straighten himself out. Don checked the semicircle. The scorpion tensed, ready to attack.

The arachnid snapped pincers. It reached out to grasp, but stopped short when Don swung his sword. The claws closed in reflex, the tail whipping over its head. Don waited like a batter for a ball, when the tail descended. He swung.

The stinger flew from the tail, but the blunt end continued to descend, sending Don sprawling, and sweeping Elves' Magic from his hands. He rolled away as the tail continued to pound the earth and raced to retrieve his sword.

Sims called from above. "Forget the blade, Weiss. Shag your butt up here, fast." Don glanced up then looked at Elves' Magic. He sprinted the extra ten feet, scooped up his sword, and raced for the ladder. The extra second allowed the scorpion to set itself. A pincer swept out knocking him off his feet. Don was up instantly only to find the rest of the creatures charging. He paused long enough to thrust at the scorpion's head. It jumped back, fowling the charge of its mates. Hissing and screeching, the arachnids commenced fighting among themselves.

Don didn't wait for the outcome of the battle. He scrambled up the bleachers where hands lifted him over the edge. Sims pounded his back and shouted, "We did it, boy. We made it."

This section of the stands was empty save for Vas bodies in small piles. Don remarked, "Appears like you guys were busy."

Nicholas shook his head. "No, waiting until you finished fooling around in the arena."

"Well, maybe you should have been doing something then. Look."

Vas appeared at the far end of the aisle. More tumbled down the arena steps and exit ramps. They had the look of riot police, carrying batons, sidearms, and wearing face shields.

Don said to Nicholas, "You've been here before. Which way to the spaceport?"

Follow me." The apeman scooped up his club and waded into a squad of oncoming police streaming from a ramp. "I've wanted to do this for a long time," he shouted to Don as he swatted away.

"What did you say?" Don yelled back. The roar of the crowd, mingled with the noise of battle, made it impossible to hear individual voices.

Nicholas broke through the line of police, sent them hurtling over the guardrail to the field below. "I said, this is fun." He took a backhanded swipe at a Vas.

"Oh." Guards attacked the rear of their formation, keeping Don and Sims busy. "If you see that slimy Count Bonsh, let me know," Don shouted back, "that'a be fun."

With a last burst of speed, the three broke through to the ramp. The remaining police hesitated, uncertain, finally deciding to retreat and wait for reinforcements to arrive before continuing the fight. Temporarily at least, the three held their escape route secure.

"Down this way, three levels, I believe," Nicholas grunted when no attack followed. He led the way down.

Away from the noise of the arena, the ramp was silent, their decent unchallenged as they made their way toward the public tunnels. When they reached the main level, they learned why.

The ramp ended in an arch with another tunnel intersecting it perpendicularly. The entrance to the main corridors. A steel grating blocked the archway. They had nowhere to run but back up.

"Damn." Captain Sims approached the barrier and kicked the bars. "I should've figured this. As soon as we made it to the stands, they sealed all the exits and closed the stadium. They have us bottled up, and I bet there's a company of soldiers waiting to arrest us."

"What do you think?" Don asked Nicholas.

The Spician shrugged. "It was a far-fetched idea at best. The only thing to do is go back the way we came." He eyed the ramp dubiously.

Don strode to the grating and shook it. He glanced around, searching for anything to use for escape. One end of the alcove they stood in was empty, except for the grating, the other end was nearly so. It contained a stack of metal skids piled one on top of the other. He investigated to learn if they could be of any use.

To Don's delight he found the machine that stacked them parked between skids and barrier. When Don saw the alien forklift, he broke out into a grin, and jumped into the seat without hesitation. After studying the controls, he twisted a key, fed gas to the engine, raised the forks and tilted them backward, and threw the machine into gear. He wheeled the forklift around and positioned the machine in front of the barrier.

"Watch out," he cautioned. "I'm going to knock that grating to kingdom come." Don tromped on the gas and the little machine leaped forward. The forks caught the metal throwing off a shower of sparks, but the barrier held. He backed the forklift up and sent it flying again, and again. He hit it a fourth time. The barrier sprang from its runners to drop on the pavement with a crash. The way was open.

"Don, you're beautiful," exclaimed Sims. "Ditch that contraption and let's get out of here." He stepped into the main tunnel.

A laser bolt flicked from the base of the ramp behind them and caught Sims in the leg. He went down screaming, the stench of burnt flesh in the air. More bolts struck the protective cage surrounding Don. In reflex, he ducked, threw the forklift into reverse, and pushed the accelerator to the floor. Tires spun, caught, and hurled the machine backward.

Don aimed at the ramp. At the last moment, he jumped from his seat and took cover. The machine bounced over the small curb and jammed itself into the gap, plugging it neatly. In the process, it crushed three of the snipers who had been slow to react.

Don crouched and ran to help Nicholas drag Sims to the edge of the main tunnel. "Damn. They nicked me," Sims groaned. He touched his leg and turned white.

"Here, lay back," Don ordered. He eased the captain to the floor and elevated his legs. Next, he examined the burn. "Not as bad as it might have been, Sims. The laser cauterized as it burnt." He patted the older man on the shoulder. "At least you won't lose it."

Another bolt flashed and struck the edge of the tunnel sending a shower of dust raining down. Don took a quick peek at the ramp and saw the soldiers wrestling with the forklift. "Nicholas, how far is it to the port?"

"About a quarter mile that way," the Spician indicated the main tunnel, "straight ahead."

"Good." Don checked the soldiers again. "Take the captain and bring him there. I'll hold these guys off and cover your retreat."

"Now wait a minute." Sims tried to stand, but his leg collapsed under him. "I'm only going to slow him up. I'll stay here and you two take off."

"Shut up," Don said calmly. "Nicholas, take him to the port. Maybe with luck you can steal a ship. I'll meet you there later. Now start moving."

The Spician nodded and picked up Sims in a fireman's carry. Without looking back, he trotted down   the   passageway.

Chapter 17

As Don watched the two go, he made a solemn vow to himself. After this mission, it was back to Luna, marry Sam, settle down and raise a slosh full of kids, and never, ever, go into space again. He drew Elves' Magic from his belt and prepared to give his friends time to escape.

Don didn't have long to wait. With a final heave, the soldiers shoved the forklift out of the way. They swarmed out of the opening, and down the ramp. More slowly, they bore down on his position. Don believed the best defense was a good offensive. If he was going to die, he might as well do it in a grand manner. He leaped into the tunnel shouting "Geronimo," and met the Vas head-on in a running attack. His sudden assault drove the point soldier back on his comrades. Before they recovered or brought their hand lasers to bear, Don lunged twice, and two Vas dropped dead on the floor. He didn't give up his advantage. He pressed harder, and another soldier crumbled.

A beam winked over Don's head and he ducked, only to sidestep as three more rays sought his legs. The laser fire came from up the ramp, but it had one good effect; whenever it missed him, it usually hit one of his attackers. The fire halted. Someone had used his head. Instead, a platoon of riflemen scrambled down the ramp, fixing bayonets as they advanced.

Don continued lunging and thrusting, shaking off a soldier who jumped on his back, but the press continued to mount. If nothing else, the Vas would pull him down by weight of numbers alone. His arms grew tired, and it became hard to keep the tip of Elves' Magic up.

At one point Don found himself fighting, Corps-A-Corps, with two bayonet toting soldiers. Both lunged at him. One high, one low. He managed to parry one thrust to his breast the other caught him in the thigh. He yelled in pain and kicked his opponent with the bloody leg. His other leg buckled and he went down. Soldiers piled on top of him. Don struggled to his knees crying "Never," and shook himself like a wet spaniel. The soldiers flew off, and he regained his feet, but he'd lost his sword.

Don still had his knife. He drew it and swung wildly.

A laugh sounded in his ear and Don whirled to strike. Just as suddenly he stopped. Puddlefoot stood there, his merry smile on his face, his shillelagh thrown over his shoulder. The smile disappeared and he cried, "Behind thee, Sire."

Don spun again and put a foot-long gash in a body. Standing back to back, he and Puddlefoot fought in silence.

"Puddlefoot, do something, quick," Don panted when the attack slackened. "Work some magic."

"Aye, Sire." The brownie closed his eyes in concentration.

A fire-breathing dragon materialized in the tunnel.

The huge crocodile head reared back and jaws opened, fire and smoke belched out, filling the tunnel and blinding them all. Gigantic wings beat a thunderous roar. The tail battered the concrete beneath their feet to dust. The monster swung around, bellowed and advanced on the aliens. The soldiers stood frozen in terror, and then, en masse, turned and fled up the ramp.

The beast ambled majestically behind and stopped short of the exit. It bent its head low, put the massive snout to the mouth of the opening, and blew a steam of fire. Grumbling, the monster turned seeking new victims. The dragon spied Don, and with fire seeping from its nostrils, advanced on him. Don fell back yelling, "Puddlefoot, stop it. Make it go away."

The brownie laughed with glee. "Sire, 'tis but an illusion, as easily conjured up as it is to make disappear. Watch." Puddlefoot scampered to the monster and placed his hand on the scaly side. Instead of stopping, his hand vanished into the dragon, all the way up to his elbow. "You see, Sire? The beasty 'tis not truly here at all."

"Great." Don examined the great lizard more closely. "Maybe we can leave him here to guard the entrance?"

The brownie shook his head. "Nay, Sire. Spells as this last only for a short while. I know a different spell, however, which will seal this way for hours."

"Do it now before the soldiers change their minds and decide to come back," Don said.

A minor explosion erupted and a flash of white light crossed the ramp. "'Tis done. What now?"

Don paused. He was tired, hungry, dirty, and covered with blood. His wounded leg ached, and for a second he didn't know what he wished to do. What was it? Something he wanted to ask Puddlefoot. Oh yeah, it was coming back to him.

"Whatever happened to that chisel you were going to bring me?"

Puddlefoot looked guilty, and then relief spread over his face. He reached in his back pocket and withdrew a two-foot long stripping chisel, made of bronze. "Here, Sire. I have failed thee not."

Don took the chisel numbly. "I take it you had trouble finding this?"

"Aye, Sire," Puddlefoot bobbed his head up and down. "Every time I discovered one I must leave it to move the *Sparrowhawk*."

"Of course, you couldn't let the ship fall into enemy hands. What?"

"Aye, Sire. The Vas patrol ships kept locating her and trying to board," Puddlefoot hastened to explain. "It 'twas stop my search and move thy ship to a new orbit or lose her."

"Huh?" Don stared in bewilderment at the brownie. "I thought you said magic didn't work on steel." The strain of battle must have mixed him up.

The little brownie looked smug. "Not magic, Sire, science. I read thy computer manual."

"My navigational books as well, I see." Don's brain started functioning. He slipped it into high gear. "What orbit are you in?" Puddlefoot told him. "Sounds good. Communication equipment still on the same frequency as before? Okay, here's what I want…"

Don gave the brownie detailed instructions on orbit and frequency changes for the radio. When he was done he said, "Now be careful. Scoot on back to the ship and be ready when I yell."

"Sire, I can take thee with me if thou will."

"Can you take three?" Don countered.

"Nay, but I can…"

"Forget it." Don contemplated introducing Sims to the brownie and decided not to chance it. Puddlefoot might not show, or worse, he might. He told the brownie, "I don't want someone to see you. Besides, it's more fun doing it this way. Now, go back to the ship and wait."

"Aye, Sire. If that be thy will." Puddlefoot studied his face with concern and vanished.

Don scooped up Elves' Magic from the floor and cleaned the blade, after which, he ripped a strip of cloth from his shirt and made a flimsy bandage for his thigh. This done, he grabbed four fallen laser pistols, examining the charge on each. One he discarded. Two he tucked in his belt, the third he held, ready to use. After all these preparations, Don trudged off to the spaceport.

***

Two armed guards lounged at the booth marking the entrance to the port. On either side, retractable steel fences stood, cutting off the port from the rest of the tunnel network. At present, no traffic came or went, the stillness broken by low conversation of the guards.

Don hurried around a bend in the passage and found himself facing the guard shack. He and the soldiers stared at each other in surprise. Before the guards could level their rifles at him, or raise an alarm, Don's pistol flashed twice and the two slumped. He approached the gate and searched for signs of hidden dangers. Satisfied, he examined the fence. A simple bolt secured the entrance. He slipped it open and entered.

Don prowled around terminals, stacked cargo, and row upon row of small vehicles, searching for Captain Sims and Nicholas, all the while keeping himself out of sight. Don was lucky the spaceport was small. The Vas were an unknown race, living in an uninhabited planet, and preferred to keep it that way. On Earth, he would have found it impossible to move about unnoticed. Here he merely found it difficult.

The spaceport rested in a cavern, half-natural, half-manmade, with a domed roof. On the few occasions when a ship departed, the dome would separate into four sections and dilate away. At no time did Don notice a loss of atmospheric pressure.

His search brought him to a small landing field pushed to one side of the complex. A lone building nestled between ships suitable for point-to-point jumps around the planet. One ship rested up on blocks, stripped for parts. In the middle of the field stood the *Dragonfly*. If Sims was anywhere, he should be here. Outside of the lone guard making a restless circle around the captain's ship, however, the field was deserted. Which meant his comrades were either hiding among the strato-crafts or hold up in the building, but which one?

Don watched from behind a dumpster while the sentry picked up a stone and tossed it across the unused field. Double-checking for other sentries, he waited until the bored guard moved away. He ignored the 'Private' sign posted on the field gate, vaulted over it, and made a dash for the cover of the dismantled craft. He dove the last five feet when he saw the sentry about to swing back, and wormed his way between blocks. His wounded leg throbbed. He cursed the limb and pushed it harder.

When Don scrambled fully under the small craft, he found most of the space occupied. Sims and Nicholas crouched there before him. Panic turned to relief as the three recognized each other. Don tucked his pistol away, while Nicholas gave a low chuckle. "We thought you were captured."

"Yeah, what happened to you, run the wrong way?" Sims added.

"Neither," Don replied. He crawled beside Nicholas to get a better view of the *Dragonfly.* "You forgot to leave a trail of breadcrumbs for me to follow. I had to search every building in this place."

Sims lost his grin. "Sorry buddy, next time I'll remember."

"So bring me up to date. Why are you still sitting here?"

"What do you want us to do, throw rocks at that guy?" The captain growled back. "There's a hundred yards of open space between him and us. Even if I could run he'd nail us before we got three-quarters of the way there."

"You're getting old," commented Don, smirking. "Here, take these, maybe they'll even up the sides." He passed out the laser pistols. "Stay here and cover us, Captain, this won't take a minute."

It took longer than sixty seconds, but in a short while the ship was theirs. The sentry lay on the landing field, cut in half by twin lasers. Nicholas hastened to get Sims while Don stood guard. When all three were together under the hull of the *Dragonfly* Don opened the hatch and entered. He found her ransacked by a quick but through search. Investigating further, he checked control boards and engine. Neither showed signs of tampering. The ship was fit to lift.

"All aboard," he called down. Nicholas passed up Sims and climbed in behind him. The small cabin proved cramped, after all three were inside. Nicholas crammed his bulky figure into the sleeper, a tight fit, but he took it with a grunt.

"Nicholas," Don waved to the dome of the spaceport. "How does that gizmo work? Does it open automatically when a ship approaches it?"

"Why, no…it's a meteor shield. When a ship wants to leave, the tower orders it retracted. There is a weak force field below. You can see the faint glimmering that contains the atmosphere. The ship breaks the field, after which, the tower closes the shield again."

So that's how they do it, Don reflected. Must have the outside of the shield camouflaged to resemble a hill or something. Then they screened their whole colony from sensors. All the volcanic activity in the region would help, also, he supposed, if held in check.

"Well, let's hope another ship leaves real soon," Don said. "The Vas are gonna start finding dead bodies and figure out where we are. Captain, can we blast our way out if we have to?"

Sims shifted in the pilot's seat and shook his head. "I don't know. If that's a meteor shield, it's built to withstand real punishment. What the heck, if we have to, we have to."

The captain prepared the ship for take-off, and then they spent an eternity of silence waiting for something to happen. When they'd given up hope, the meteor shield opened, another ship was ready for departure. He nudged Sims who nodded. "All set, boys?" Sims asked as he fed power to the engines and swung the little craft around.

"Give it a few more seconds to open fully," Nicholas cautioned. "It will be a tight squeeze with two ships flying through."

Don searched for the other ship lifting off. Instead, two truckloads of soldiers pulled up to the gate of their landing field. "Oh-oh. The shows up, Sims, if you're going to do it, do it now."

Sims goosed the *Dragonfly* and she sprang into the air. At the same time, the meteor shield began to close. The Vas had shut down their port.

The captain changed their angle of flight and increased the thrust. Acceleration squashed Don back. The shipped bucked. With a tug broke through the force field. The jaws of the shield lay beyond. The ship flashed through, entered and exited the thermosphere in a blink of an eye, and was in space. Conditions returned to normal as Captain Sims cut the boost to one gee. "That's it," he cried jubilantly. "We're gone."

The sky blackened and the stars glowed. The captain started punching keys. "I'm not even gonna figure out a proper course," he declared. "We'll head straight out of this system and do that later."

"Drop me off with the *Sparrowhawk* before you do," Don said.

Sims glanced up from his console in surprise. "Uh-uh…what are you, crazy? If a mess of ships were up here before, this place will be swarming with them now. Forget it."

Don glowered at him and then studied the overheads. "No can do, Sims, I still have a mission to complete."

The captain twisted in his seat and stared at Don in disbelief. "*What?* You must be crazy. We know where their planet is. We can build a fleet and take care of them later. Besides, how am I going to find your ship?"

"Captain," Don said carefully, "my last orders before leaving Earth were to make friends with the Vas or destroy them. So far, I have done neither." He picked up the radio mike and changed the frequency. "Dragonfly *to* Sparrowhawk...trigger your radar beacon."

On the 'scope a light started flashing on and off. Don pointed to it and remarked, "There she is, Captain. Match orbits with her or I will. it's easy enough to compute."

"How did you do that?" Sims asked. He worked a vector in his head and set the controls.

"Preprogrammed it into the computer and set it off with a code word," Don lied.

They chased behind his ship, slowly closing the gap. After detailed maneuvering, Sims docked with the larger craft. Don wasted no time, they were short on minutes, but before he left, he shook Sims hand. "I'll be all right," he said.

"Good hunting, Weiss, but I still think you're being stupid. You're gonna get your ass shot off."

Don winked at him and asked Nicholas, "You don't mind going to Earth?"

The Spician replied, "I cannot go back to Spica until things cool down. Earth is as good a place as any, and it's a lot better than a Vas prison."

Don patted him on the shoulder and entered the airlock. Once inside his ship, a worried Puddlefoot greeted him.

"Hurry, Sire. Ships approach." The little brownie gestured to the 'scope. Three blips moved with purpose toward them. A fourth, the *Dragonfly,* darted away.

Don took his seat and commenced pulling webbing around him. "Strap down, little buddy. I think they'll try and board. Let's see if we can sucker them in."

One blip broke away from the rest and went after the *Dragonfly*, but in a flat out race, nothing could touch the little craft. The other two ships continued to descend on the *Sparrowhawk*, not knowing what to expect.

"Sire, they are near." Puddlefoot's voice broke the quiet.

Don kept his eyes glued to the radarscope. "I know, but I want to let them get closer." He watched tensely. "That's right," he said to the 'scope, "Come to papa."

One enemy cruiser was drawing close to investigate. Now if they would drop their screens, he could send a warm welcome.

The craft hailed them with no response. It drifted nearer, the glow surrounding it faded as it prepared to launch a lifeboat.

Don fired.

Even before the blast ended, he triggered his screens and accelerated. The cruiser disappeared in a blaze of vaporized steel. In response, the remaining enemy ship swung about and blasted as the *Sparrowhawk* showed her heels.

Don's defensive shield flashed white but held. The *Sparrowhawk* banked left, right, and nosed down into the thin atmosphere of the planet. The two ships streaked across the sky, Don zigzagging as he flew. The alien cruiser pursued, following every twist and turn with ease.

"Okay, Puddlefoot," Don rasped, "now we're going to find out what kind of a hotshot pilot I really am."

Off in the distance a high range of mountains loomed. He picked out a spot between double peaks and headed for them. He dropped low in the pass and followed the snaking progress of a frozen river as it ran through the crags. The walls of the valley narrowed, and he found himself with fifty feet of clearance. It became a war of nerves as to who would break off battle first.

Don won. The cruiser slackened its speed and ascended. Don waited in suspense until the ship climbed high in the atmosphere, then he rose. He crossed his fingers and prayed the enemy would not notice, and slipped into another, smaller valley. Discovering an outcropping of granite large enough to hide the *Sparrowhawk*, he taxied his ship beneath its cover. There he hovered, waiting to see what would happen.

"What does thou propose to do here?" Puddlefoot asked, biting his lip as he watched the harried look on Don's face.

"We wait," Don replied. "Wait until they leave, or find us." He did something against the manual of ship handling, and against all common sense. The *Sparrowhawk* was a deep space vessel, meant for point-to-point travel in outer space. Earth technicians re-outfitted her for landings, but on her fins. He was about to attempt to put her down as she was. Flat. Nevertheless, the ship's tremendous weight, megatons of it, might crush her belly plates if landed in such a manner.

Don landed. More, he cut the gyros and turned off all power.

Don prayed as the ship settled. The hull groaned and sank into the frozen tundra three feet. "This had better be the right move, Puddlefoot." The ship was still creaking in protest. "I'm hoping that cruiser won't spot us down here and figure we escaped, but if we can't lift off again, we've had it, the Vas have won."

Puddlefoot replied with conviction, "Sire, thy ship hast never abandoned thee. Why should she start now?"

Don crossed his fingers. Maybe the little guy had something. In any case he wouldn't worry. Problems would be dealt with one at a time as the cropped up. He didn't have to look for them.

After a long time he dug out a spare pressure suit, also picking up a pair of high-powered field glasses, and with an afterthought, Elves' Magic. "Be right back," he told Puddlefoot. "I'm going to take a look-see."

"Sire, do you think they know we are here?"

"I don't know. That's what I'm going to find out."

Don went outside and stepped to the edge of the rocky overhand. The frigid wind cut through the insulation of his suit like a laser through ice, freezing his side, and making his eyes water in his helmet. He hastily put the glasses to his visor and scanned the sky. He saw nothing, but that didn't mean they were free from spies. The cruiser could be miles out in space watching with powerful telescopes, or blowing the next valley out of existence on the theory his ship lurked there.

Don's right side went numb. He searched the heavens once more and, posthaste, re-entered his ship. "I didn't see anything," he reported to Puddlefoot, "but I'm still not sure they're gone. Can you go in space, real quick, and double check for me?"

"No sooner said than done, Sire." Puddlefoot disappeared. Don paced for an endless time and consulted the ship's clock twice. After five minutes, the brownie was back. "Nay, Sire," he answered Don's unspoken question, "there be ships, but not close by, and none appear to be watching."

Don smiled. Calm filled him like the ocean after a storm. It was over, or beginning. Either way the time was right.

"Good. We'll chance it, Puddlefoot." Don's voice was ice. "It's time to stop running and being pushed around. Let's carry out our mission." He switched the power on and engaged the gyros. With powerful thrusts from the belly jets the *Sparrowhawk* lifted, groaned, and rose unhurt. She was bent, nicked and chipped, but as Don eased her into the air and ran test after test, she replied in words only he understood.

Don performed one last test, figured a quick trajectory in his mind, and fed the results to the computer. The ship banked and gained speed, pointing her bow at the horizon.

Before the ship reached its destination, he assumed manual control. From the edge of space, the colony was like any other desolate part of the planet, the hemispheric dome of the port a slightly rounded mountain with small hills surrounding it. In the distance, the volcano supplying heat to the colony smoked. The ship settled over the port, stopped, hovered.

"Puddlefoot, this is it. Hang onto your seat."

"Aye, sire. Shall I man thy viewing scopes as well?"

"Right," agreed Don. "When we start, the Navy will come along fast. You're my prime defense."

He returned to his console, and with careful aim triggered the blaster. A stream of incandescent destruction stabbed from the ship striking the planet.

At first, nothing happened. The rock cover of the dome melted away, exposing the meteor shield underneath, but the dome itself remained unharmed. It stood, a mailed fist lifted defiantly to the sky, and taunted them to do their worse.

The blaster finished discharging leaving the shield exposed. The ship dropped fifty miles and Don tried again. This time the shield glowed ruby and softened, it sagged here and there, bubbled, and flowed.

The port defenses awoke, returning fire with beams of destruction no less incomparable than that of the *Sparrowhawk's*. Electron beams and spears of immeasurable energy surged up from hidden bases. The ship's screen flared and climbed the spectrum as more bases added their fire.

"The ship can't take much more of this," Don grated to Puddlefoot between clenched teeth. "We have to knock out those gun emplacements." A thought struck him. He was surprised he hadn't considered it before. "Puddlefoot, when we first met you said you like to take things apart. What can you do with those bases?"

The little brownie's eyes glowed with a feverish look. "Aye, Sire that is what I do best."

"Good, do it. I'm going to take the ship up. I'll see you in a couple of minutes."

Puddlefoot threw him a three-fingered salute and vanished. Don broke off the fight and soared, climbing high into the upper reaches of the atmosphere. As the distance from the planet increased, the force of the enemy fire faded. After retreating two hundred miles, Don stopped his flight. The ship hung in space like her namesake, watching for some sign she could strike again.

Far below, the port defenses hurled energy. Flashes of light came from a circle surrounding the spaceport, and at a farther distance, from the colony. The beams shrank in number and soon disappeared entirely. The defenses stilled. A 'pop' echoed in the cabin and Puddlefoot stood beside him. "All done, Sire, as you asked."

"Just like that?" Don asked, incredulous.

"Aye Sire." Puddlefoot said with a satisfied air. "When you are doing something you like, you do it quickly and well."

"I guess so." Don agreed. "Let's take her back down and try again."

The *Sparrowhawk* descended in a fast glide, this time without return fire from the outlaying bases. The meteor shield still smoked faintly, while below it, the force field winked through. The ship's battery spoke and the shield vaporized, the force field burst like a soap bubble, but the ray did not stop there. The blaze hit the main landing field, smoke and fumes belching upward to turn the earth beneath to molten lava that bubbled and flowed.

The blaster fell silent. In the wake of the attack, nothing of the spaceport remained but fire and slag. Puddlefoot gazed at the scene and said in a small voice, "Sire, truly the fires of hell hath fallen on this place."

"Yeah," Don replied grimly, "but we're not done yet."

He shifted the position of the ship by ten miles, northward, to the vicinity of the smoldering volcano, the central portion of the Vas colony. Don unleashed his weapon again and let its raw power bore into the planet. A mile wide section of frozen rock commenced to glow ruddy and bubbled, but when the blast faltered, he was not satisfied, for the destruction he wanted hadn't taken place. He knew this from experience. The Vas tunnels ran deep. With all the energy expended, he had scratched no more than the surface of the colony. If he was going to end this conflict, he had to do more than destroy a sports arena and a few passageways. He must end the colony's capability to wage war and the colony as well.

The blaster was not strong enough. What remained? Nothing, except for Reggie's farewell gift. The blockbusters. Don didn't know what they'd do, but he was going to find out.

Puddlefoot hovered at his elbow. "Ships Sire. They approach by the hundreds."

The brownie exaggerated, but ten ships that were close enough to intercede in the battle closed on the *Sparrowhawk*. They were still far away but moved swiftly, meaning to overrun the ship by sheer numbers and strength. Don glanced at the radar, irritated by the interruption. "Don't bother me with details, Puddlefoot. Can't you take care of them?"

The little brownie looked crestfallen. "Of course, Sire, but I thought thou wouldst be interested."

"Not at all. I'll leave the riff-raff to you." Don scanned his board and switched over to the rockets. Sighting in on the molten landscape, he loosed two at it, and with an afterthought, sent one flying at the enemy ships. Puddlefoot would need all the help he could get. With a sigh, he sat back and watched for the results of the bombardment.

The rockets struck with but a faint shaking of the lava. It was deceiving. The tremor did not stop. It grew violent and spread in a radiating ring, which expanded even farther as Don watched. The circle stretched itself into the air, blossoming into a tremendous cloud.

Don was use to atomic explosions. He'd used them in the Academy, but what occurred then was minuscule in comparison. Five thousand miles of the planet's surface heaved up in angry violation. Don threw the ship into overdrive and lifted her away from the blast.

"GOOD GOD ALMIGHTY. Puddlefoot, did you see what happened?" he breathed to the brownie. Then he remembered, Puddlefoot was gone, he'd left to stop the attacking ships.

He'd fired one of those missiles to help the brownie.

Don checked his 'scope to see what happened. It was clear. No blips appeared on the radar, no ships hovered out in space. Don tried the radio, but all he received was static. He shifted his attention back to the view scope to see what was occurring on the planet, expecting Puddlefoot to show up shortly.

The cloud dissipated revealing a new crater. Blazing rock boiled into the air from the lava bed underneath, turning the colony into a super volcano. Black ash rained from the sky.

Don shrugged. The mission was over. He started plotting a course to take him to the outer reaches of the system.

It annoyed him that Puddlefoot hadn't shown yet. The brownie always got lost like this. It was time to return home. The Vas fleet was still around and the *Sparrowhawk* was in no shape for a space battle. The generators made a grinding noise, and she lurched where she use to flow.

Darn that brownie anyway. Where was he?

When Don reached the edge of the system, he threw the ship into orbit around a small planet to do housekeeping, small repairs, and wait for Puddlefoot. The grinding he fixed. The lurch he couldn't do anything about outside of crossing his fingers. He swept, mopped, polished brass, and waited.

He waited a long time.

***

Don stretched out on the pilot's couch, two cans of beer beside him, one open, one closed, both frosty. In the background, the ship played a Wagner Overture. *The Ride of the Valdrikes.*

He reached a decision. Puddlefoot never returned and he could wait no longer. Vas ships-of-war had hailed him twice, and he'd managed to escape by the slimmest of margins. Perhaps Puddlefoot was back in Fairyland, or, Don thought sadly, been destroyed in the last battle. Perhaps he never existed at all, but Don was sure that if he did not leave now, the Vas would use his ship for target practice tomorrow.

He had one chore left. Don pondered what to do with the remaining blockbusters the ship carried. He still possessed seven. Earth wouldn't need this type of weapon for a long time, and he didn't want to be the one to introduce them. In the view scope, the world of the Vas appeared as a faint star. It would take a while, he mused, for the rockets to reach there, but it was better to do that than to take them home. He strolled to the fire control, set it on automatic, and pushed a button. Seven missiles streaked from the *Sparrowhawk* into the starry void. It wasn't until months later that the planet became a star for real. A short-lived star.

Don didn't see this. By that time, he was home.

Part 4: Sepulture

Chapter 18

"Weiss, before you leave on your vacation, I want you to know there's another promotion in the works for you."

"Ma'am, do you mean I won't get a crack at the assignment you promised me?" Events were moving too rapidly for Don. For two weeks since his return to Luna, he'd been busy with debriefing, conferences, meetings. Parliament already proposed trade negotiations, and ships were in route to Arctutus. The State Department was hastily throwing a team together to follow and setup diplomatic relations.

Don assumed, wrongly, once his report was finished, the job offered to him almost a year earlier would vanish, and he'd be back herding sky junk through the solar system. Apparently, it wasn't to be.

"Huh? Oh no, my boy, no," Hershey assured him, with a flick of her hand, "nothing could be more from the truth. A change in pay grade and title. You don't have to worry. Your new assignment still needs you, maybe more than ever."

Don could attest to her statement. When he'd talked to Sam on his return, he learned new planets and systems were being opened up by Spaceways as quick as ships became available. With the end of the menace from the Vas, Hershey planned a galaxy-wide campaign.

"Thanks, Ma'am," Don replied, relieved. "Are you sure you can't spare Samantha for a couple of weeks? I'd like to take her down Earthside with me."

Hershey smiled wickedly. "Not on your life. I need Sam here. Go to your cottage, and enjoy the last of your bachelorhood. Samantha will follow when I'm done with her. She'll make it there on time, I promise."

The General Manager stood and made a shooing motion toward her door. "Now go. We'll call you when we need you."

Don's parting with Sam was sweet but brief. Yes, she loved him, and yes, they'd get married, but she had a few things Hershey needed attending to first.

"Darling, we've waited this long. Don't be mad," she said when he pouted. "A couple more weeks more or less won't matter when we'll be spending the rest of our lives together. The poor woman has been running for twenty-four hours a day for months, and I can't leave her right now." Sam frowned and hugged him tight. "I'm afraid she'll have a nervous breakdown or something. After the new campaign is running smooth, I'll join you. It won't be long."

They kissed. The next day Don left for his cottage. Stepping inside, it was as if he'd never left, except a thick layer of dust covered everything, and the fireplace was filled with ashes.

A month passed.

The first few days in the cottage, he'd simply relaxed and let his body grow accustomed to Earth's gravity again. Afterwards he rambled through the woods and fields, swam in the streams, and once, at the urging of his neighbor, and old man named Sonny, gone hunting.

It was early morning and they chased squirrels. When the opportunity presented itself, Don couldn't bring himself to shoot the creature. From the moment he saw the shadow tail twitching its whiskers, he stared at the animal. Finally, he picked up an acorn and threw it, scaring the squirrel away. "And don't come back, dummy," he shouted.

After that, Don spent increasing amounts of time lying on the sofa, staring out the cottage window at the lake beyond. He kept wondering what happened to Puddlefoot.

He hadn't seen the little brownie since the last battle with the Vas. This in itself wasn't unusual, but a nagging feeling kept tugging at Don's brain, somehow he'd destroyed the elf. If it were possible to kill an immortal creature, Don amended to himself.

As the days passed, however, and he still saw no sign of his friend, he became increasingly worried. Would Puddlefoot every return? Had he died final battle? At first, Don kept a bowl of milk on the back porch, and it turned sour after a day and a night. He kept replacing the contents until, finally, it started disappearing. Afterward, he perked up, until the morning of the hunt. When he stepped out to meet Sonny, he discovered a raccoon at the bowl.

From then on, he kept the milk inside. It went untouched.

Sonny thought he was crazy and told him so. "Why you keep a bowl of milk there." They were sitting at the kitchen table drinking a beer. He touched the bowl and said, "Don, you don't even have a cat."

"What? Of course I do," exclaimed Don, turning red. "She's in Luna, staying with a friend."

Sonny went round-eyed. "Don, you ain't make no sense, and you know it. You have a problem there."

Sonny didn't talk to him much after that incident, but maybe he was right. It reminded him of a part of a conversation with Doc Thomas at the end of his debriefing.

This was his post-flight physical. Don didn't worry, he was in perfect health and knew it. The Doc conducted some tests, studied Don thoughtfully, told him to relax. He would return in a minute. It was closer to a half hour, but Don dismissed the delay, he was glad for the rest. When Doctor Thomas did stroll into the examination room, he carried a thick stack of papers.

"Don, remember I told you we were going to go over your profile at the end of your mission?" He dumped the papers on his desk and sat.

"Yes, sir," Don replied, his chest clenching. This was supposed to be a warm body examination. What did he have up his sleeve?

"Well, a lot has happened since then," Thomas rumbled, picking up the top paper and glancing at it. He placed the note back on the stack. "I have not really had the time to study all the records since your return, but I did listen to the recoding you made about your adventures." His eyebrows rose. "I must say, I'm amazed."

"How so, sir?"

Now Don was more curious than nervous. The Doc wanted to talk. He would let him, anything to keep the nut chasers happy. Besides, there wasn't anything amazing in what he'd done. He carried out his orders.

Doctor Thomas stared him in the eye. "In certain high risk, dangerous, situations you appear to be two persons acting like one."

A shiver ran up Don's spine and the tightness spread throughout his body. He knew what the doctor was referring to, now. He'd tried hard to reconcile the facts while leaving Puddlefoot out. He would have to be careful, the Doc might throw him in the looney bin yet. "Are you saying I have a split personality, sir? I'm schizo?" Don snorted. "You're being ridiculous. I'm as sane as you are."

"No, not at all," Doctor Thomas hasten to say, putting up his palm in denial. "Besides, they're not synonymous, and there is one other thing…"

"What, sir," Don said, cautiously.

"A year ago you were defensive, almost antisocial. Now you are not." He smiled. "At least, not *as* antisocial as before. Did you follow my advice?"

"Huh?"

"Did you daydream?"

Don was at a loss what to say. This conversation was getting way too out of control. He half rose out of his chair and exclaimed, "Are you trying to imply I lied about happened out there?"

"Not at all," declared the doctor. He added with a chuckle, "You misunderstood me. What I meant to say is did you construct stories to amuse yourself in the periods of isolation during the voyage, for therapy?"

"No."

"No?" Thomas's eyebrows shot up. "Then how did you pass the time?"

Don thought about it. "Read…Listened to music…Drank."

Doctor Thomas nodded as if he expected Don to say that. "No stories?"

"Never," Don replied firmly. "I use to, but I stopped when I was a cub."

The doctor kept his gaze fixed on Don. "You're lying to me." He fiddled with the papers for a moment. "You either cracked apart somewhere along the line and put yourself back together again, made a good adjustment to your circumstances, or you're worst than ever, a walking time bomb waiting to explode."

Don started to protest. Thomas cut him off. "No, I know what I'm talking about, and I know pilots. Anyone else I might slap a label on and tuck them away, but not with your kind. You are special, the cream of Earth's civilization."

In spite of himself, a smile flickered on Don's face. "Well, I wouldn't go as far as to say the best. Good may, but…"

The doctor laughed.

"Don't try your humble act on me," Thomas chuckled. "I meant what I said. The Naval Academy takes four hundred young men and women and winnows them until there are forty left. Some stay with the Navy, some resign and go to the Merchant Marines, and some, a very few, end up like you. Doing great things. When you crack you crack big." He paused, took a breath, and shuffled his papers again. "I just wonder what really transpired out there."

As Don stared out over the lake, he wondered also. Was Thomas right? Was he a time bomb waiting to explode? One day to start jabbering about brownies and locked away forever?

Puddlefoot was real. He'd seen him, talked to him, shared his food.

Had he? Was Puddlefoot a figment of his mind springing to life when he needed him? Was he a superman, like Doctor Thomas made him out to be, and Puddlefoot the boyish part emerging to play, now and then, but always ready to help?

Don tried to contact Nicholas, and then remembered Nicholas never saw Puddlefoot, nor did Captain Sims. Frik talked to him, but the Arcturian disappeared into the depths of space on some secret mission. Don possessed no way of verifying what he thought was true.

***

As time passed and the milk continued to go sour, he came to believe Doctor Thomas right. Somehow, against his will, his mind daydreamed, thought up Puddlefoot, and continued his existence throughout his adventures in space.

When Don arrived at that conclusion, he rose from the couch and went to bed. He'd laid around long enough. Sam would be arriving from Luna in a few days and he was getting married. Life marched on, and so would he. If it were necessary to confess his delusions to Thomas and take his medicine, or therapy, he winced at the thought. He would do so. Weren't the stories what the Doctor told him to create, though, construct dreams? Puddlefoot certainly was a daydream.

He tossed his clothes on the floor and sat on his bed, feeling better than he had for many days. As he slipped between the crisp sheets, he recalled he hadn't put out a fresh bowl of milk, and started to rise. He stopped when he was halfway to the door and laughed sadly.

Stupid habit. Leaving an offering out for brownies was the first thing to break. If dreaming was good he dreamed, but now the dream was dead. It was paradoxical. He lay back down and fell asleep.

Sometime during the night, he woke. Outside, a cricket chirped and farther away, a barn owl cried. He rolled over and put his arms under his pillow. The sounds of the night continued, but he paid no attention.

He slept.

The noises dimmed, but one continued. It crept into his bed and spoke softly.

"Sire, thou hast not left my bowl of milk tonight."

About the author

I am an army veteran and graduate of Florida State University. A former police officer and plant manager, I moved from Long Island in 2000 to hot and sunny Florida where I live with two puppies, a lazy Siamese named SnoopyCat, and my beautiful wife Sue. Published works include – *B.E.V.*, *Valley of Shadows*, *Rod of Reality*, *Dragonkiller*, and *The Girl Who Rode Dragons*.

If you enjoyed this title, you might like:

The Girl Who Rode Dragons
By: Arthur Butt

All Jackie wanted was equal treatment and to ride a dragon. When her cruel brother-in-law takes over as head of household, and makes her quit school, she is forced to do all the chores, and collect wood in the forest. Jackie finds a dragon's egg, and although law forbids girls to ride dragons, she secretly hatches the egg, and dons boy's clothes. After she brings the gift of fire to the dragonriders, she becomes an accepted member of their band.

Civil wars breaks out, dragonrider against dragonrider. Jackie leads the loyalist faction against the rebels. The stakes—the fate of the kingdom and the life of her and the man she has grown to love.

For more titles like this, visit us online:
www.solsticepublishing.com

www.ingramcontent.com/pod-product-compliance
Lightning Source LLC
Chambersburg PA
CBHW051143030726
47504CB00004B/1020